Amsterdam Traffik

Kelvin Robertson

Published by Keldaviain Publishing

The rights of Kelvin Robertson to be identified as the author of this work have been asserted in accordance with the Copyright, Designs and Patents Act 1988.

A CIP catalogue record for this book is available from
The British Library.

ISBN 978-0-9928599-6-1

Chapter 1

Evening Standard, London, November 8 2013

*Five girls are standing topless in skinny jeans, heeled
boots and flower crowns yelling into the camera.
One is complaining that she is late for her job as a
history teacher at the Sorbonne. Four of the five
women here are French, although they regularly
switch into English— the common FEMEN language
– around Inna Shevchenko, their unofficial leader.
Shevchenko, 23, is the only Ukrainian here and the
co-founder, alongside Anna Hutsol (still in Kiev) and
Alexandra Shevchenko (now in Germany), of the
original movement, which started as a post-Soviet
protest and has grown into an international
phenomenon.*

The look on Katja's face told a story: she was beginning
to have second thoughts. Several of her companions
were already taking off their jumpers and tee shirts,
laughing with excitement. Those not prepared to bare
their chests helped with the posters and theatrical
paint, writing slogans across naked stomachs in thick,
black script, others transferred bright blues and yellows
onto the girl's naked breasts.

'What's the matter, Katja, do you still want to do
this?' Katja blushed with self-consciousness and looked
up at Magdalena, a tall, well-built girl who was her
inspiration, and one of the reasons why she had agreed
to join the group. Magdalena's gaze held hers, dark,

piercing eyes virtually commanding Katja to join them.

'Come, Katja, I know this is your first time but I also know that you are committed to our cause. Look, Rayechka has some nice colours. Why don't you get her to help you? This is an important day for us and you can be a part of it.'

Katja knew that she would go through with it. She had thought about joining them for some time – it was something that might be useful for the future. The women of The Ukraine did not have a voice, finding it almost impossible to change things for the better in their impoverished, corrupt country. She pulled her tee shirt over her head, her long blonde hair cascading onto her shoulders, her bright blue eyes focusing on the task in hand.

'Here, Katja, let me help you,' said Rayechka, who was already naked to the waist, her breasts and nipples painted in blue and yellow and bright red, the red of bloodshed, the word FEMEN across her stomach in bold lettering.

Katja reached behind her back and unclipped her bra, allowing it to fall free; Rayechka giggled at her embarrassment but before Katja had the chance to change her mind Rayechka began to daub the theatrical paint all over Katja's breasts.

'There, look at you, I think you will do very nicely. Girls I think we are ready. Put your jumpers back on, get the posters and we will give that President of ours something more to think about today,' said Magdalena, thumping her fist into her open palm.

The girls cheered. Eight of them had bared their chests, and the other ten had remained clothed, ready to support their sisters with well-rehearsed chants and carrying the placards. It was not many voices for a serious protest but their tactics were more important than their numbers and if their previous brushes with authority were anything to go by they could expect some serious publicity.

'Here!' Magdalena handed each of the girls a headband of coloured flowers. 'I made these last night, they will make us look even more feminine and, with luck, will be splashed across the world's news programmes tonight.'

The young women took their headbands, picked up the placards, filed out of the room and walked across the City towards the Government buildings. Their President was to make an address in person in a short while; journalists and media from across the world would be there, so it was a good time to make everyone aware of FEMEN.

The financial crisis had hit the Ukraine as hard as any country. Unemployment was rife, wages and pensions were unpaid, and the political turmoil was worrying Western leaders. Foreign governments needed Reassurance, donors and investors, were beginning to question whether the country could pay its way, maintain stability and avoid coming under the influence of Russia.

The girls arrived at Hrushevsky Street at the edge of the square surrounding the Parliament building; already there were 20 or more activists waiting for them, carrying banners, decrying the coercion of Government officials in the latest scandals.

'Katja,' called one of the girls.

It was Oksana, Katja's cousin; she was younger, too young to join the spearhead of the movement, too young to be removing her clothing, perhaps next year.

'Hello,' Katja grinned, her fear evaporating as more of her friends surrounded her, friends with the same outlook, the same disgust at the regime's corruption.

'There is already a large crowd in front of the
Verkhovna Rada. Can you hear them?' asked Oksana.

'Oh yes. Have you seen them?'

'No, not yet, but I do know that they are angry with the deputies for taking bribes from the Russians. We will stir them up, Katja.'

'We will,' said Magdalena, overhearing them. 'Come on girls, up with your banners and down with the President.'

'Down with the President and down with corruption,' the girls began to chant as they made their way across the road.

They walked, singing, chanting and determined, towards the Parliament building where a large crowd was gathering. The girls threaded their way towards the front to the whistles and catcalls of the coarser element who knew what the girls were about to do and had come to see them, more interested in the female form than in politics. A door at the front of the Parliament building opened and a party of dark-suited men made their way towards the makeshift stage erected for the event. The leader of the group, the President of the Republic, climbed the three steps onto the platform, a single sheet of paper in his hand, and he looked over the crowd. After a short pause, he tapped the microphone

4

for effect, glanced over his notes before he looked up to begin to speak.

'People of The Ukraine, today will mark a milestone in the history of the Nation...'

He got no further. The crowd's roar of disapproval swept over him, booing, shouting slogans, decrying the deals with the Russians. They were complaining about the oligarchs, the corruption, but most of all they were venting their anger on the President, a tough man shaped by the rough and tumble of Ukrainian politics. He showed little emotion, simply standing there, implacable, waiting until the crowd subsided and then he spoke again. This time he took the initiative, firing his words like a machine gun at the crowd. He knew that a large section of them would support him once the initial anger had subsided; they had to, they had cost him a lot of money.

'We have, with the former Soviet Union, Russia, our neighbour and protector for many years, recently concluded an accord that guarantees security of gas supplies and cheaper prices. This will keep you all warm next winter and it will boost our industries, create jobs and bring a better life for our citizens...'

'What about their Navy?' shouted someone from the crowd?

The President ignored the comment and was about to carry on with his statement when the shriek of female voices cut through the clamour.

'What of the corruption surrounding this accord?' they called out, unfurling their banners. 'Where is all the money going, why do the citizens never see any of this wealth?'

'Follow me,' Magdalena called to the other girls, ripping off her coat and jumper, exposing her naked, painted chest for the entire world to see.

From scaffolding erected for the world's media, cameras swiveled and focused on the women cheered on by their clothed sisters. Topless protesters gathered in front of the podium, parading banners and chanting slogans. Many in the crowd applauded and encouraged them, but not the President, acutely aware of the watching media. He gave a pre-arranged signal to his security men surrounding the stage and withdrew back towards the building.

From somewhere amongst the assemblage of security men came an order, several of them moved forward, from the side of the parliament building, uniformed police appeared and began to break up the crowd. At the same time, the watching media received statements about troublemakers infiltrating the meeting, accusing the topless female demonstrators of fermenting a riot. Once the police had dealt with the troublemakers, the President would return and then his supporters would prove his popularity.

Katja had protested before and been slightly envious of the half-naked, painted girls who drew the attention of the police. At those protests, she was merely part of the crowd but this time she was at the forefront and an easy target. Perhaps she was not as alert as she should have been when the uniformed police appeared; a warning shout from Magdalena caused her to turn and run. Magdalena had earlier noticed the police arrive in their vans and watched them move towards the topless girls. She had experienced the situation more than once but somehow something was different this time.

Were the authorities about to treat them more seriously than on previous occasions? The gas deal with the Russians involved not only vast sums of money but also a re-emergence of Russian imperialism. Today the world's media were watching and she guessed that the President was not prepared to allow their protest to escalate.

Katja heard her warning shout, but she was too slow, feeling a hand grab hold of her naked shoulder, and then an arm caught her round her neck and she was unable to move. She hit out, squealing in frustration as the greater strength of a burly police officer held her prisoner; within seconds she found herself being bundled into the back of a waiting police van.

'In here, put them in here,' and after a scuffle she was

reunited with two of her friends from the protest.

'Animals,' said a familiar voice. It was Magdalena.

'Animals, if you ever wondered why we do this, then you have surely witnessed the reason.'

Katja sat up, in the gloom her eyes adjusting and she recognized her companions as Magdalena and Lyudmyla, a fat girl with droopy breasts who was crying.

'Oh shut up, Lyudmyla,' said Magdalena. 'They won't do anything to us, they just want us out of the way but it's too late, I saw the television cameras pointing at us when we stripped off. Yes, it's too late, the world knows what's happening and will be keeping an eye out for us.'

'Where will they take us do you think?' asked Katja.

'Probably a detention centre and then they will let us go tomorrow when things have calmed down.'

They heard the doors to the front of the vehicle slam shut. The engine started and the van began to move off. After a ride of no more than ten minutes, along bumpy, potholed streets, the vehicle finally came to a halt.

'Out,' shouted a voice as the doors to the rear of the van burst open.

The girls had lost their tops during the mêlée and climbed out a little less confident than they had been only a short time earlier. Each girl had her arms across her breasts, thankful for blankets handed out to cover their modesty.

'You're in for it this time you troublemakers,' said the grim looking policeman. 'Come on, this way.'

To Magdalena, this sounded ominous. On the two previous occasions they had arrested her she was kept in a cell overnight 'for public order reasons' but this time it felt different. Still, if the authorities sent her to prison she would have made her statement and with the group's growing notoriety that statement would reverberate in places that mattered – she hoped.

'Name?' asked a police officer sitting at a desk, a large ledger open in front of him and watching as the girls shuffled into the detention centre, each accompanied by a policeman and Katja wasn't sure exactly what to do. She looked up at the man.

'Name?' he said again.

'Katja.'

'Katja what?'

'Pavlychko.'

'Go and sit over there,' he said, pointing to a wooden bench.

'Next.'

It was Magdalena's turn and Katja noticed how uncomfortable she looked. Perhaps this was not going to be as straightforward as she expected. A door opened and a ranking police officer came out to inspect the prisoners. He looked them up and down and paused for a while chewing his bottom lip.

'You girls are in big trouble, the authorities are fed up with your mischief making. You have become a thorn in the side of the President's office and he wants me to make an example of you so do not expect to be leaving here very soon. In fact it could be years before you go home.' Katja froze, things were beginning to appear more serious than she could have imagined, and she found herself in a situation she had not expected. She began to feel fearful, wondering what she would tell her mother but they had taken away her mobile telephone and she had no means of contacting anyone. She cleared her throat,
coughed nervously and spoke to the officer.

'Erm, Sir, can I call my mother to tell her what has happened please?'

'Certainly not, my orders are to keep you here until it's decided what to do with you. I expect you will be allowed a lawyer before the trial but other than that, no communication with anyone.'

Katja's heart sank. For the first time in her life, she was in serious trouble, the police were about to lock her up and she had no way of letting anyone know.

Across the City, not far from the square, Oksana had found a small café and was sitting alone outside. She tried to make it appear that there was no connection between her and the protesters, playing with her mobile phone as if nothing was amiss. She had run as fast as she could when she had seen the police arresting Katja, found the coffee house and decided to sit and try to hide for a time. Alone and frightened, her mind re-living the events of the past hour, she waited for her coffee to arrive and wondered what to do.

When the police had appeared she had felt no alarm: it had happened before; they often watched the protests and occasionally made token arrests. However, this time it was different; they had appeared in greater numbers and were much more aggressive. It did not take long for the majority of the girls to realise that something was wrong and they had scattered across the Square, disappearing into the crowd as fast as they could. Some though, had not appreciated the danger and had not moved quickly enough allowing the police to catch up with them and take them into custody. Katja was one of the unfortunate ones. Oksana knew that she must contact her Aunt Kateryna and tell her what had happened.

Her coffee arrived and she exchanged her phone for the cup, picking it up with both hands, trying to stop herself shaking. She took a sip, her eyes flitting here and there as she looked around for any sign of the police, but there was none and she began to feel better. Warming her hands on the cup, she managed to drain half of the drink before placing the cup back on the table. Invigorated she reached for her telephone and, with nervous fingers, scrolled through her address book until she came upon the number for Aunt Kateryna and pressed the call button.

Two miles away, Kateryna sat at her desk reading some papers, and watching her closely from the other side of the desk was a slim, dark-haired woman dressed in a sober Harris Tweed suit. The woman had a pair of expensive silver-rimmed spectacles on the end of her nose; she too was reading some papers, and every so often, her eyebrows twitched as she wrestled with an unfamiliar Russian word.

'What's this word – укрывательство?' she asked,

pronouncing the syllables slowly and precisely. 'Ookra- why-tistla?'

'Ah... harbouring, yes. Let me have a look, Anita.' Kateryna took the piece of paper and read where Anita indicated.

'It says that "the recruitment, transportation, transfer, harbouring or receipt of persons, by means of threat or use of force or other forms of coercion..." It is a standard description of abduction and people trafficking. Is preamble to the next section of the agreement.' She passed the paper back across the desk.

'Of course, I...' she did not get the chance to finish her sentence, as Kateryna's mobile telephone began its shrill tone from deep inside her handbag, the private phone.

'Excuse me.'

'Of course.'

Kateryna picked up the bag and rummaged for the phone, listened for a few moments and nodded.

'Mm... mm...' was all she said in reply.

The speaker at the other end carried on for a further minute before Kateryna finally said, 'Oksana, you have done the right thing calling me. I will see what we need to do but please promise me you will tell no one you have called me. Yes... yes... goodbye.'

Her expression did not change, her face unreadable, as it would be on a woman who had been in the profession as long as she had. It was second nature to her not to give anything away, but Anita sensed that something was wrong, very wrong.

'Anita, I must ask you to bear with me for a while, I have had some news, as you have witnessed, and it requires my immediate attention. Please can we stop our meeting? Will you return to your hotel until I contact you, probably later this evening?'

The English woman nodded, asking no questions: it would do no good prying, and Kateryna would tell her only what she wanted her to know. She shuffled her papers together, slipped them into her briefcase, said goodbye, and left the room.

Kateryna watched her go and then she herself tided her papers, put them in the safe and left her office and slipping through a side door in the headquarters building, she headed out to the car park to where she had parked her battered Zil. She climbed into the driver's seat, switched on the engine and with a grim look on her face raced off across the City to the detention centre.

'Who's in charge here?' Kateryna asked as she walked into the building.

The police officer at the desk looked up from his newspaper.

'And who might you be?' he sneered.

Kateryna flicked her wrist to reveal a leather wallet and opened it to expose the badge of a Colonel of the Secret Service. It had the desired effect. The policeman almost fell from his stool in shock, his newspaper falling untidily across his desk and as he stood up he knocked the seat over, the commotion spreading across the corridor and reaching the ears of his superior. The officer in charge emerged to investigate the disturbance, and was met unceremoniously by a badge that he recognised very well.

'Colonel, please, will you come to my office. What can
I do to be of service?'

Kateryna did not do anger, but she could feel it, a cold, hard anger she controlled like a surgeon's scalpel.

'You have arrested some female protesters. On whose orders may I ask?'

The Captain's throat felt dry, he licked his lips and tried to speak. 'Erm... we received orders from the President's office to attend the gathering outside the Verkhovna Rada. The Parliamentary Security Guard expected the FEMEN women might turn up and told us to arrest them. The order came from someone on the President's staff.'

'Well we are not happy about the situation, I'm reliably informed the world's press were watching and what they witnessed today could prove costly to the reputation of Ukraine. I will need your name, rank and number and the names of all the police involved in the operation.'

The Captain's knees felt as if they would not hold his weight for much longer. For the Secret Service to ask for such personal details often meant a long holiday at some camp or other up in the mountains, or a stint at Chernobyl, something he did not relish. Kateryna watched
his terrified eyes; she had the leverage she needed.

'Captain, I will confide in you a little, to avoid any further embarrassment to the State. I have responsibility for internal security and I must make quite sure no further mistakes are made. These women may well be a danger to the State but we do not know who funds them, or who their leaders are and it may be that we can use one or two of them, turn them, encourage them to work for us instead of against us. Do I make myself clear?'

The police officer nodded, more concerned about his
own immediate future rather than the fate of the women.

'I have a Secret Service officer with me, you will hand the women over to us for interrogation and you will hear no more of it. Release them into my custody.'

The Captain was sweating. He reached to pick up his telephone and call one of his men for assistance.

'What are you doing?'

'Calling the sergeant to come and open the cell door.'

'No, do not do that. We need to be as discreet as possible. Just you and I will move them to my vehicle.'

The officer opened his desk drawer and removed a plastic swipe card, stood up and motioned her to follow him. The security in the detention centre seemed lax; they saw no one on the way to the cells and the Captain quickly released the prisoners. Kateryna motioned for them to follow her and the three girls, still wrapped in their blankets, dishevelled and with worried looks on their faces, trooped out of the cell.

'You will remain quiet and follow my orders to the letter or you will regret it,' she hissed at them.

Who was the woman who seemed to outrank the Captain? Only when they were outside the detention centre and Kateryna opened the car door did Katja realise it was her mother. She was so shocked she almost called out 'Mother!' but had enough sense to remain quiet. She knew her mother worked in a Government department but never which one; she had always said she was an accountant, but an accountant would not be able to pull a stunt like this.

'Get into the back seat of the car,' she said, holding open the door of the blacked-out Russian Zil.

Kateryna leaned further in, out of the line of sight of the Captain and said 'Leonid, you will need your gun and call headquarters to tell them we are bringing them in. Thank you, Captain, you have been very helpful,' Kateryna said, turning to the policeman lingering a few metres away.

'Colonel, I will need a receipt for the prisoners,' he ventured to say.

'Of course, Captain, as soon as Leonid has handcuffed the prisoners I will come and sign your receipt. Might I suggest you return to your office and type it up and I will be with you shortly.'

'Of course.'

The police officer turned to the door just as two other police officers emerged and Kateryna swallowed hard before climbing into the driver's seat to watch the Captain disappear back along the corridor. The two other officers walked past; it was now or never, she switched on the engine, gunned the throttle, and the big powerful car leapt forward. She swung it round in a half circle and within seconds had turned a corner onto the main arterial road. She had done it and with a stony face, zoomed along at
120 kph. In the rear seat of the car the three girls sat, quietly stunned by the events of the past few minutes.

Only Lyudmyla's sobbing and the rhythmic throbbing of the six cylinders broke the silence.

Anita finished reading the papers she and Kateryna had been going through, took off her glasses and rubbed her eyes. In the two days since she had left London Heathrow on the four-hour flight to Borispol she had hardly stopped. Kateryna had met her off the aeroplane and whisked her straight to her office in Volodymyr Street where they had immediately set to work over cups of thick Turkish coffee.

Anita had worked with Kateryna several times before,
in Kiev, in London and at various conferences in European capitals. The two women were experienced operatives who paths had crossed during their younger days as field operatives, when both had spent their time gathering information in hostile environments. Both were skilled in the art of survival, pitting their wits against each other's secret services but time had moved on and now they were working together, allies in the fight against organised crime, money laundering and human trafficking. Their meeting today was to draw up an agreement to share information, to permit access to each other's flight passenger information and to use data trawling techniques to expose spikes in behaviour patterns that would eventually lead them to international criminals.

She opened her laptop computer and for two hours documented her progress, detailing the computer systems and telecommunication centres that would be used once the system and their respective committees' ratified protocols were in place. She took her smart phone from the pocket inside her suit jacket and Blue-toothed the encrypted file from the computer, compressed it with new classified software and emailed it to GCHQ. The transmission time was less than a second and then she shredded the file on both machines. Her work completed, Anita sat back, normally after a hard day's work she would enjoy a relaxing Gin and Tonic and was about to call room service when the sound of her mobile phone suddenly interrupted her thoughts. 'Hello, Kateryna, have you sorted your problem?' she asked cheerily.

'Listen carefully, Anita,' Kateryna spoke in a deadpan voice. 'A car will pick you up in exactly 12 minutes from the rear of the hotel. Bring your bag and tell no one.' The line went dead.

Anita felt cold; she had not been in a situation remotely like this for quite a few years. So much for office work, papers, computers, negotiations, she was back in the field.

The car raced through the darkening streets of Kiev, along the riverside and across the Pivdenny Bridge towards the Martyshiv Lake shore and there amongst the trees, the car came to halt. They were outside a small wooden dacha and with only a cursory nod, the driver indicated that this was her destination. She swung open the door of the car and as soon as she had both feet on the ground, the car drove off. She side stepped into the cover of some bushes and looked around. She did not have a gun; her superiors felt it was too sensitive; but she did have a knife sewn loosely into the lapel of her coat. Made of a new type of plastic, almost invisible to airport scanners and as deadly as any steel blade, she at least had a weapon. Feeling along her lapel, she worked the knife out through the narrow slit and gripped the smooth handle, lowering it to her side, concealing its presence.

'Anita,' whispered a voice some ten metres away in amongst some trees.

She turned her head to see the shadow of Kateryna, beckoning her, and cautiously, looking around, she made her way through the trees towards the house. It was dark by the lake, the only light in the house coming from a solitary candle, but it was enough. The two women entered via the rear and Kateryna shut the door behind them drawing the bolt and pulling a thick curtain across the window.

'We are safe enough for now. Put your bag down, I will switch on the lights.'

Anita obeyed; slipping the plastic knife unseen into her pocket, she gripped the back of a chair, alert for anything and when the lights finally came on, the sight of a homely, simple dacha met her eyes. The wooden furniture was rustic; a small table and chairs, a settee with thin flowery cushions, but the most striking feature of the room was a girl sitting on the settee. She looked about 19, blonde hair and blue eyes, wearing a white cotton dress with a pleasant orange and black motif. In her hair, the girl wore an orange ribbon, the significance of which was not lost on Anita.

'This is Katja, my daughter. Katja, this is Anita, my very good friend from England.'

Katja stood to her feet and held out her hand in greeting. She was a stunningly pretty girl but her eyes seemed to betray something deeper, something faintly mendacious, thought Anita.

'Katja's English is good; do you want to speak English or Russian?' Kateryna asked Anita.

'Россия прекрасна, Russian is fine.'

'Good, then make yourself comfortable and I will make some tea, do you want a cake?'

'Er... yes, that would be nice.'

'Katja, entertain our guest for a few minutes. Tell her about this morning outside the Verkhovna Rada.' She turned to Anita, 'I have not been keeping a close enough eye on my daughter.'

As her mother walked towards the small kitchen
Katja's blue, embarrassed eyes turned to Anita.

'I have caused my mother some trouble today. Have you heard of FEMEN?'

'Yes, I know the name. It is a women's protest group
I think.'

'Yes, but we are women, weak women in a strong man's world. This country is so corrupt and there is very little we can do about it but we have come up with the idea of baring our chests to draw attention to our cause and you know it works. We have gained so much publicity and today we believe our images were broadcast all around the world but...'

Kateryna returned from the kitchen. 'But they have been a bit too successful and are beginning to stir up a hornets' nest amongst the governing clan. They think they are like your suffragettes, and maybe they are. Katja did not tell me what she was doing at the University outside of her studies but now I have found out the hard way.'

The kettle began to whistle; Kateryna stopped talking and went back into the kitchen to make the tea.

'So Katja, what happened today? I was with your mother when she received a telephone call that cut short our meeting. It must have been about you.'

'Yes, she told me that my cousin Oksana called her. Oksana was with me at the protest and managed to get away unharmed.'

'You were arrested?'

'She was arrested,' said her mother, returning with a tray of tea and cakes.

Kateryna put the tray down on a small table and poured the tea, her eyes flicking towards her daughter. Anita had been faintly aware for some years that Kateryna had a child but it was something she had never talked about. Neither had spoken much of their private lives; she knew very little of Kateryna, other than she had once been a formidable enemy of the West and now she was a valuable friend.

'My daughter knows nothing of my work. I tell no one, you know the rules Anita and please forgive me if I am dragging you into all this.'

Now it was Anita's turn for the implacable look, allowing her a moment to reflect on the developing situation. Why would Kateryna suddenly confide in her? What did she want of her?

'Katja, I think it is time I told you some things, things you ought to know about this dangerous world we live in. With your permission, Anita, I will tell my daughter a little about my work and then both of you about the danger I believe we are in. May I?' she said looking at Anita.

Anita nodded; their own States' Official Secrets Acts bound them both, and they had been in the game long enough to know the unwritten rules. She would say as little as possible but if Kateryna wanted to talk, then that was not a problem and she might learn something.

'Katja, I work for our country's Security organisation.' She refrained from using the term Secret Service. 'I am at the top of my profession and I have access to many things and many people, which is how I was able to get you away from the detention centre this afternoon. I have discovered that the President's office was planning a show trial to try to rid the country of your fledgling organisation, before you have any real voice. I wish you had told me what you were doing. I could have made sure you were safe before all this happened.'

She took a drink from her cup and offered the plate of cakes to Anita and Katja.

'The President is a dangerous man when he is crossed and I know it will only be a matter of time before he points his finger at me.' She paused to watch her audience's reaction.

The other two were hanging onto her every word, Katja because to hear her mother talk like this was a revelation and Anita because she was a professional.

'Anita, I have never told you much of my private life and Katja, you have never known who your father was. Well this may come as a shock to both of you but at the end the cold war, when relations between the former Soviet satellites and the West began to thaw significantly, I was posted to London.'

Anita nodded slowly, her memory of her first encounter with Kateryna clear in her mind. She remembered vividly the night she had followed Kateryna through the back streets of Kensington to the house of a Member of Parliament, a well-known Tory cabinet minister, Sir Malcolm Oakley. Anita's work had been instrumental in exposing him as a spy but nothing seemed to come of her investigation and it was not until almost two years later that she became aware of the truth. Sir Malcolm was the one obtaining information from his mistress – Kateryna. Sir Malcolm had been having an affair with Kateryna and she was providing him with intelligence. Anita looked at Katja: the same blue eyes, the same straight nose. Could it be... ? Kateryna confirmed it.

'Anita, I have been a good friend to your country since the Soviet Union collapsed and asked for nothing in return, satisfied simply in the knowledge that we were escaping the clutches of Russian imperialism. However, the events of today have changed all of that. If you have not already guessed, Sir Malcolm Oakley is Katja's father and you probably wonder how I managed to keep it secret. Well, how could my superiors have never wondered that I became pregnant whilst working in London?' She paused, it was not in the nature of security people to tell much but this was important.

'I was married to Sergey at the time and he too was a double agent. He agreed to let the world think Katja was his daughter. When it suited us, we parted company. I do not know where he is now. Katja knows that Sergey is not her real father but it is only now that I reveal his true identity and I ask you both not to tell anyone.'

She stood and walked to the panelled wall at the far side of the room, ran her fingers down the coving and sprang open a small secret panel, reaching inside she pulled out three envelopes, replaced the panel and returned to her seat.

'Our President has a history, a chequered history, and I have followed him for many years, collating evidence against him when he was involved in organised crime and when he was in opposition. I have carried on with this task even when he became President and now I have enough evidence in here to send him to prison, in many countries, for a long time. This is my daughter's life insurance and mine.

'Anita, will you please take these two envelopes, they are identical, and give one to Sir Malcolm. He knows about Katja and he will take care of his daughter, the other I want sent to the Prosecutor's office in The Hague, with strict instructions that no one should open it unless some harm befalls my daughter or me. And this – she handed a much thinner envelope to Anita – is for you and your Government. We have worked together Anita for a year and a half on our project and it is about time we showed some results. This envelope contains the names of the most dangerous of The Ukraine's international criminals, particularly those involved in drugs and people trafficking. I hope you can make use of the information because they are immune here in Ukraine. Money is a powerful tool in a corrupt country such as ours.'

Anita took the envelopes. This would do nicely; Kateryna had what appeared to be some serious intelligence on the men running the crime organisations out of the Caucasus, their tentacles spreading right through the European Union. It would be a feather in her cap when she returned to London with this valuable information.

'Thank you, Kateryna, I will call my Embassy if you don't mind and arrange to stay there tonight. I will get them to send a car for me. Excuse me.'

She stood and walked towards the kitchen, taking out her smart phone as she went. After a hushed conversation in which she revealed her identity, she returned to wait for her transport and as they waited, the three women made small talk. Anita learned about Katja's desire to visit London and study textile design; she was to take her degree at the Ukraine State University in a few months and then she wished to find work in England. Kateryna was silent for the most part, thoughtful until the crunch of tyres on gravel announced the arrival of the car and 20 metres away, concealed in the trees, a lone figure pressed a button on his mobile phone and reported witnessing the arrival of the car outside the Colonel's dacha.

Chapter 2

The woman looked pretty in her linen smock, its intricate pattern of colourful flowers contrasting with the stark surroundings. On her head, she wore a band of crochet knitted orange wool and in her hand, she carried an imitation designer handbag. She walked slowly along the street of the small town, her eyes flitting from one decrepit building to another, until, eventually, she found what she was looking for, a small café with a rundown façade, a few tables and chairs out in front and no customers in view.

The road was potholed through years of neglect, the street was drab, a result of tired Soviet architecture, and in the distance she could see the last of the working chimneys belching out smoke from some State enterprise. The one or two pedestrians she passed were dressed in cheap worn-out clothing and did not give her a second glance. Elena reached the café, sat down in a quiet corner of the veranda and closed her eyes for a minute, feeling the pleasant spring sunshine on her face.

'What would you like?' asked a soft female voice. Elena opened her eyes and looked at the waitress, a smart girl of about 20 years old, well developed and statuesque.

'Good morning, I would like coffee.'

The girl disappeared and returned with a Turkish style coffee pot and placed it on the table for Elena to serve herself.

'Are you from this town?' asked Elena.

'Yes, I grew up here and went to school here and I expect I will die here.'

'Oh, come, that does not need to be the case. I came from a small village near Zhytomyr,' she lied. 'I thought the same as you until I took the plunge and went to Kiev where I found a job. I saved up for a while and used the money to visit Germany where I found a job working, at first in a factory and then as a receptionist in an American hotel. The money was good, good enough for me to return home and buy my own house.' She smiled sweetly at the girl, whose expression reflected her thoughts. Was an escape route from the daily grind and poverty of this backward town really possible? She looked at Elena; here was a woman who had found work in Germany. She was well dressed and smart, carried a designer bag, and she envied her.

'How do you get a job in Kiev?' asked the waitress.

'Not too difficult. The first thing is to find an agency, who charge only a very small amount, and they will look for you, enquire with businesses throughout the City. But listen, if, when, you get a job you will only start dreaming of a better one in the West, Germany or Sweden or even America.'

The girl's eyes lit up, she had dreamed that maybe one
day she could move away and find a better life and she was not alone in that dream; many young people felt trapped and looked to the West for a better life and Elena felt the tug on her line. The girl was taking the bait.

'Why don't you come to Kiev on your day off and I can introduce you to people who can help you find work in the West. It might only be as an agricultural worker or in a factory to start with but it will give you some money to buy time until the job you really want comes along.'

The waitress took only seconds to make up her mind, she would do it, she would make the 60-kilometre journey to Kiev and find one of these agents who could get her work in a Western European country. She had a small amount saved up and hoped it would be enough.

'How will I find you?' she asked. 'How much will it cost?'

'Here,' Elena rummaged through her bag. 'Here, I have a pen, give me that napkin and I will write down a telephone number. You have a mobile phone don't you?'

The girl shook her head.

'Never mind, you can use a public telephone and get yourself a mobile when you start your job,' she said, smiling again.

'Thank you, oh thank you for that,' said the girl, clutching the napkin. 'How much will it cost, this agent?'

'Oh not too much, I'm sure you will be able to afford the fee on a waitress's pay,' said Elena, dodging the issue.

The girl looked pleased and she was still dreaming when she returned to the kitchen.

Elena drank her coffee and wondered if she might
find another girl or two in this town before she caught the train back to the City. A quarter of an hour later, her coffee barely touched, Elena waved for her bill.

'How much do I owe you for the coffee?'

'Oh, that is all right, it's on the house. Can I call you next Thursday? That's my day off.'

'Of course you can. I look forward to seeing you again.' Elena rose from the table picked up her bag, shook hands with the beaming waitress and left the small café in search of another victim.

When The President was told that a high-ranking woman from the Secret Service had spirited away three of the girls arrested during the previous day's demonstration he was livid. He had intended to make an example of them, a show trial, and a prison sentence. Not too long, a year or two perhaps, enough to deter them from constantly exposing themselves to the media and long enough for him to push through his reforms. This woman, one from his own Secret Service, had thwarted his plan, making him angry, and as his anger boiled over he thumped his desk in frustration.

'Who is this woman who disrupts my plans? Who is this woman who thinks that she can do as she likes?'

The Chief of Police together with the head of the President's personal Security force stood in front of his desk unable to answer.

'Sir, we don't know, we haven't managed to conduct a thorough investigation yet,' replied his Police Chief. 'But we do have a lead and we are following it up.'

'What lead? Tell me about it.'

'One of the arrested girls is called Katja Pavlychko, a student at the University.'

'That seems easy enough to find out. What's the significance?'

'With some difficulty I have discovered that there is a Colonel in the Secret Service of the same name, Kateryna Pavlychko.'

The President frowned; had he heard that name before, he wondered?

'Go on.'

'I have had to call in favours from colleagues but it seems that this Colonel is working with several European Secret Agencies on organised crime and for the past two days has supposedly been in meetings with a representative of the British Embassy.'

'What do you mean, supposedly?'

'As with all visits by foreign personnel, friendly or not, a watch is kept on their movements just in case any of our people are giving away more than they should.'

'And has she, this Colonel Pavlychko?'

'We don't know but what we do know is that a car from our Secret Service was used to take the British agent to a dacha on the bank of Martyshiv Lake. She was tailed, as I have already said, and two hours later she was picked up by a car flying the diplomatic flag of the United Kingdom.'

'What has this to do with Colonel Pavlychko?'

'The dacha belongs to her.'

'And the girl, the one arrested here yesterday?'

'We have checked with the University and she has the same address.'

'It doesn't look to me as if it's a lead, more like a smoking gun. Get this Colonel here; let me have words with her. She won't be in the Secret Service much longer if it is her.'

The two men left, the Security man to his office and the policeman to arrange for the arrest of Colonel Pavlychko. The President himself had other business to attend to and after closing the door to his office, he thoughtfully picked up his telephone.

Markov Kalaman stepped from the shower, reached for the towel hanging over the hot rail, and quickly dried himself, glancing admiringly at the mirror as he did so. He pulled on a pair of shorts and walked towards his study where the phone was beeping; he raised the receiver to his ear and spoke.

'This is Markov.'

'Markov, I have a job for you. Come and see me tomorrow at... let's see. I have meetings until three. Come at three tomorrow afternoon. You can arrange it with Ivan my Security chief – I think you know him,' said the President.

'Yes, Mr President, I know Ivan.'

'Good, I will see you tomorrow then.'

Markov replaced the receiver. What could the President want with him this time? He mentioned that he had a job for him so with luck there would be money involved and some ready cash would come in useful for next weeks' vacation at the Swiss ski resort of Verbier.

'Vladimir,' called Markov. There was a knock at the door and a big, thickset man in a light-grey suit entered. 'When are we sending the next load to Holland?'

'The consignment will be ready in a week. I think maybe ten or 12 days and the minibus can leave.'

'What about my sister, have you heard from her?'

'Yes, she is coming today with another girl.'

'Good, good, that will make six I think. What about the men?'

'There are 52 of them at the farm ready and waiting to go west, we just need to know where you want them to go and then we can get rid of them.'

'Very good Vladimir, I will make some calls to Holland and Germany and let you know where they should be sent. It should be a profitable few weeks for us and I will make sure you are well rewarded.'

Vladimir half smiled. He was not prone to showing his emotions, a bull of a man, pugnacious, a useful lieutenant for Markov. Vladimir left the room, made his way down the wide staircase of the dacha, one built in the old style of the grain barons of 19th century Odessa, Markov's hometown, and went to check on the men housed in the largest of the outbuildings.

The house was set on 5,000 hectares of hilly and wooded land, on the edge of the Carpathian Mountains, secluded but within reach of the road between Lviv and Kiev. The Polish border, the gateway to the markets of Western Europe, lay to the north-west and to the south, an endless supply of the raw materials needed for Markov's business – people. Not only did he trade Ukrainians but Romanians, Turks and refugees from the conflicts in the Middle East. He traded in other commodities as well: gold from India, drugs from Afghanistan, all flowing through his secluded estate where he kept a small army of thugs. Although his crime organisation was not large, he did not control a bank or deal with the Russian Mafia, his enterprise was successful and, more importantly, he had the ear of the President.

Elena led the waitress up a flight of rickety stairs to the first floor of a grubby, run-down building.

'This way, Sveta,' said Elena opening the door to a room where two men were sat playing cards. When they saw who was entering they immediately stopped their game and stood up to show the respect their paymaster deserved.

'This is Sveta; she wishes to join the next party going to Holland. See to it that she completes the paper work and make her comfortable until the transport arrives.' Elena turned to the girl. 'I will leave you with these two for now Sveta; I will probably see you in Amsterdam. I have to return to my job in a week,' she lied.

Sveta, alone with the two strange men was beginning to feel isolated, having second thoughts and it showed on her face. The men were used to the situation; it was part of their job to make the women passing through the hands of Markov's organization feel relaxed and one of them came towards her and held her hand.

'Would you like a cup of tea?'

Sveta hesitated and then accepted and before long they had her at ease, showing her photographs of young men and women working in the fields and factories of Holland and Germany, happy and smiling, all the time convincing her of their sincerity.

'Here, sign this contract. Do you have the money for your accommodation and transport to get you into Holland? We will take care of your entry visa and we will get you a passport to allow you to travel freely once you have a job and are settled in.'

Sveta's confidence returned and she thought of her new life, a job in the West, money of her own and the chance of some real happiness. She was a simple, good- hearted girl from the rural backwaters and knew nothing of the outside world.

Markov had moved quickly after his meeting with the President. He had expected the conversation to centre on the drug shipments coming in from the East. The Turks were becoming difficult; coerced by the Americans they had tightened up their security and forced his couriers to cross the Turkish border twice when returning by the southern route. But they had to come that way, the northern route through Azerbaijan and Georgia was no longer possible – it was just too dangerous.

'Markov,' the President had said, 'we have a small problem that I would like you to take care of. It is a bit of a favour from me to you, really. There is a young woman living by Martyshiv Lake, a University student who has caused me much trouble.'

'I should kill her?'

'No, no, nothing so crude. No I want you to take her west, to your friends in Holland or Germany, and find her work, the kind a woman is best at. It will make her grow up I think.'

Markov had understood and summoned Vladimir and two more of his men to outline the President's request together with a brief description of the girl and her address.

'The girl has upset someone in a high place and we are to make her disappear for a time. They tell me she is young and good-looking, ideal for my friend Caas in Amsterdam. Bring her here to the farm and keep her locked up, keep her away from the other women. I don't want them upset just yet.'

The journey to Kiev took place mostly in silence, one or other of them speaking only to confirm directions and before long; they had found the small dacha. Parking the car amongst the trees, they spent several minutes observing the house and its surroundings and drifting towards them through the still night air, came the sound of American pop music.

Vladimir stepped from the car and, as so often with big men, was surprisingly silent as he made his way towards the house. Staying amongst the foliage and trees he made a circuit of the building before returning to the waiting car instructing the driver to stay put and the other man to keep a lookout at the roadside. Leaving them, he moved back through the trees to the rear of the property where he gently pushed aside some bushes for a better view of the house. The music was stemming from a well-lit room and through slightly parted curtains he could see a pretty girl dressed in a dark-blue tracksuit dancing around to the music.

Vladimir walked amongst the trees, towards the back door. Moving swiftly he stood under the rear porch and grasped the door handle, turning it slowly, applying pressure to swing it open, but it did not move. The door was locked, probably bolted. He stood still and listened again to the music.

Katja was as mad about American pop music as she was about the FEMEN movement; she was familiar with all the current stars and their output and danced about the room as if at a Hollywood Oscar party. She imagined mixing with all the stars, and of the lecturer at the university, his proposal and the chance for her to visit the west, when suddenly, there was a loud crash.

Katja called out, afraid her mother, working in the kitchen, had had an accident; but Kateryna instinctively knew that trouble had arrived and cursed herself for having left her gun in her handbag.

Dropping the cutlery she was holding, except for one knife, she rushed towards her daughter's bedroom and met a startled Vladimir face to face in the narrow corridor. Having burst in, he was making his way towards the girl's room unaware that there was a second occupant in the house. When he saw the middle-aged woman barring his path he simply shrugged her aside and went for Katja.

'Stay in your room, lock the door,' yelled Kateryna, but it was too late; Katja was already in the passageway and with one swipe of his powerful arm Vladimir held her in a grip of iron.

'Leave her alone,' said Kateryna in calm and calculating voice, a tone that should have warned Vladimir.

He took no notice and pushed past her but a karate chop from Kateryna connecting with his throat slowed his progress and changed his opinion of her. At last, he focused on Kateryna, but was unable to avoid her kick to his shin, the pain forcing him to drop to one knee. It was time to defend himself and defend himself he did; he threw Katja forwards towards her mother before lurching after her and crashing into both women. Kateryna lunged at him with the knife, catching his jacket forcing him to retreat out of range, but the pause allowed him time to recover just enough to swing his huge fist at Kateryna, missing her by a hair's breadth. She swung her knife again, this time at his face, the blow glancing off his shoulder and then there was nothing but blackness. His second punch connected, knocking Kateryna senseless and clearing the way for his escape.

Katja began screaming as Vladimir, one hand around her waist, grabbed her, the other cupping her mouth as he dragged her backwards, arms and legs flailing. The sound of the commotion alerted his henchmen who came running, and between them, they managed to wrestle Katja into the boot of the car. The doors slammed shut and the vehicles wheels squealed on the dry tarmac as they made their getaway. Racing through the dark and deserted streets of Kiev the car finally reached the main highway heading west towards the Carpathians and Markov's lair.

In the boot of the speeding automobile, feeling overwhelmingly claustrophobic and frightened, Katja tried to understand what was happening. What had they done to her mother, her brave mother who had tried to save her from the overgrown thug who had burst in on them? Too traumatised even to cry, she lay in the dark, cramped box that was her prison and stared into the darkness.

It was deathly quiet in the dacha, Katja's American pop music tape had run down and it seemed as if the whole of Kateryna's body was in pain. Her head throbbed from the vicious blow she had taken; the side of her body on which she lay had become numb and she could not move. At first, she had no idea of where she was, or what had happened, and it was only after lying still for ten or 20 minutes that her head finally cleared and her memory began to return. Her body convulsed in pain as she struggled to turn over, but it was no good. In her mind, she felt over her body, trying to assess her injuries, wondering if her jaw was broken – but far more painful was the knowledge that they had taken her daughter from her.

For more than an hour she lay on the floor until finally she found the strength to turn face down on the floor and force herself to her knees, and it was another ten minutes before she was finally able to stagger to her feet. Holding on to the sparse furniture she made her way to her handbag lying beside the armchair and fumbled Inside for her gun, oh, if she had only had the foresight to keep it within reach... but she had not and she could not change what had happened – not yet. She fumbled further and found her mobile telephone, her lifeline, and rang a special number.

'Hello, how are you today caller?' said the voice.

She had neither the strength nor the inclination to play the game and went straight to the critical part of the coded conversation.

'Today ish furshday shixsh of Novembah.'

'No caller, you have the date wrong.'

'Ah, itsh the sheventten of February and it's been a rainy day,' Kateryna struggled to say, her broken jaw hindering her speech.

The code was correct, the operator was satisfied and she had cleared the first hurdle.

'Putting you through caller.'

Kateryna did not wait for the voice at the other end to quiz her on passwords, simply quoting her service number and saying she was badly hurt. It was enough; the agent at the other end of the phone was experienced enough to understand her predicament and quietly asked questions that required only a yes or a no.

'I will get someone to you straight away, Colonel. I
know you do not have your car tonight.'

The line went dead and Kateryna managed to slump, exhausted, onto a chair where she remained semi- conscious until she felt a hand on her shoulder.

'She's hurt badly, better get the ambulance here,' said a man's voice.

'Colonel, Colonel Pavlychko, can you hear me?' Kateryna lifted her head a little and opened one eye.

'I will bring you some water. We have sent for an ambulance, you will soon be taken care of.'

Her head slumped forwards once more until she felt the cold rim of a glass against her lips; the water reviving her somewhat and during the next half hour, as they awaited the ambulance's arrival, she regained some composure.

'The ambulance is here. Tell the medics to look after her whilst we have a better look round. There has obviously been a violent break in but I have no idea what they were after.'

For the next half hour, the two Secret Service men trawled over the debris of the violent attack, noting anything of interest before finally entering Katja's room.

'Look, there, it's a picture of one of those girls in the news. Lively little things don't you think?'

The other man grinned; the girls' ploy of going topless during their protests gained attention everywhere every time.

'So where is this girl, the Colonel's daughter? Didn't even know that she had one, did you?'

'No, she's too high ranking for me to mix with. I have only ever seen the colonel at work and I know very little about her. But if it is her daughter, then she is a very good-looking girl.'

The other man nodded.

'Wonder if this is what it's all about, FEMEN. I heard a rumour this morning that someone from our department spirited some FEMEN girls out of a detention centre a couple of days ago. Let's take some pictures of this mess before we go back and make our report.'

The two agents watched the ambulance slip quietly
away before returning to finish their inspection and return to their headquarters. Their superior officer was in some kind of mess but they knew better than to speculate on what that might be.

'Put her in there on her own,' said Markov, running his eyes over the shivering Katja. 'We don't want her upsetting the others do we? They are going voluntarily, this one isn't.'

He waved his arm towards a shed on the edge of the compound, one they used for the occasional troublemaker, and told his men to leave her. There was a larger structure nearby and this was where they kept the 'others'. The
'others' were a group of women, five young and attractive women, all who had paid a considerable sum of money to Markov's organisation to secure for them well-paid work in a Western European country.

'When will you be ready to move, Vladimir?' Markov poured vodka for himself.

'We still have one more to come. Elena has done well; she has recruited almost all the girls for this consignment, five here and another one who should be here within the week so I would say that the minibus can leave on the
16th.'

'Splendid, here have a drink, you deserve one. Now about our new arrival, we will keep her separate for the journey to Amsterdam and I still have time for the skiing trip to Switzerland. We leave first thing tomorrow. I will tell my sister to take charge whilst I am away and when I return we will visit Amsterdam. We should take the girl with us in my car; we can drug her to keep her quiet From what I have seen of her, she is too pretty to mess up. I think Caas will be pleased with her; she is one for his Middle Eastern customers I think. Those oil sheiks will pay good money for a blue-eyed blonde.'

Vladimir bared his teeth in a weak grin; if they did manage to get rid of the girl to an Arab he could expect a bonus. Markov always gave him and Kostyantyn a bonus when they sold a girl to the Arabs.

The aid placed a piece of paper in front of the president before leaving to usher in his visitor. The President read through the few lines of text, his eyebrows rising in mild surprise and then he looked up as the door opened again and a stocky, middle aged woman in a business suit walked in. He turned his head and looked up at her, slightly shocked at what he saw. One side of Katernya's face was a mass of red and purple, bruising from Vladimir's punch, even so, he looked her straight in the eye with a threatening glare. Kateryna was impassive because, although her injuries were still causing her distress, she had welcomed the chance to confront the President. She was determined to state her case before the man whom she believed had stolen her daughter

'Colonel Pavlychko, take a seat. Colonel, I will come straight to the point. I believe you know why you are here. Two days ago, I gave a speech, an important speech to the world's media, interrupted, unlawfully, by this group of women who call themselves FEMEN. They were disruptive and we arrested three of them, took them to the new detention centre in Lukyanivska Prefecture. A pity they were not in the old prison because you, my dear Colonel, would never have managed to get them out of there.'

He stared hard at Kateryna, his piercing dark eyes attempting to cow her. He was a powerful man and always got his way: resistance to his will was not an option for most people. However, Kateryna was not most people and still she remained unmoved by his threats.

'We have investigated the crime of releasing prisoners without authority. We know it was you who entered the detention centre and removed the three women, one of whom is your daughter, is she not?'

Kateryna said nothing; she had interrogated many prisoners during her time with the Secret Service and this pig was not going to intimidate her so easily.

'Answer me, woman, did you release those prisoners unlawfully?'

'Mr President, I received notification from an informant that the women had been arrested and taken to the detention centre. At that time I had no idea my daughter was one of them and I saw it as my duty to investigate the matter in my role as a Colonel with responsibility for internal security.'

The President thumped the desk, his usual response when angered.

'Look, these women are becoming a problem and need to be stopped. You have thwarted the police and the court in bringing them to book.' He paused for a few moments, letting his words sink in. 'I want these women back in prison and I want them on trial for their crimes. Do I make myself clear?'

'Mr President, you make yourself perfectly clear. But
I know my daughter; she is not an agitator or a terrorist
– she is simply a teenage girl in University where ideas like this take root. Within a year or two, they get a job or marry and it is all forgotten. Can you not let the matter rest... Sir?'

'Let the matter rest? I should say not. I have told too many people that I want them locked up and no way will I lose face over this. I want those other women behind bars by tonight and you, my dear Colonel, can expect a severe demotion – if I decide that you can even stay in the Service.'

The president's threats dismayed Kateryna but in no way defeated her. 'Mr President, I think you should look at this. It could well make you see things in a different light.' Kateryna reached inside her jacket and pulled out a brown foolscap envelope. She placed it on the desk and waited, her heart beating a little faster than perhaps it should. The President picked up the envelope, ripped it open and removed the single sheet of closely typed text.

'What is this?'

'I suggest you read it – carefully.' There was no hint of respect in her voice, no 'Sir' at the end of the sentence, simply the implacable look of one who knew what she was doing.

The President of the Republic of The Ukraine put on his glasses and for several spellbinding minutes read through the text.

'Where did you get this?' he asked curtly.

'For many years I have been following your career. In the beginning, under instruction from my superiors, latterly out of interest and the possibility that your activities might compromise State security. I have documented your petty crimes as a young man, the beatings you meted out to rivals, the murders you and your associates committed and the organised crime in which you have been, and still are, involved. You have threatened my daughter and me and so I have taken out an insurance policy, an insurance policy I have lodged with friends I can trust and with lawyers in The Hague. Each is under instruction not to open their envelopes, which I might add are much thicker than the one you have, unless any harm befalls me or my daughter, and harm has befallen myself and my daughter'

The President's blood ran cold. He had met with Markov only the day before and instructed him to find this woman's daughter and make her disappear as retribution for Kateryna's insubordination. He had not decided what he would do with Kateryna until he had met with her and now that he had, things were not quite as he expected. His rise had not been without some effort on his part, working with unsavoury characters from Ukraine and Russia, eliminating rivals. Now, in his hand, was a synopsis of his criminal activities and, from what he could see, all true. If she had logged evidence of his wrongdoings with the right people, then it could spell the end for him. And there was the other sheet of paper lying on his desk, the one from the Foreign Intelligence Service.

The President was no fool. He had not reached the position he was in without carefully weighing his options before making his moves. This was no different and his brain was busy computing a solution.

'You are a clever and resourceful woman, Colonel, and I salute you, but you cannot be allowed to get away with this scot-free. For the moment we will maintain the status quo, we will sit on this and await developments.' He paused and looked thoughtful. 'There is one thing though Colonel, if you wish to see your daughter safe once more then I suggest you take a seat for a while longer, his tone softened, and listen to what I have to say'

Kateryna left the President's office, walking purposefully, her eyes looking straight ahead and after emerging into the fresh air, she took a deep breath. The president's proposal was daring and extremely risky but it had possibilities and she did want to see Katja safe and well again.

Chapter 3

The mountain air was clear, cold and refreshing, surprisingly so for the beginning of April and it made Jane's eyes water. She left the ski lift near the top of Mont Gele and walked the few metres to begin the 20-minute hike up the steep slope of the Stairway to Heaven, a pathway leading to the mountain top where she could tackle the particular off-piste run she had decided to try. She was not alone as she made her way up the first few metres; in front of her several skiers were steadily making their way in single file up the track, skis strapped to their backs, ski sticks moving methodically.

She joined the few stragglers and began the ascent, her eyes drawn towards the horizon and the vast, overwhelming view of the Alps. Across the craggy snow- laden valleys she could see the Matterhorn and Mont Blanc, a view that still mesmerised her after all these years. She blinked in the strong sunlight before pulling her sun goggles over her eyes and she began to climb. Starting a little too quickly, her lungs began to labour in the oxygen sparse air and after 50 or so metres she had to stop for a few moments, digging her ski poles into the snow for support to allow her body to catch up with her breathing.

'Are you all right, my dear?' asked a deep, foreign voice behind her.

Jane turned to see a tall, well-built man dressed in a red and white ski suit and a red headband across his forehead.

'Perfectly well thank you.'

'Good, I'm pleased about that. Would you mind if we pass you? It seems you are not in hurry.'

'Of course,' said Jane leaning to one side to let the man and his three companions pass by.

He spoke again, his breath forming a white cloud. 'I may see you later in village. You look an exciting and life- loving woman and I look forward to meeting you again.' Jane both hated and loved attention and could not help a wry smile as she listened to the charm of this over confident – Russian? Yes, his accent was Russian.

She managed not to show any emotion as the men passed by, big men, unsmiling men who headed up the slope at a pace she could not hope to match. She watched them go and had to admit he was an attractive man and his manner suggested a successful one, but she would not allow him to see that his charm was having any effect on her. It was late in the season and from experience, she knew that often the late arrivals were successful people, ones who had been so busy making money that they had almost let the ski season pass them by. It had not passed her by though; she had purposely come skiing to escape, to get away from London for a while, to spend some time alone and to reflect. She had been involved with several men over the years but this last one, Michael, took the biscuit for inconsiderate behaviour. The bastard had used her, taken her for a ride for the past two years, pretending their relationship was strong. True, she had some happy memories but two months ago, he had announced that he did not want to continue seeing her. He said that they were drifting apart – incompatible, he had said. The bastard, she could not think of any other word that described him so fully. She paused again to catch up with her breathing and readjusted her skis, switching shoulders as she thought as many bad thoughts about Michael as she could. She remembered the voodoo stories, how the priests stuck pins into dolls to harm people; where might she find a doll that looked like Michael she wondered?

Jane was a successful Human Resources Manager with the bank and she had met Michael at a private party in the New World Gallery where she had been looking for an agreeable painting to finish off the redecoration of her flat. She liked modern art; she had studied it in her late teens and had intended to follow a career in art until her father had persuaded her to take a degree in Human Resources and Management. He had said there was more chance of her making a decent living and being independent than trying to find an arty farty job, as he called it, and he had been right.

Michael – where was she? Oh yes – he had charmed her, told her he was in banking, was looking for opportunities and invited her to dinner. She remembered that first date, the fancy dinner at some celebrity chef's place and then on to the Royal Opera House. He had seemed a well-read, clever person who would do well in banking, and he had, but not under his own steam. She had helped him to acquire a good job on the Investment Banking side, she had helped him at every opportunity to advance his career and he had taken those opportunities.

Within months, he was a high-flyer earning close to the million-pound bonus level and then he dumped her, left her flat, and only three days ago she found out that he was engaged to some floozy from Berkshire. She tried to forget him and breathed in the clean air, which was what she was here for, to clear her mind and start again. She looked out across the snowfields, watching some of the skiers ahead of her put on their skis and others already launching themselves down the slopes. The swish of the dry powdered snow was music to her ears and made her unable to contain herself; she could not wait for her turn to leap into space.

Now girl, she said to herself, skis together, knees bent and 'whoopee' as she launched herself over the crest of the first drift and down the off-piste run towards the village far below. Her 207 skis felt a good snug fit, and within the first 50 metres she had reached 80 kph. Twisting, turning, she kept her speed safe, slowing a little as she slid sideways through the powdery snow. At times, her descent seemed to be almost vertical, forcing the adrenalin through her veins, the feeling of exhilaration banishing all other thoughts from her head.

She was alone; the other skiers had taken their own lines, disappearing behind drifts and outcrops leaving her a solitary figure against the white landscape. She pushed herself forwards over a small ledge and down she went again, a great shower of sparkling white snow in her wake. She really felt as if the mountain belonged to her as she crouched low, the ski poles tucked tightly under her arms. She sped down the mountainside and then out of the corner of her eye, she spotted another lone skier on a converging path, wearing a red and white snowsuit, a contrast to her light green. She kept an eye on him as he gradually came closer: could it be the Russian, she wondered.

It was, and he appeared to be an expert skier, at least as good as she was, so graceful in his turns, and as the gap between them closed, she could see him grinning, almost challenging her to race him. With the mood she was in it was an instant trigger: here was another man trying to outwit her, and she would not let that happen. She crouched so low her head was almost touching her knees, she skied in a straight line, increasing her speed to well over 100 kph – but she could not shake him off.

Markov had been skiing all his life. As a young man, he had harboured ambitions to represent his country; he never quite made the cut, but he was good, very good, and relished the challenge that this slight woman had taken up. With flurries of snow in their wake, they closed to within 20 metres of one another and with nothing more than the odd sideways glance, weighed each other up. Any more than that was dangerous.

They hurtled down the mountain, first one in the lead,
then the other, plumes of powdered snow tracking their progress. Jane felt exhilarated; she rarely had competition on the slopes, preferring to ski alone, but for once she was glad of the company. She was not reckless though, executing several sideslips to control her speed, letting the big Russian lead for the final few hundred metres before both took to the air over a hump in the track, finally coming to rest in a flurry of snow on the outskirts of the town.

'May I congratulate you on some fine skiing,' called Markov.

'You're not bad yourself.'

'Why thank you, can I invite you for an après-ski?' Jane frowned; he was very forward but what the hell, after all wasn't this why she was here?

'Yes,' and a smile returned to her lips. She raised her goggles and hoped she did not have great red rings around her eyes. 'I'd love a drink after that. It was certainly exhilarating.'

'It was. By the way I am Markov, and you?'

'Me Jane...' Oh she must stop doing that.

'Me Jane? I do not know that.'

'Sorry, a silly joke – me Jane, you Tarzan.'

Markov looked puzzled, uncomprehending and Jane decided not to pursue it even though this man did look something like the original Tarzan.

Markov returned from the bar and placed the two schnapps cocktails on the table. He sat down opposite Jane, slid one of the glasses to her and raised his own in a toast.

'So what brings a beautiful woman to Verbier alone?' he asked.

'It's a long story and I don't really want to talk about it, thank you.'

'Ah...' Markov understood exactly why she was here.

'And you, Mr Markov, what brings you here?'

'My name is Markov Kalaman; you will call me simply Markov.' He smiled and lifted his glass. 'To good skiing.' Jane lifted her glass and completed the toast.

'Where are your friends Markov, were there not four of you earlier?'

'Yes, we are four. One is driver; the others work for me also.'

'And what is it you do?'

'I am trader in many things. You want something, I get it for you.'

'Such as?'

She is inquisitive, he thought. 'Farm equipment, earth movers, tanks.'

'Tanks?'

Markov laughed. 'Not for army, for farms and factories. What's it you do? Let me guess, you are model?'

'Don't be stupid, I may have been a model, but that was a long, long time ago.'

They both laughed.

'Where are you from, Markov? You sound Russian' Markov feigned hurt. 'Russian, I am not Russian, I am Ukrainian.'

'Oh, funnily enough my ex-boyfriend was dealing in grain futures in the Ukraine the last I heard.'

'So you are here to wash a lover from your soul?' he said, his eyes narrowing slightly.

'That's a funny way of putting it.'

Markov laughed. 'Come, I see in your eyes I am right but I also see that really he was not so important to you.' Jane blushed; she did not want to talk about Michael.

He had hurt her at a time when she needed support. Her aged parents were suffering and she had to think about care for her father who was ten years older than her mother and in the early stages of dementia, but Michael was a selfish, arrogant pig who thought of no one but himself. She banished thoughts of Michael and laughed again; she was enjoying Markov's company. Perhaps the healing properties of the high mountain air were having their effect.

Markov's mobile phone began to ring and he pulled it from his pocket.

'Ah, you will have to excuse me, business. Will I see you in the Farm Club this evening, Jane?'

'Maybe,'

Jane smiled a smile that said neither yes nor no.

'Excuse me.' Markov had his mind on other things.

'Yes Elena... '

Jane watched him go and finished her drink, looking round at the other skiers enjoying the après-ski. Would she go to the Farm Club to see this Ukrainian stranger? She did not even know herself. A hot shower and a good meal in the hotel restaurant might decide for her.

The phone on her desk rang and Anita looked up from her work. She had been back in London for two days, briefing her boss on her meeting with Kateryna, surprising him with the envelopes she had brought back.

'This one is to go to the firm of lawyers in The Hague and this one is for Sir Malcolm Oakley.'

'Really,' said her superior with some surprise. 'You know the Director is retiring?'

'Yes, it's been on the cards for a month or two, I understand.'

'Well while you were in the Ukraine we have had a change at the top and our new Director *is* Sir Malcolm Oakley. He started yesterday morning.'

'I haven't really seen anyone yet, Sir, I haven't even had a chance to access my emails. This comes as a bit of a shock.'

'I'll bet. Tell you what, write up your report and bring it to me personally and I will arrange a meeting with the Director and then you can tell him what you know. Bring your envelopes and we'll see what he wants to do with them.'

The two loud explosions still reverberated round the confined space of the underground, windowless room as Anita lifted her handgun and flicked on the safety catch. She placed it on the metal shelf and took off her safety spectacles.

'Good shooting,' said the armourer. 'You haven't lost any of your ability. That was as good a practice session as I've seen all week.'

'Thank you, I thought I might be a little rusty after all this time.'

Anita looked at her wristwatch and turned to leave the shooting range deep in the basement of the building. Her appointment with the Director was in another half an hour and she needed to collect her papers from the safe. Along the way she stopped at the bathroom to wash her hands, face and to get the thin oil of the gun off her skin. She looked in the mirror and decided she needed a minimal amount of make-up, enough to make her look respectable and finally, she walked into the Director's secretary's office.

'He's expecting you, take a seat and I'm sure he won't be long.'

The red light flashed on the secretary's desk panel, she looked towards Anita. 'Impeccable timing don't you think? The Director will see you now.'

Anita stood up, with her papers and envelopes tucked under her arm, went and knocked lightly on the door.

'Come,' said a voice from within.

Anita closed the door behind her and came face to face with Sir Malcolm for the second time in her career.

'Ah... Anita, you don't mind me calling you by your first name do you? I like to keep things reasonably friendly. Do take a seat.'

He had not changed much she thought; his hair was thinning and turning grey but he looked fit and was still a handsome man. She could see what Kateryna saw in him.

'We've met before have we not?' He held her gaze.

'Yes, Sir, we have.'

'I seem to recall that one or two members of the Firm were concerned I was playing for the opposition. Well, as you can see, I would not be sitting here were that true, would I?' he said with a twinkle in his eye.

'No, Sir, I was simply following orders, keeping an eye on you and your visitor. I learned afterwards that you were working closely with the Director of the time.'

'Quite, anyway water under the bridge. So, what can I do for you. Your section chief said it was important that I see you. I've only been here a couple days so they must have prioritised you.'

'Yes, Sir, thank you for seeing me so promptly. I don't think you will regret it.'

'Oh,' he said, raising his right eyebrow in mild surprise.

'Sir, I have just returned from the Ukraine where I have held meetings regarding organised crime emanating from that country and its impact here. My opposite number in Kiev is Colonel Kateryna Pavlychko.' She paused to allow the significance of the name to sink in; his only reaction was for his right eyebrow to rise a little higher. 'Sir, I know about your daughter Katja and this is the main reason I have come to see you... '

Sir Malcolm Oakley's right eyebrow rose even higher but other than that he showed little emotion.

'Go on.'

Anita began to explain in detail the clandestine meeting at Kateryna's dacha and the significance of the material held in the two envelopes. The Director was very aware of the situation in the Ukrainian President's office, the corruption and the Russian involvement. He listened carefully to everything she said, nodding and clasping his hands, his elbows resting on his desk.

'How are Kateryna and Katja? I have never seen my daughter you know – what does she look like?'

'She looks like you Sir; you can tell she's your daughter. Colonel Pavlychko is well also, but she is worried for the safety of them both, that is why she has asked me to give you the envelopes. She said that you would know what to do in the event of any harm befalling them.'

He took a deep breath through his nose, compressing his lips in thought.

'Thank you for bringing me this, I will consider carefully what I need to do. You may leave.'

In an open plan office at GCHQ, the signals centre for the British Government, an RAF corporal signalman watched as an icon on his computer flashed, announcing an incoming signal. It was red.

'Sir, an urgent message has just come in from our embassy in Kiev.

'Thank you,' said his controller, 'email me the signal and I will take it from here.'

The corporal copied the signal across to his superior's workstation, who took note of the addressee and its security level before he encrypted the signal once more and transmitted it to another secluded room in the basement of the SIS building in

London and ten minutes later, there was a knock on Anita's office door.

'Come in.'

The signaller walked in, saluted and placed a slip of paper on her desk before he left without saying a word. She picked it up, noted the security classification and
began to read.

'Damn it,' she gasped, shocked that the thing Kateryna most feared had happened – and so soon. Her eyes flicked over the page as her mind raced, assessing the situation and trying to decide what she should do. She sat for a few minutes, thinking, it was quite simple: unknown assailants had kidnapped Katja and the finger of suspicion was pointing at the President's office. Why would he risk exposure? The papers she had delivered would, she guessed, be damning for him and, by association, the Republic of The Ukraine. Would he really risk that, was he mad? She picked up the telephone.

'Sir Malcolm, I need see you – urgently?'

The noise was not loud enough to drown out a conversation but there was definitely a party atmosphere in the Farm Club. Jane left her coat, alpine hat and mittens in the cloakroom and brushed back her hair with her hand. She looked in the mirror and wondered if she should reapply her make-up; just a little, she thought, not now though, perhaps later. She walked into the main area, full of noisy skiers and flashing lights. The music was a little too electronic for her taste. She made her way past the bright young things, and those not so bright, gyrating on the dance floor, went towards the long stone-sided bar and ordered a Martini. She took a sip of the drink and looked around; no sign of Markov and his friends. She felt a little self-conscious but she had been here many times on her own and soon found a seat where she could sit, unnoticed, and watch the dancers.

'Good evening, Jane.' It was Markov. 'So you decided to come?'

'I had nothing better to do and anyway, I know so little about the Ukraine that I'm sure this evening you will enlighten me.'

Markov flinched, that was an ungracious comment to start the evening off. Normally he would simply dump a woman who spoke to him like that or slap her across the face, but she was good looking enough for him to overlook it this time.

'Is a little noisy just here, shall we find a seat over there?'

'What about your friends, where are they?'

'There look, talking to those girls.'

'You seem to like the girls, you Ukrainians.'

'Ha, when they are as pretty as you, can you blame us?' He pulled out a seat for Jane.

'And a gentleman too I see.'

'Of course.'

She seemed to mellow somewhat, became a little more at ease and he wondered why. Perhaps he would find out later and for a while they sat talking and watching those on the dance floor until Markov stood up.

'We have not had dance, do you dance?'

'Why yes, I'd love a dance.'

For the next hour, they both talked and danced; small talk and Jane drank a little too much Martini and Markov watched her with interest. She was an intelligent woman, attractive but of no particular significance to him other than as a companion for the evening but she was English and that at least attracted him. He looked at his watch, how long until they made the trip to Amsterdam? Elena had called him twice more that day, once to inform him that they were almost ready to take the women across Poland and the other to say the President had called. 'Has he not got your mobile number, Markov?' Elena asked and he had told her that he was on vacation and would ring the President when he got back. If there was a real problem he was sure his sister would either cope or contact him so, please, let him enjoy his few days of skiing.

'It sounds important, Markov, you should call him.' Markov had tried but there was no answer and it had slipped from his mind. He just wanted to ski for two more days before he had to return home.

'It is getting late,' said Jane, 'I should be going, otherwise I will not get up in the morning and I want to try the Mont Fort run tomorrow.'

'Let me see you home then.'

'No, it's okay, I am only round the corner at the Nevaï.'

'What about tomorrow, can I treat you to dinner?'

'Yes, all right, that would be nice.'

'Eight o'clock. I will book a table at Le Rouge, they say they have a new French chef and his food is wonderful. I will pick you up from the Nevaï at seven.'

She stood and he kissed her on each cheek before she donned her warm outer clothing and walked the few metres to the hotel musing to herself. 'A date already, and with a handsome Ukrainian tycoon.' She was only here for a few days and she was beginning to have the good time she had promised herself, so what the hell.

Flight BA0726 touched down on time; Geneva airport had not changed much since the last time she was here – still one of the worst airports in the world. Anita struggled to retrieve her baggage and managed to push her way through the crowds of people arriving, leaving or just there to meet someone before she reached the glass doors to the outside world and saw what she was looking for – a smartly dressed man holding a placard with her name on it, Mrs Simms.

'Mr Rollins?' she enquired.

'Mrs Simms?'

'I was delayed in Luton, what a rush to get here,' she said, completing the phrase.

The driver from the British Embassy was convinced and held out his hand for her bag.

'This way, Madam,' he said and when they were away from prying ears, 'I am to drive you to Verbier where you are booked in as a Mrs Simms. I have a passport and papers in that name for you in the car.'

'Good.'

He opened the door for her and placed her bag in the boot. It had been a busy 24 hours for her since the second encrypted message had arrived from Kateryna. Anita knew nothing of her injuries but could imagine the stress she was under worrying about her daughter. Reading between the lines of the half-page message, she guessed Kateryna had had a showdown with her President, either by telephone or in person and Kateryna had not been idle in passing onto her some valuable information in a second, longer message.

She had a name, Markov Kalaman, a criminal who was not yet on the radar of most police forces in Western Europe but Kateryna certainly knew of him. Her department had been keeping an eye on him and men like him for some time, but when it came to arrests, higher officialdom always seemed to intervene. She had learned that it was likely that Markov's organisation had abducted Katja and that he was out of the country by now. She said that she hoped Anita and the British Secret Service might locate him and that he would lead them to Katja. She guessed that her daughter would still be alive, for the intention would not be to kill her. However, that might change – a strong hint to Sir Malcolm to help her and their daughter. Shaking her from her thoughts the driver said.

'Everything you should need is in there, passport, fictitious travel documents and a telephone number.' He reached into the glove compartment and passed her a large brown envelope. 'Should you need assistance, two of our people will be in Verbier for as long as you are, oh, and here is your gun. We are advised that you requested a Berretta Nano.'

'Thank you,' she said.

Her mind was racing, going over events of the past few hours and planning for the next. Since Sir Malcolm had become involved, things had moved rapidly; the extra power he wielded had begun to tell.

'Gentlemen, madam,' he had said at the briefing meeting. 'We are becoming a little worried about the situation in the Ukraine. Not only is there a strong Russian presence trying to influence events but a worrying political situation. The Ukrainian Government is keen to join the rest of Europe, but the

Russians still want them within their sphere of influence. In amongst all of this there is a group of young women activists who are attempting to disrupt their President's cosy relationship with the Russians – organised crime, prostitution and everything else that is rotten in that country. Recently, only four days ago, there were a series of arrests at a gathering outside the Parliament building and since then one of these young women has disappeared, we believe abducted on the President's orders. Normally the police would investigate but we believe that organised crime is involved and we, as an organisation, are being asked more and more to gather intelligence about the activities of these cross border criminals. Some Eastern European gangs are infiltrating friendly governments: look at the case in Israel, where it is known that a gang infiltrated the Government, their banks and even Mossad. We have to stop them and I believe that this case is part of that fight and a successful conclusion will lead us to other cells operating within our borders.' He made no mention of his connection to the kidnapped
girl, simply passing on information and authorising the operation. Because Anita had already set up a co-operation agreement with the Ukrainian Authorities and was one of the Service's best operatives, he had asked her to take charge. She had set to work immediately and armed with the names provided by Kateryna, had trawled through travel bookings and itineraries held on the Ukrainian State computers, proving within minutes the new agreement's worth. Markov and three fellow travellers were in Switzerland at the ski resort of Verbier, and now she was on her way to find him.

Anita dropped her bag on the bed, took a quick shower to freshen up, put on clean clothes and a little make-up, and went in search of Markov Kalaman. Pulling up her collar against the cold, she took out her smart phone, called up a GPS app, and keyed in co-ordinates from the piece of paper she had brought with her – a ski lodge on the outskirts of the town about a mile away from her hotel.

Advised to take warm ski clothing, she was pleased she had, glad the colours she was wearing were not nearly as loud as some she saw appearing inconspicuous and forgettable. Her breath floated freely about her in the cold late afternoon air, a white cloud of frozen droplets trailing her like a jet's exhaust she walked. She was acclimatising to the cold, invigorating air and occasionally glanced down at the GPS map on her smart phone. A signal appeared at the edge of the map flashing red and she zoomed in a little to identify the street names. Her target, Chemin des Vernes, was less than a kilometre away and what was this, she zoomed in some more, ah... cable car Médran, which should be easy to find. She slowed her pace and looked up to find her bearings and, sure enough, in the distance, she could see cable cars and pylons stretching up towards the ski slopes.

After less than a quarter of an hour, the flashing red indicator moved firmly into the centre of her phone's screen and then she saw it, an impressive three-storey wooden chalet with an overhanging roof, a balcony running the full length of the first floor. There were lights on inside and as she approached she saw two men appear on the balcony; still 50 metres away she was sure they had not seen her, but it would be foolish to let anyone connected with her target see her and recognise her later. She halted and moved into shadow, put her phone to her ear as if in conversation and watched from a distance until the men finally returned inside the building.

So, the chalet was occupied and she was 90 per cent certain she had the right one – but she needed to make absolutely certain. She pocketed the phone and looked round; a man and a woman were leaving the chalet opposite and further along the road a group of young people appeared from an apartment block. None seemed to notice her as they passed, a good sign, she thought. It was six o'clock and would not be dark for another two hours at least, so she could be visible to anyone who might come out onto the balcony. She needed to find cover for her surveillance but could see nothing but residential properties and it seemed difficult to loiter here without suspicion. Perhaps she could break in somewhere; that was a possibility if she could pull it off. She would only have one chance to survey the area from out in the open, one reasonable chance of walking past the suspect's chalet without drawing attention. Then she saw it, a for sale notice on a property not far from the Ukrainians' chalet, facing it from the opposite side of the street and it looked as if she would have a reasonable view of them from there. Quickly she slipped between two buildings and headed towards the one for sale, casting her eyes over every part of it, searching for an entry point. She had not formulated a plan of entry as she reached the gate and then some loud music started up from a nearby chalet making her jump.

'Dammit, girl, keep cool,' she said to herself. The noise had had made her look looked around and she noticed a small door at ground level, tucked into a corner, a boiler room or a rear access to the garage perhaps, fairly well concealed, ideal.

She looked around for one last time and, satisfied no one was watching, made her way through the gateway and moved towards the door. It looked secure and it had a Yale type lock – good, it was possible. She felt inside her trouser pocket for her wallet, pulled it out and thumbed through the credit cards; locating one seldom used, she set to work. Slipping it carefully between the door jam and the lock, she worked the door handle and within seconds, she was inside, the door shut behind her. Controlling her breathing, she remained there for several minutes, calming down and listening. The house was for sale and appeared unoccupied but there was still the chance that there was someone here. She strained her ears but apart from the muffled sound of music from the nearby chalet, there was nothing: not a sound.

It was dim in the house, the only light coming from the front and it was to there that she moved next, watchful, on guard. Still there was no sound; she moved noiselessly through the hallway, looking in the rooms one by one and saw dust covers over the furniture. Sighing with relief, she got to work. The first floor offered the best vantage point and provided she kept away from the windows, she should be safe enough and able to watch the targets. She reached inside her jacket and pulled out the digital camera with the enhanced sensor. She could take pictures from almost half a kilometre away with this baby and still a face could be blown up and made recognisable. There was a large chair in one of the rooms facing her subject's chalet, away from the window but with an excellent view and it was here she settled down to wait.

For an hour there was no movement until eventually, a man appeared on the balcony with a glass in his hand. She pointed her camera at him and took three shots in quick succession. He was looking towards her but not at her and she was sure she had good images; then another man appeared and she took more shots, and then again, with a third man, before they disappeared, and for a further 30 minutes, she waited for their reappearance.

'Where are they?' she wondered, and then suddenly the three of them walked past her vantage point. They must have left through another door out of sight and now she believed that she was in danger of losing them. But wait, where was the fourth man? She had to decide what to do, and quickly; should she wait to see if the fourth man appeared to follow them?

She decided that she would follow the three of them, and, pocketing the camera, she went to the back door and looked around for something to keep the door from jamming shut. She saw a waste bin and quickly rummaged through it, finding a discarded cereal packet and tearing off a corner, she slipped it between the lock and the jam ready for an easy entry should she return. Pulling the door closed behind her, she hurriedly walked towards the road, taking out the phone as she went to take pictures of the chalet and the surrounding area for future reference.

Markov was not in the chalet, he had left unnoticed whilst Anita was busying herself breaking in. He was on his way to meet Jane, his date for the evening. He reached the lobby of the Nevaï Hotel and found her by a window looking out towards the mountains.

'Good evening, are you planning tomorrow's skiing?'

'Markov, no, just admiring the view.'

'Shall we go, it's a bit of a walk but I'm sure you can manage.'

'I'm sure I can,' snorted Jane.

'Ha ha, I like girl with spirit. So tell me, what was the skiing like today for you? I was back up the Stairway again. I like the near vertical, off-piste runs up there.'

They walked together towards Le Rouge, exchanging views on the state of the snow and skiing in general and Jane was pleased eventually to enter the warmth of the restaurant and leave her outer garments in the cloakroom.

'Table for Mr Kalaman, certainly, Sir, if you will follow me please,' said the maître d'hôtel.

'Let me help you, Madam,' he said, pulling back her seat. 'Would Sir care for the champagne to be opened now?'

Markov nodded and pulled his chair forward, smiling broadly at Jane.

'I think you will enjoy this champagne, it is rather special.'

Jane could see that it was special, a Dom Perignon 'Ninety five, a good vintage, expensive too, 1,000 Swiss francs at a guess. If he had gone for a '96 she would have understood, they were a mere two or three hundred a bottle, expensive enough, but with the '95, she knew he was making a statement. She had seen it with Michael and his friends, showing off at bonus time, throwing money away as if it was going out of fashion

66

– nasty people when it came to the wire. Was this Markov a nasty person underneath his smooth veneer?

Anita was 200 metres back when she finally made it to the road and decided she would be as well keeping that distance. One of the men was unusually alert and regularly turned to look back. They were heading into the centre of town along the Rue de Ransou and Anita wondered if she could take a different route and catch up with them later. She took out her phone and scanned the GPS map, quickly computing their route and where it might take them and an alternative path she might take. There, she had it, turn next left and then right and she could take a parallel course to reach almost the same point in town, La Rouge restaurant by the look of it.

'What do you think of the duck?' asked Markov, as he cut into his steak.

'Very good, the sauce is delicious, and your steak?'

'Very, very good, tender, as rare as I like it. He is good chef. I must employ him one day,' he mused.

Jane looked up from her plate. Just how wealthy was this man? She had heard the traders talk of the Oligarchs, East European billionaires; she did not believe he was in that class, but during the conversation it seemed that money was no object. Then Markov looked up and waved his knife, Jane turned and saw three men and she recognised them.

'My friends are here, I told them I would be dining with you tonight and we might join them for a drink later.' Jane nodded a tacit approval but she was not keen on the idea of sitting in the company of four Ukrainians, three of whom might not even speak English.

Behind them, Anita noticed the brief communication as she ordered tonic water for herself and when it arrived, she melted into a corner of the bar to observe her quarry. So, this was the mysterious fourth man: but who was the woman with him? As she wondered how she might handle things, a stroke of luck presented itself when, from around the room, the sound system struck up the English version of *Happy Birthday* and from the corner of her eye she saw the swing door of the kitchen open. A waiter with a cake, topped with a ring of burning candles, appeared and like all good Brits the birthday crowd began singing the birthday song. She watched as some of them stood to take pictures with their digital cameras and mobile phones, flashes popped, there was a great deal of commotion and very soon Anita was in the thick of it, snapping away, congratulating everyone though not one of her pictures contained the birthday boy.

As things settled down she stood with her back to the wall, ostensibly watching the antics of the partygoers and, through their midst, Markov's henchmen. Across from them, at a table near the picture window, she took note of the man she believed to be Markov and the mysterious woman with him. However, she could do no more; it was too risky to remain here, more pictures were out of the question, but at least she had located Markov, found his residence in Verbier and obtained images of him.

Then it occurred to her: might Katja be in the chalet? No, that was highly unlikely. They would have had difficulty bringing her here and why would they? She decided to leave that idea and to pursue another line of investigation. She collected her ski jacket and went out onto the street and away from passers-by; she punched in a local number from the piece of paper given her by the Embassy driver; the phone hardly rang before a man's voice answered.

'This is Mrs Simms; I have an urgent message for Mr
Rollins.'

After a brief exchange, the line went dead and Anita began to walk slowly along the road towards a junction where a man asked her directions to her hotel.

'Mr Rollins?'

'Yes, Mrs Simms?'

She had made contact with the men from the Embassy and now it was time to hand the project over to them. The man escorted her in the direction of her hotel, but before they reached it, he turned down a side street and led her into a small chalet where she met his partner.

'I have some images of the suspect; can you send them securely to London?'

'Yes, Bluetooth them to my laptop and I will do it while
you two talk,' replied the first man.

'I have found where they are staying and broken into a chalet opposite. I got a good view of them. Can you bug their place and eavesdrop on them? There are pictures of the chalet in the Bluetooth stream to help you locate the building.'

'No problem, we'll get straight on to it.'

In La Rouge, the evening was ending; revellers had begun to disperse and Markov paid their bill and was helping Jane on with her thick ski jacket.

'I'll walk you back to your hotel, Jane, you will not mind if my friends accompany us? They are, er... are here anyway and we shall all be going back to our chalet.'

'No, don't worry about that, I will call a taxi, it's not far, I know, but I think that would be best.'

'I understand, thank you for a lovely evening, perhaps we might meet again someday?'

'I think the Ukraine is a little too far for me,' replied
Jane.

She was becoming a little uncomfortable in his company; all his talk of getting what he wanted, how he had the ear of people in positions of power, how they would help him made her feel she was back amongst the self-serving traders and bankers in London. She was conscious of being evasive and tried to moderate her comments; perhaps it was his three friends, tough and sinister looking; she did not want to antagonise them.

'I will be in Amsterdam in the middle of the month, if you would like to meet. I can show you the sights. I often go there on business and my contacts there take me to places the tourists never see. Here is number.'

Markov took a pen from his inside pocket and scribbled a telephone number onto a napkin he picked up from the nearest table.

'Amsterdam, are you into diamonds as well?'

'Not quite, I must be going, we have early flight tomorrow morning and I need to sleep.'

He took her hand, kissed it in an old-fashioned way, and with a cursory nod of the head to his men to follow him, walked towards the doorway leaving Jane alone.

Not far away Anita was returning to her hotel room to rest after having left the men from the Embassy to finish transmitting her photographs to London. She felt that she had made at least some progress in tracking down the whereabouts of Katja but there was still a way to go. She had discussed the situation as far as she could with Reg and Andrew and ordered them to set up a surveillance station in the chalet to keep an eye on the Ukrainians. Reg and Andrew said goodbye to her and once she had left, gathered their equipment.

'This isn't going to be a long job, Reg, I think a couple
of stand-alone listening devices should suffice.'

'We can set them up before we install the directional
sound amplifier in the chalet,' said Andrew.

'Good, I've finished sending. Give me just one more minute and I will check the batteries on these babies,' said Reg

He closed the lid on his lap top and opened the battery compartments on the tiny devices, checked the power levels and finally they were ready. They soon left their base dressed in warm ski apparel carrying miniaturised equipment and prints of the observation and target chalets in their pockets. The walk to, Des Vernes was not a long one and the streetlights reflecting off the snow made identification of the chalets easy. Although it was brighter than they would have liked, the moonlight made for an easy entry into the observation chalet. Slipping into the shadows at the rear of the property Reg found Anita's card between the lock and frame, pushed the door open and went inside, sprinting up the stairs gun in hand to clear the way for Andrew to set up the listening device and a high definition camera.

'All done Andy?'

'Yes, I'm happy.'

'Good, come on then.'

They slipped out into the street, covering the ground to the Ukrainians' chalet in quick time. Like Anita, they were skilled at breaking and entering; it was part of their job. Reg, the leading hand, was the most experienced and carried a small bunch of oddly shaped keys which, one by one, he inserted into the door lock. Twisting them this way and that he finally heard a faint click, gripped the handle and depressed it gently until the door opened and they were in. Next, he directed Andrew to the rooms to the rear of the chalet whilst he entered the one with the balcony to keep a lookout. Reg moved about silently, planting his listening devices and within five minutes, they were back outside and crossing the road.

'What time is it, Andrew?' asked Reg holding a pair binoculars to his eyes.

'Eleven thirty-five.'

'Hmm... wonder how long they will be? If they are partying it could be a long night for us. We had better start a watch system, one hour on, one hour off, starting at midnight, okay?'

'Yes fine,' replied Reg, fiddling with the fine control
on his listening device.

At midnight, Reg handed his binoculars to Andrew and sat back on the settee to rest his eyes whilst Andrew scanned the road for the Ukrainians. It was always the worst part of the job, waiting, and even when their subjects came within range of their equipment it could be equally as dull. Nevertheless, they were here for any snippet of information they could get; just one item could make it all worthwhile to the department. Folding his arms he settled down to wait and half an hour later his patience was rewarded by the sight of a group of four men approaching; they were spread out a little, but they were a group. He lifted the miniature night binoculars to his eyes and scanned their faces, matching them to the images the agent had supplied, and he felt sure that this was it.

'Reg,' whispered Andrew.

Reg was not asleep; you did not sleep in these situations – you simply rested your eyes and because Reg had undertaken dozens of such missions and knowing that they usually fell into the same pattern, he was instantly alert and came to kneel beside Andrew's chair

'There, look.' Andrew passed him the binoculars.

'I reckon that's them, all hands on deck,' he muttered. The four Ukrainians passed by on the street, entered their chalet and the lights came on. For half an hour, the two Secret Service men eavesdropped on their conversation and took pictures whenever they appeared at the window. Reg held one earpiece to listen in while he fine-tuned the receiver and made sure the conversations were being recorded whilst Andrew used the tablet to remotely focus the camera and take pictures.

'We will need to be leaving here at six o'clock in the morning,' said Markov. 'Let's not be too late. Bohuslav, he said to the newest of his employees, a man recommended to him, take a look round.'

It was not unknown for a rival gang to attempt sabotage: a small packet of drugs, a gun, anything incriminating slipped into their baggage and subsequently found during the airport screening process could cause untold damage to their organisation, especially if the Swiss police arrested Markov.

'The bags are clean, Markov,' said Bohuslav, returning.

'Where's Kostyantyn?'

'Still in the other room.'

The ever-vigilant Kostyantyn had found something and was investigating. He knew not to disturb the small device he had noticed sticking to the underside of the coffee table or to call out, even so, Andrew picked up the sound of his breathing and pulled off one of his earphones to whisper too Reg, 'Someone is pretty close to the microphone in the front bedroom.'

Alerted, Reg lifted the binoculars and scanned the room in the chalet opposite, but he was too late; Kostyantyn had realised what was going on and had rolled away from the eavesdropper's line of sight. Reg relaxed.

'It's okay, there is no one near the mic.'

They settled down once more to wait, Andrew listening and Reg lying on the settee; if there was a development he would be instantly on the job. Opposite them, Kostyantyn walked into the room where the others were sitting and nonchalantly tugged at Markov's sleeve as he passed. He poured himself a drink and walked back out of the room. Markov understood and his glance was enough to alert his men to watch their tongues. Kostyantyn poked his head round the door a few minutes later.

'Boss, I am running your bath for you.'

'Very good, I will be there when I finish my drink.'

After one final swallow, he placed the empty glass on the low table, the sound of glass on wood making Andrew jump, and rose to his feet to walk towards the bathroom where Kostyantyn was waiting for him. The two men stood very close together and, covered by the sound of the running water, Kostyantyn whispered into his ear.

'Boss, there is a listening device under the table in the sitting room and there must be more I think. It was not there when we left because I did my routine check. Someone is nearby listening to us.'

Markov felt cold, who was it? Which of his enemies had followed them to Switzerland? There were a few options: the gangs from Eastern Ukraine were a problem, trying to muscle in on his territory and the Russians, they were far more dangerous and resourceful, particularly his archenemy the Blue Russian, a man not unlike himself. He made a snap decision, the alcohol playing no small part in it, but he would probably have reached the same conclusion if he had been stone cold sober.

'Find them, find out who they are and kill them.'

Chapter 4

The flight back to London had been a difficult one for Anita; she had spent much of it looking out of the aircraft's window and reflecting on the events of the morning. When she had asked the two operatives to carry out the surveillance of Markov and his henchmen she had expected it to be a routine assignment. Rising early that morning she had breakfasted briefly, scanned an English newspaper and then attempted to telephone Reg for a briefing on the night's work. Unexpectedly, there had been no answer; she waited a few minutes before trying again – still no answer. The alarm bells began to ring, not loudly but enough to galvanise her into action. Hurriedly, she threw on her over garments and made her way to their chalet. Knocking softly on the door she had been surprised that there was no answer and presumed they were still carrying out the surveillance. She tried their mobile once again and still there was no answer. She had heard the ringing tone yet there was no sound coming from the room.

The alarm bells had begun to ring louder and she had felt decidedly uncomfortable, and hurrying to the surveillance chalet, she had found the rear door open. She tried Reg's number one more time and this time, heard a faint ringing from inside the building; now she was sure there was a problem. Feeling for her gun, she had flicked off the safety catch and gingerly entered through the swinging door, along the dim corridor and silently up the stairs. What she found still shocked and horrified her. It wasn't the first time she had seen dead bodies, it wasn't the first time she had experienced misfortune, but the two men were there on her orders and their deaths made her feel guilty. She had known that the Ukrainians were dangerous people but she had not expected to see what confronted in that room. When the announcement came to fasten seat belts she had promised herself there and then that she would exact retribution.

The Director took a personal interest in the case; it was his daughter and although he had never seen her, the desire to catch her abductors was suddenly stronger. Spread out in front of him on the polished oak desk the images relayed from Verbier left him with a grim expression on his face. Opposite sat an equally regretful Anita quietly bracing herself for the questions that would surely come.

'Sad that we should lose two good men. What exactly happened?'

Anita leaned forward a little.

'Sir, I contacted our personnel as agreed. I had limited equipment with me and I saw no point in risking the targets seeing me. I thought it more appropriate that our people observe them from a distance and try to collect some intelligence.'

She described in detail how she had gained access to the chalet close to the suspects and how she had photographed them, followed them and observed the one identified as Markov with an unknown woman. The logic seemed simple: all-night surveillance with high tech equipment without them suspecting that we were observing them, but the operation had gone wrong she told the Director. She had suspected something was amiss early the following morning, yesterday, and had gone in search of the two embassy staff, finally finding them with their throats cut and lying amongst the debris of the chalet living room. They had not died quietly.

'Before I left the chalet I took the images you have in front of you and then I called the Embassy for the clean- up squad. I met their car about an hour later and gave them their instructions before I caught the flight back to London. By the time I found the bodies the Ukrainians had left; whether they left because of the incident or they were leaving anyway, I don't know, but now they are aware that someone is watching them.'

'Who might they suspect, their own Government perhaps?'

'Quite possible Sir, our men had no identifying marks, standard procedure.'

'Mm...,' he paused. 'Hard to say who they might suspect, these people have many enemies. We are sure it is this this man Markov that has my daughter and now we have an idea of what he looks like. As I say, these people have many enemies, plenty within the criminal world as well as law enforcement agencies. The thugs with him are probably his bodyguards, there for protection. It can be easy money dealing in drugs and prostitution and it can create mayhem amongst competing organisations if they believe another outfit is moving in on their patch they will not stand idly by. Look at the Mexicans. For the bigger outfits the rewards are great and they let no one stand in their way. Okay, what to do? First let's find out who this woman is.'

The Director pushed an image of Markov and the woman to the fore.

'Then let us find out where Mr Markov Kalaman is holed up and try to predict his next move. Now the mess in Switzerland, through our own channels, we have informed the Swiss as to what has happened and they are releasing a concocted story about two Z-list celebrities taking a drugs overdose. They will keep it low key to avoid upsetting their precious hotel industry.'

'Markov, we have had an expert look at the device I took from under the table but he cannot say exactly where it came from or who specifically uses this type of equipment; anyone with the right connections can get hold of such devices. The two men died quickly without giving us any information but I checked their clothing before we left and the shirts and underwear were from a British chain store – the name was plain to see. My guess is that they were British intelligence,' Bohuslav advised.

'British Intelligence, that is a surprise, what would they want with us? We have not been near the British Isles.'

'Maybe not, but these days there is a lot of cross-border co-operation between police forces. Maybe they are working for some other country, maybe they just live in Britain but work for some other organisation that wants to bring us down.'

'Let me talk to one of my contacts, perhaps I can find something out. Find Vladimir will you, ask him to come and see me.'

This was puzzling, what if it were a Government agency, what could he do to protect his interests? There was a knock at the door and Vladimir walked in.

'You wanted to see me, Boss?'

'Yes, after that episode in Verbier I want things to happen a little quicker than we originally planned. When can we move the women?'

'We will have them all here this week and can send the minibus to Holland. One week from now, you take your profits, Boss. Vladimir shrugged his shoulders, 'Perhaps a little fun with them first though?' He half smiled; it was as much as he could ever manage.

'Mr President, this is Markov. I have a little problem.'

'What problem? I do not want to know about your problems. You did not return my calls last week and now it is I that have a problem.'

'Mr President, while I was in Switzerland I was spied on by the British Secret Service.'

He was uncertain as to who had actually been watching him but the British were favourites and maybe the President could shed some light on the matter; better still, he might be able to call off the British.

'The British Secret Service, don't be preposterous. You are too small a fish for them.'

The President's blood ran cold, Colonel Pavlychko was behind this, he was sure; he had moved too quickly in having her daughter abducted and now she was calling in favours but she had agreed to his proposal. Was she playing some other game?

'Markov, I know nothing of any British Secret Service, you are imagining things. Better that you should look towards your Russian enemies I think. Goodbye Markov.' He put the phone down, sweating, worried, things seemed to be going wrong already and it might indeed be the British Secret Service. That was a problem, the girl was somewhere with Markov's men

and as long as he moved her to Amsterdam the Foreign
Intelligence service could take care of things but her
mother had hard evidence against him and if she was
playing her own game then it was more prudent to look
to his own protection. For now,

Markov was on his own.

At the other end of the line, Markov looked into the
silent telephone and slowly replaced the receiver.
Could it be the Russians after all? He supposed the two
dead men could have been Russians, or even Poles,
living in England, plenty of them did. According to
Bohuslav, they had not heard them speak before the
fight and it was over too quickly for them to have said
much anyway; he would get one of his men to trawl the
internet for any news. Surely, he thought, the local
police would have been involved and maybe the local
newspapers in Switzerland would have run a story,
perhaps there would be a clue there.

Katja sat head in her hands, her eyes red with tears
and worry. She had no real idea where she was nor
who had abducted her and wondered why no one had
come to take her home. Her only contact with other
human beings was twice a day when a man brought her
meals of porridge or borscht and potato dumplings.
She slept on a well-worn mattress on the floor and if
she needed to use a toilet, she had to call out for
someone to escort her across the courtyard outside.
She was beginning to lose track of time, imprisoned, as
she was in the wooden shed alone with her thoughts.
Bundled into the boot of a car when they abducted her,
she had neither seen nor heard of anything that might
give her a clue as to where they had brought her. The
journey had seemed interminable, noisy and bumpy,

leaving her disorientated; and now they had incarcerated her in the windowless shed. Her only contact with the outside world was the short trips to the primitive toilet, a simple pit amongst the trees. She kept her head down in case of violence but had glimpsed distant mountains on occasion and guessed she was somewhere in the Carpathians. The Carpathians were to the west of The Ukraine and a long way from Kiev.

She knew that she was in a difficult position and saw little or no possibility of escape; her only hope was that her mother might find her. She had not realised that her mother was part of the Secret Service, and she had been very surprised when she had informed her that she was a high-ranking officer. She cast her mind over the events of the past week – was it a week? Her antics with the FEMEN movement were the cause of her troubles; her mother must have upset someone badly for things to turn out in such a way.

Not far away from Katja, in the larger of the sheds another young woman, Natalia, sat on the edge of her bunk flicking through a well-worn and out of date glossy magazine. She had been here more than a week; she had expected they would have left long before now and she was becoming concerned. She had made friends with some of the other women in the dormitory, all young like her and eager for work in the West. In the compound, they could move freely but if they felt the need for exercise, always at least two men would escort them in small groups beyond the perimeter. The men said it was because of the wild animals still roaming these parts and they would not be safe on their own.

'I heard that we will leave for Holland very soon,' said one girl. 'One of the guards likes me and when we are out walking he tells me things. He says that our transport is arranged, they are just waiting for one or two more women to arrive and then we leave.'

'That's good news; I'm getting fed up sitting here with nothing to do. What kind of work are you looking for?' asked Sveta.

'I want to be secretary. I study at the night school to work a computer. What about you?'

Sveta thought for a few moments. She had no real

skills; she could not expect to find work in an office.

'I don't know anything that earns lots of money. I can work in the fields or a restaurant. Elena said there is plenty of work in factories.'

'Ah, yes, Elena, she told me the same. Where did you meet her?'

'One day she came to the café where I worked and told me about work in countries where I could earn lots of money,'

'The same for me. I was working as waitress when she came to café.'

The two women talked for a while, swapping stories of their experiences, surprised at how similar they were, surprised that Elena had said exactly the same things to them both. They talked about their hometowns, poor backwaters, and of their aspirations until the door opened and Markov walked in. He stood at the threshold assessing the merits of each girl, deciding to which customer he would deliver them.

'Ladies, you will be pleased to know that your transport is arranged. It will be here the day after tomorrow. I hope you will all be very happy in Holland,' Markov added without a smile and leaving as quickly as he had appeared.

'There, you see I was right, we leave soon,' said the woman, beaming.

Markov closed the door behind him and nodded to the guard leaning discreetly on the fence outside before he walked back to the house where Vladimir was packing small bags of white powder into the lining of several suitcases. They would loan the suitcases to the women for the journey west, another aspect of their kindness.

'What do you want us to do with the one in solitary, Markov?'

'I haven't really thought about it yet. It will not be a good idea to send her with the rest of them; I do not want to upset them before we reach Amsterdam. She needs to travel separately, with us I think. We can drug her and take her in the Mercedes; we will be there in 16 hours if we do not stop much on the way. Send the rest of them in the minibus, you and I and Kostyantyn will take her in the car. I have spoken to Caas and he assures me that an Arab acquaintance of his will pay a good price for a blue eyed blonde girl.'

Typically bleak and wet British weather greeted Anita as she drove to work and after leaving her car in the underground car park she passed swiftly through security and made her way towards the offices on the top floor. After pressing the lift button several times she waited impatiently, glancing at her watch. She had an important meeting in less than ten minutes and she did not want to be late.

'The woman is British, her name is Jane Bennett and she lives in Woking,' said Anita, spreading the photographs she had taken of her across the table. 'She works for a large investment bank in the City, Head of

Human Resources. I can't believe she is mixed up with Markov.'

The Director's eyebrow raised a little, as it did when he disagreed with someone. He was not prone to argument, more a side step and an encircling movement until his point of view prevailed. He picked up one of the pictures taken in Verbier and studied it for a few moments

'So, she works for an investment bank. They deal in many things, move money around, commodities worldwide, and a perfect cover for money laundering so don't be too sure she isn't involved. Go and meet her, find out whose side she is on, see if you can use her. Any news of my daughter yet?'

'No, Sir, I'm afraid not, although I have heard from Colonel Pavlychko. She is convinced that Markov's organisation snatched her daughter and she has put a tail on them. Most of the things you might expect a criminal organisation to be involved in appear to be commonplace to our suspect. He brings drugs in from the East and ships them all across Western Europe, he is suspected of several armed robberies in the Ukraine and he is involved in people trafficking.'

'Now wouldn't you expect someone like that to require connections in the banking industry to help with money laundering? '

The Director looked at Anita to make his point and she nodded.

'You may be right, Sir; I personally do not think this woman is involved – her body language, the way she seemed to behave, but I will make sure.'

'Good, so this Markov is the prime suspect, he has

Katja you think.'

'I'm afraid it seems so, Sir, but we don't know where she is. There's a strong possibility they will try to smuggle her out of the Ukraine to somewhere in Europe or the Middle East and Kateryna believes it will be soon if they have not already done so.'

Anita did not want to say more, it was speculation; she needed more evidence before they could move in on Markov and his gang. Before she could say anything further the Director's phone rang. He picked it up and spoke briefly in monotones, which told Anita the meeting was over. She collected the photographs together and stood up. Sir Malcolm cupped his hand over the mouthpiece and said that she should pursue the case as she saw fit and to report daily to him.

Anita, looking thoughtful, left the Director and made her way back to her own office. So, they had established the mystery woman's identity, British and in banking and with no obvious connections to any criminal organisation; she did not have a criminal record, even her driving licence was clean. However, what if the Director was right and she was somehow involved with Markov. Anita looked out of the window at the rain and pondered. If she was involved, she had an idea how to change the woman's mind.

Three hundred kilometres to the north, the weather was not much better; the sky was overcast, the sea grey and foreboding. Roger shrugged his shoulders and turned away from the Yacht Club window towards some of his fellow yachtsmen sitting round a table.

'Looks like four boats are coming from Hartlepool this year, which makes it 20. Not as many as last year, but not too bad a turn out and I think that it should be a good race. As long as that bloody North Sea behaves itself,' he said, sitting down next to Neil.

'Aye,' said Neil, draining his glass, 'other beer lads?' Four empty glasses shot across the table towards him.

'Thought you would never ask,' replied John.

Neil grinned and gathered the glasses together to carry them to the bar for refills.

'You will be coming with us this year won't you, Paul?' asked Lee, the skipper of a yacht entered in the race.

'Of course, wouldn't miss it for the world.'

'Good, that means a full crew, so we had better start getting our act together; it's only two weeks to the race.

'Ay up Amsterdam, 'ere we come.'

Neil returned with the first two of the pint glasses to overhear the conversation turn to the boat and its seaworthiness for the trip. Each year the fleet of yachts from the Club made the voyage to Holland, a race that was the highlight of the Club's calendar and he wished he could go with them – but this year, unfortunately, work got in the way.

'I hope you've changed the oil and the filters, Lee. Remember last year, the rest of the fleet was going out for the start when you decided to change the filter,' said Roger.

The others laughed, Neil brought the last of the beer and together they ribbed Lee a little more. Each one of them had sailed the race several times on his 12 Metre yacht, a fine example of Swedish boat-building, a boat suited to the conditions in the North Sea: but Lee's maintenance programme was woeful and that worried them. Lee grinned; the banter was a large part of the fun of sailing and after downing the greater part of his glass of beer, he made an announcement.

'I have a surprise for you all. I have sold our house and we are moving to a smaller one. Sharon says she is fed up cleaning a five bedroomed mansion when there are only two of us living there now. Our eldest is working in Canada and the youngest only uses his room for a couple of weeks when he's home from University. Says that he plans to spend the summer working in a Kibbutz, so we will not see much of him this year.'

'Kibbutz?' exclaimed Roger, 'I didn't know you were

Jewish.'

'Jewish?' said John, 'I think he must be, have you seen how infrequently he buys a round?'

'Infrequently, that is a big word, what does it mean? I'm from Barnsley and we don't use big words like that,' grinned Lee broadly. For all his bravado, he was relieved they had finally committed to crewing his boat on the race. 'Let me finish, I said we have sold our house and I can afford a new set of sails so this year we should have a good chance of winning.'

'About time,' Roger laughed. 'I don't know how you ever expect to do well with those worn out ladies' knickers you call sails.'

Jane was puzzled. Who was this Mrs Simms she had to see so urgently? She had received a telephone call from one of the directors of the bank, no less, asking her to see a Mrs Simms and the woman was due at her office in a few minutes. She tidied up some papers on her desk, filing several away in the cabinet against the wall. The financial crisis had worked its way through the bank, costs had been cut, there had been redundancies; everyone believed the worst was over but nothing is ever that simple. The world was feeling the aftershocks, the bank had not cut deep enough and a department would have to close, and one of those sheets of paper contained the names of those who were to leave, willingly or not. It was with a grim satisfaction she had seen that Michael's name was on that list.

There was a knock at the door.

'Come in.'

A slim woman with dark hair and smartly dressed in a dark-brown business suit and carrying a briefcase appeared.

'Jane Bennett?' asked the woman.

'Yes, you must be Mrs Simms.'

Anita, smiled slightly, the name seemed to have stuck.

'Yes, pleased to meet you.'

'Take a seat, what can I do for you?'

Anita had decided on a full frontal attack. She needed to move quickly and shock tactics could well be the best way to reveal on which side of the fence Markov's lady friend sat. She flicked open her briefcase and pulled out a small leather wallet with a clear window to one side revealing her identity card and held it up for Jane to see.

Jane looked at it incredulously.

'Who are you?'

'I work for the, er... police; I can tell you no more than that at this stage. You have recently been skiing in Switzerland I believe.'

Jane's jaw dropped but she said nothing, she was not hiding anything, simply stunned. What did the police want with her and why was it important that she had been to Switzerland?

'You met a man there called Markov,' added Anita.

'Yes, I did.' So was this what it was all about, Markov?

'Do you know him very well?'

'No, I only met him skiing; we had dinner together one night.'

'We know that,' and Anita reached into her case to produce photographic evidence of that evening.

Jane's jaw dropped a little further.

'Where did you get those, who took them?' asked Jane.

'I took them.'

'Then you must have been in Verbier, in La Rouge. I didn't see you.'

'You were not supposed to see me; neither was your friend Markov.'

'He's not my friend, I hardly know him. One dinner date, that's all.' Jane was becoming a little alarmed and perplexed. What would a British police officer be doing taking pictures of her in Switzerland? Was she really police?

Anita saw her anxiety, speculating on the cause and she wondered if she did have something to hide, or was she genuinely shocked. She would find out soon enough.

'Look at these pictures.' Anita placed several images on the desk in front of Jane. 'These two men carried on the surveillance I was sent to initiate.'

Jane looked at the photographs, the dead men, their throats slit, the blood, and her eyes widened in disbelief. She held the back of her hand against her mouth in horror,
her eyes flicking back and forth over the gory detail.

'Did Markov do this?' Jane asked in a quiet, quivering voice. 'Was I so close to this?'

Anita was convinced. 'You had no knowledge of this, did you, and I think you are telling the truth. Tell me what you know about Markov, anything you can remember from your conversations.'

'Can we have a cup of tea? I really need something.'

'Yes, of course.'

Jane picked up the phone and asked for two cups of tea, replaced the receiver and looked at Anita. Anita returned her gaze and the two women sat reflectively until a few minutes later there was a knock on the door and the tea arrived.

'Milk, sugar?' asked Jane.

'Just milk please.'

They each picked up their cups and took a refreshing drink, the hot liquid working wonders for Jane as her mind raced to reconcile the facts newly presented to her.

'I didn't like the look of his friends. They seemed like bodyguards, thick set, tough looking.'

'They were his bodyguards, thugs, and they will have killed our men, not Markov. No, he will always make sure he is beyond the law, at least in his part of the world.'

'What do you mean?'

Anita ignored the question.

'What can you tell me about him? How does he make his money? Where is his base of operations? Anything you know about him we want to know.'

'He is from the Ukraine; he deals in commodities I believe.'

Hmm... thought Anita, commodities.

'Did he say what part of the Ukraine?'

'Not really. I know nothing of the country but he did mention the mountains once or twice. He liked to go hunting in the mountains he said.'

'Anything else? Did he say what he might be doing in the future?'

'Yes he did.'

Anita's ears pricked up.

'He said he was going to Amsterdam and maybe we could meet up again.'

'And will you, have you his telephone number?'

'I have no intention of ever seeing him again after what you have told me.'

'What I have told you is governed by the Official Secrets Act by the way. You must never divulge any details of this meeting to anyone,' Anita instructed.

'I understand, but who are you really? Your identity card did not mention police.'

'All in good time, but as far as not seeing Markov again, I wouldn't be too sure. We may need your help in the near future. We can't force you but you can get close to him and any help you give us will not be forgotten.'

'I... I... don't know, what would you want me to do?'

'Not a lot really, just help us find him. I am authorised to tell you a bit about the background to this operation. I believe your story and I think that you could be of great service to us.'

Anita finished her cup of tea and reached into her bag
for another small pack of photographs.

'This girl,' she said pushing a picture of Katja towards Jane,
'has been abducted by our friend Markov and his gang and we believe that... '

On the lower slopes of the Carpathian Mountains, Markov Kalaman's estate sat nestled out of sight on a small plateau, the fine house and newly constructed out buildings testament to his criminal activities. The crime boss was relaxing, sipping a glass of vodka, smoking one of his favourite Djarum Black cigarettes and looking out at the woodland in front of the house when Vladimir came to see him.

'Everything is arranged, Vladimir?'

'Yes, the minibus will be here in the morning. I have two of our men working the shift at the border crossing at the end of the M10. If there is a problem they should be able to smooth things over, maybe it will cost a few Hryvnia or Zlotys but it will be a price worth paying.'

'And the women?'

'They will be at the border crossing within a couple of hours after leaving here, with luck they will be in Poland before midday.'

'Good, good.'

Markov was happy to hear the news; at last, they were ready. Markov's men would move the women across the Polish and German borders and then to Holland the day after tomorrow and there he would get a good price for them and the drugs they were smuggling. He could expect, he guessed, maybe two million Ukrainian Hryvnia.

The yachtsmen of the north east of England were out in force, the weather had improved and, for once, the North Sea was looking inviting.

'Roger, get the spinnaker out, the wind's right for a hoist before we go back.'

Roger smiled at his skipper. He had always said that Lee's knowledge of sailing would fit on a postage stamp and his look seemed to convey that thought. Lee read his mind and laughed, he had heard it so many times before and, being a thick skinned Tyke, the insult simply bounced off him. The crew were working well together, they knew their jobs and after the morning's workout he felt pleased with their performance.

'Might win this year, particularly with these new sails,' Lee commented to Paul.

'Let's hope so Skip. Are you ready for'ard?' he shouted to Roger who had moved forward and was busy clipping lines to the downwind sail.

'Gimme me a minute.'

The crew took their positions ready to start pulling lines as soon as Lee gave the word. He looked towards the top of the mast, judged the wind direction, and as the boat came round a few degrees Roger gave the thumbs up and Lee gave the order to hoist sail. The crew began pulling on lines; the spinnaker came out of its bag a jumbled mess of coloured sailcloth and rapidly ascended into the sky. Paul and John hauled in their lines, setting it and with a muffled crack the jumbled mess turned into a thing of beauty.

'Roll in the foresail,' ordered Lee, 'let's see what she'll do.'

Sails were trimmed, eyes became fixated with the log, five knots, six, and seven and before long the boat was ploughing through the sea touching eight knots. For an hour they sailed parallel to the coast, the sails full and the white water spilling past until Lee finally called a halt.

'Look at that, eight point two knots. She is going well boys. At this rate, we could be in Holland before the pubs shut. Drop the sails and let's head back in for a beer. I reckon we can win this race.'

'You say that every year and look what happens,' said

Roger.

'What?'

'Last year we nearly finished up on the Dogger Bank and the year before I thought we were going to finish up in Harwich. That could have been useful though, we could have caught the ferry to Holland.'

Chapter 5

The border guards in Poland were often finicky and seemed more so than usual as Markov's car joined the long queue waiting to cross. The guards were meticulously searching each vehicle entering Poland and the line of vehicles had grown to at least a kilometre in length leaving Markov feeling uncomfortable. Behind the wheel, an impassive expression on his face, Vladimir stared out at the line of traffic in front of them and in the rear of the car, an equally expressionless Kostyantyn sat beside the sleeping Katja. Polish border guards were well known for being fussy and intrusive and would be poking their noses into the car at some stage and so they had drugged her to keep her quiet. At the crossing Markov had hoped that they would pass through without incident and the guards would not ask too many questions, but in front of them the queue stretched a long way and at the rate vehicles were passing through the checkpoint, half the day would be gone before it was their turn.

'Is there nothing we can do? Look at it, a snarl-up worse than I've ever seen.' Markov's patience was wearing thin but unknown to him the congestion was the result of a dispute between the border guards, unhappy with their hours, unhappy with their pay and unhappy with anything else they cared to mention, and the Polish authorities. They were working to a go slow to nudge their Government into conceding better pay and conditions and the result was the snarl-up of traffic.

'I have had enough of this,' growled Markov. 'Where are our men, Vladimir, where will I find them?'

Vladimir's face hardly changed but he felt like cautioning his boss against any rash move. The border guards could be a difficult lot if they were upset and they could use wide ranging powers of detention should they so wish.

'One moment, Boss.'

He took his mobile phone from his pocket and flicked through some numbers in the directory. He dialled one and listened for a few moments, made the connection and spoke for a few minutes with one of their men working temporarily as a guard and after he finished he placed his telephone on the dashboard and turned to Markov.

'He says be patient, Boss, he will have a talk with a superior and see if we can be given some priority.'

'I hope so! I do not want to spend the night here – I need to be in Amsterdam tomorrow to make arrangements before the women begin arriving.'

Vladimir's phone rang.

'Ja... ja... okay I tell him.'

He put the phone in his pocket and started the engine 'You will need some zlotys, Boss; there will be a couple of guards up ahead waving us into an inspection bay. We will jump the queue but they will need paying.'

Markov said nothing; it was the way of things. If it meant getting through and on their way sooner rather than later then he was very happy to oblige and as the car moved forward along the emergency lane, the sound of one or two angry horns greeted them. They crept along to the front of the queue until, sure enough, a guard waved them down and indicated that they should enter the green lane for an inspection. Vladimir obliged, bringing the car to a standstill in front of a Ukrainian border guard who he knew very well but declined to acknowledge for the moment. The man looked into the car and asked who was in charge.

'I am,' replied Markov. 'We have urgent business in
Holland and we need to pass through faster than this.

'It can be arranged. The price is 1,000 zloty. This is not for us you understand, but if you want to get through quicker we have to bribe the guards on the other side for it is they who are holding things up.'

Markov lifted out his wallet and took out the money. He had zlotys, euros and American dollars ready for just such an eventuality. He lived within a system of bribes and favours, saw no wrong in it. He would recoup his money elsewhere when someone else asked him to perform a favour for them. He passed the money through the open window and shrugged his shoulders, a small price to pay for not wanting the guards looking too closely. Not only were they abducting Katja but also hidden in the car in several secret compartments were 50 kilos of heroin, another million Hryvnia for him. Then the deal was done, the bribe paid, and they were speeding along the E40 towards Krakow and the German border. It would be another eight hours before they crossed into Germany; there they could simply drive through without even a showing of passports and on to the Netherlands.

On the E40, seventy kilometres further ahead, the minibus was making good progress and the women were becoming excited. The driver had passed a message back that they were nearing the German border and each one pressed her nose to the window to catch the first glimpse of the west they had heard so much about. As soon as the vehicle crossed the border, it became instantly apparent they were in a prosperous country. The roads were smoother, the buildings more attractive and there was no sign here of the Soviet debris that had surrounded them all their lives. They were heading towards that new life they had promised themselves. The dream was becoming reality.

'I wonder where we will stay in Holland,' Sveta asked the girl next to her, a good looking girl with Slavic features, light-haired, translucent blue eyes.

'I want stay in a hotel. I never stay in a hotel. Hot water for bath is what I dream of,' she said.

'Oh yes, that would be nice, a hot bath after that pig farm we have been in for the past ten days. You came only a few days ago didn't you?'

'Yes, I travel from Mazyr in Belarus. I come with two other girls. We save money for more than a year for guides to bring us over the border at night and now I am here for new life in West.'

'Where are your friends?' asked Sveta.

The girl became silent and looked down at her feet.

'We caught by border guards. My friends not pretty like me. I do what they want and they let me go but my friends I think are still in Belarus.'

The women stopped talking for a while, tired from the long journey and lulled by the drone of the engine they drifted into fitful sleep. Most of the passengers did the same, sleeping or looking out of the windows in silence, as the minibus ploughed its way across Germany.

The rain seemed as if it would never stop and Anita was glad she had brought her umbrella. The car park at GCHQ was enormous and she would have a walk of at least
100 metres before she could enter the doughnut shaped building looming in the distance. Passing the security post, she drove to the unsecured visitor's car park and left her car before running the gauntlet of the English weather towards the security kiosk.

'Good morning, Madam, may I see your pass?'

Anita handed him her security credentials whilst a second officer appeared with an electronic sensing device to sweep over her and her bag. He asked to see inside the bag and for a short time inspected the contents. Satisfied, he signalled to his partner to raise the barrier and Anita passed through to make her way towards the main reception area. Today she was meeting a cyber and communications specialist for some instruction on the use of a tracking device she would need in locating Markov's whereabouts.

Kateryna had been just as busy. She was recovering from her injuries and tracking Markov whenever she could but he was elusive. Using pay as you go mobile phones, regularly discarding them to avoid detection and, unknown to Kateryna, he now suspected the Ukrainian Secret Service of perpetrating the spying incident in Switzerland and had begun to take more care when contacting his business associates. He had learned that it was possible to trace a mobile phone but was a little taken aback to realise just how accurate the technique was, and he had become much more cautious.

Part of the reason was that Kateryna had overstepped her authority in her pursuit of Markov and his gang, detailing some of her subordinates to keep an eye on anyone she suspected who was connected to him. She was as certain as she could be that it was he who had abducted her daughter; becoming firmly convinced when she had obtained a photograph of Vladimir, the one who hit her when they took Katja, it was the President who had ordered the abduction. For his part, the President had soon realised his mistake and to make amends he had drip fed Kateryna small snippets of information, appearing to be working with her, helping her to locate her daughter. He had allowed her to discover Markov's base a dangerous but necessary ploy so early in his plans.

'I will show you a short introductory video, Madam,' said the communications officer. 'It will give you a general idea of how people operate with mobile phones these days and it will also give you an insight into what we can do about it. First, I need you to sign this paper to indicate which information we have given to you, and for your file. I'm sure you understand.'

'Of course, have you a pen?'

The video lasted no more than fifteen minutes and when it ended Anita quietly mulled over what she had learned. She knew that the possibility of tracking a mobile phone existed but was astounded to find that it was possible to track a mobile phone without recourse to the phone operator and further, that tracking is possible in real time with a statistical build-up of a user's movements over a specified time. A tool useful for proving where a target had been at a particular time and with the prediction software, equally possible to calculate, with reasonable accuracy, the future movements of a target. It also told her that when a Sim card was de-activated and then later re-activated, a signal would alert those watching. A technique developed to locate the whereabouts of mobile phone activated explosive devices.

'Are you happy so far?'

Anita nodded; things had certainly moved on since her last instruction only three or four years before. She expected that it would be difficult to locate Markov in Amsterdam, and had hoped the boffins could come up with something to help her. She may be lucky to come across him in the street, but she needed to be on his tail as quickly as possible, keep close and hope that he would lead her to Katja. The communications expert let her think for a few moments. He had dealt with her type many times, bright, intelligent people that got up to things he could only imagine; it was his job to give them the tools to make the job easier and safer, and he took that responsibility very seriously.

'I have laid on a small demonstration for you in the workshop. I thought I would show you some of the magic boxes we have come up with and I suggest that we have lunch after the demonstration and then I'll introduce you to a very clever chap who will tell you a little more.'

'Sounds good. I can see I have a lot to learn in a short time: lead on please.'

The rest of the morning was fascinating, Anita learned more about mobile telephony, tricks and dodges criminals and terrorists employed to avoid detection and, more importantly, they loaned her a small, tracking device that would work in the street.

After lunching in the canteen, her host took her to another part of the building and passing through more security, she entered a workshop area. The place had an almost tangible air of secrecy about it, rooms with benches, oscilloscopes and computers, filled with men and women in white coats moving about, quietly, purposefully.

'Let me demonstrate this little gem.' Her guide walked towards a small office. He beckoned Anita to follow and inside they found a young man busy typing instructions into a computer.

'May I introduce Albert, he is our top programmer.' Albert grinned and stood to shake Anita's hand.

'A man of few words, aren't you, Albert?' The young man nodded.

'But he has some brilliant ideas. He came to us from Cambridge where he worked on his doctorate. What he doesn't know about mobile phones and their inner workings is not worth knowing.'

Albert's grin grew broader.

'I am not completely mute,' Albert offered, 'but I have to admit I find it more satisfying talking to a computer than human beings. Well, some human beings.'

Anita liked him; he was obviously very bright and steeped in his work. A real live boffin, she thought.

'This lady is here to learn about tracking mobile phones. She has the highest clearance and is authorised to receive a copy of your latest software, Albert. If I leave her with you, can you show her how to use it and provide a copy for her laptop? You did bring your laptop, didn't you?' he asked Anita.

'Yes, it's in my bag.'

'Good, we will have to load the software; it has a self- destruct routine in case someone tampers with it. The security access is quite high and you will need to memorise some of what Albert tells you.'

'I understand.'

'I'll leave you here for a while. Call me when you are finished, Albert,' and then he left them alone.

'My software will work on any laptop running windows Vista and above. It's designed to track and extract information from multiple devices,' said Albert He closed the lid on the computer he had been working with, reached across his desk to another, smaller machine, and started it up. As it whirred into life, he opened the desk's side draw and lifted out a jumble of wires and several small devices. As the operating system loaded onto the computer, he began assembling wires and a mini- receiving aerial together with a USB stick and central hub that he plugged into a port on the laptop.

'There, we are just about ready for the demonstration. I will tell you the codes for entry; we write very little down in here. There is a copy in a safe somewhere but I do it all from memory – it is more secure that way.'

Anita hung onto to his every word; this young man was a serious boffin.

'The software interrogates as many as four mobile devices at once. I do not know if you will need that function but it is possible. Right, now technically speaking we can communicate with the operating system of the device and extract some or all of the information automatically. This is useful but sometimes it is not enough. Suspects will regularly delete data to avoid incrimination just in case the police apprehend them. Where my software really comes into its own is that we can bypass the operating system and extract old deleted data. The data may not be complete and may have been partially written over but there is always something useful in there and with the memories of mobiles becoming larger and larger the deleted data is often still in one piece. Are you following me so far?'

'Ye... s, I think so.'

'Good, we'll have a demonstration then.'

For the next three hours Albert and Anita ran the software through its paces, interrogating several mobile phones, each with a different operating system, and Anita gradually became familiar with its functions. She learned the codes for accessing the software and when Albert had shown her all he could, and was satisfied that she was able to use the software proficiently, he loaded her machine with a copy.

'This stuff has one of the highest classifications going.

Don't let it fall into the wrong hands,' warned Albert.

Anita assured him that she would not and when her instruction was finally complete, she shook hands with Albert and said goodbye and her escort from earlier in the day returned to guide her back through the security rings to the main reception. The day had gone, it was beginning to get dark and when she finally left GCHQ to return to London her head was swimming with the information she had taken in. The codes were difficult though, and as she sped back towards London, she ran through them repeatedly in her mind.

Bypassing the City of Apeldoorn, the minibus headed along the A1 towards Amsterdam, its passengers tired, but excited. Every road sign they passed now had the legend 'Amsterdam' in bold letters. They passed by smart industrial areas, canals with boats moored in front of pretty houses and here and there a windmill. It fuelled the women's feelings of exhilaration, they were nearing their journey's end and all of them hoped that this would be the beginning of a new life, a job with enough money left over to send home to aged parents.

'Look, the signpost says Amsterdam 50 km,' said Sveta.

'We should be there soon.'

The woman next to her, who Sveta now knew as Yana, looked wide-eyed out of the window, her hair dishevelled from the travelling and her escape over the border to the Ukraine. She must have been aware of this because she began to smooth her hair back with her hands and pulled her jacket sleeves to straighten them, but it was of little use.

'I will need some new clothes and a bath; perhaps I can borrow some money from someone. I will need to be better dressed if I am to get a good job.'

Sveta looked at her and felt some pity. 'I have some spare clothes in my bag you can borrow until you get a job.' The girl looked at her with thankful eyes. She had been through a lot to get this far and inside she was feeling the strain, feeling she might not be able to go on, but Sveta's kindness gave her just the lift she needed and her eyes brightened up.

'Thank you, Sveta; I will not forget your kindness.'

Driving through increasingly built-up areas, the minibus finally reached the outskirts of the City, turning off the motorway, heading for the south-eastern suburbs, winding its way along narrowing streets, past grim four and five-storey buildings before coming to a halt outside a rundown 1960s apartment block.

'Get your things you women and follow me,' instructed the driver, leading them to the entrance of the building.

The door opened and there waiting for them were two of Markov's men who walked past the women, keeping watch on them and anyone else out on the street. As the women entered the building other men eyed them. They were Dutch associates of Markov, men with more than a passing interest in the women. Their boss was paying good money for them; he wanted only fit women and girls who could carry out their new trade without difficulty.

'The blonde one, she looks good. I have her first,' said one.

The other man grinned, his eyes flitting across the faces and bosoms of the new arrivals, deciding which one he wanted first. It was always the same, the highlight of their working days.

'Follow them, they will take you to the apartment,' said a man in Russian.

One of the Dutchmen led the way up the stairs, the women trooping after him, clutching their meagre possessions, eventually reaching the top floor where the man unlocked the door to a flat. It was reasonably spacious, two bedrooms, a living room and a tiny kitchen, suitable for a small family but cramped for the women. The flat was too small for the six of them; surely some would be housed in another apartment?

'Where do we stay?' asked Sveta innocently.

'You all stay here,' Kostyantyn said.

Just then, the driver appeared and rolled out a sleeping
bag on the floor.

'Bohuslav, is Markov here? I want to know where I bring the next lot.'

'Markov will be here soon I think, just bring them here. These women will be elsewhere in three days' time. We will break them in and take them to their buyers.'

Sveta heard the tone of the conversation and her head whipped round. She did not understand the words but something in the tone did not feel right.

'You three in there and you three in there,' Bohuslav pointed to the two small bedrooms.

'What about a shower?' asked one of the women.

'You can shower in here,' and he opened the door to a small bathroom.

'Have you towels and shampoo?'

Bohuslav simply shrugged his shoulders, walked away and left the women to fend for themselves.

Later that evening four men arrived at the apartment. Cleaned up a little the women looked presentable, Kostyantyn had told them some people would come to offer them jobs and they should look their best. The first of these men looked over the women, who by now were becoming worried; all was not as it seemed and when the man fondled Sveta's breast she recoiled in horror. The man simply laughed and did it again. Sveta lifted her arms to protect herself and that is when reality dawned for the first time. The man struck her hard across her face sending her reeling against the wall.

'You have spirit,' he said in Dutch. 'I will have you first. Take her to the car and this one and this one,' he pointed to Yana and another of the girls.

It was bewildering for the women; they could not understand the language nor resist the violence. They were helpless and they knew it. One by one the chosen three were led away down the stairs and out to two cars waiting in the street. Sveta was bundled into the first car with two of the Dutchmen and the other two girls into the one behind with the remaining men. After a short journey of no more than a kilometre, they arrived at another rundown apartment block and the men ushered them inside.

'This is your home now,' said the leader in broken Russian, spoken well enough for Sveta to understand.

'You work for us now. You owe us 10,000 euros for your travel and keep; you will pay for rent and some clothes out of your earnings. First, you need to learn the trade. In there,' he indicated a small, darkened room. 'We see what you are like.'

He pushed her backwards through the open door until she fell on the small, hard bed and he stood over her.

'Yes, you are pretty; you will make us a lot of money. Take your clothes off.'

Sveta had understood some of the broken Russian he spoke, and when she tried to get up, he hit her across her face and began pulling off her clothes. She tried to resist and might have succeeded for a while if he had not called out to his accomplices. In the other room, Yana and Olenka heard everything and when it was their turn, they did not resist.

Across the City, in an expensive apartment on the first floor of a building in Damstraat, Markov was relaxing with a large glass of vodka, and watching television.

'Bohuslav has rung; he says they have collected the

first batch.'

Markov nodded.

'Very good, Vladimir, I will call Caas, I know he will be happy with these girls, they are perfect for the work, good figures and not bad looking. I am seeing him at the casino at 11. Keep an eye on the one in there while I am gone. She is a bit special and I want a good price for her.' In a small, locked and darkened room , Katja was slowly coming round. Bewildered and disorientated, she had no idea where she was, no idea what was happening to her.

Chapter 6

'Are you really sure this boat will make it to Holland?' Roger asked in his acerbic, invariably provocative, tone.

'If you had helped me when I asked you then you would see that this flying machine, tuned to perfection, will have no problem whatsoever in crossing the North Sea. This year we are going to win,' said Lee.

'You said that last year,' John chipped in.

'And the year before!' added Paul.

'Well if you lot pull your weight then we will win. Who wants a drink?' asked Lee, turning from the Yacht Club window overlooking the small harbour.

The start of the race was less than 24 hours away; the crews of the participating yachts were busy loading stores, fuel and carrying out last minute maintenance. Their work would go on right up until the time came to leave the harbour ready for the start of the race, and the crew of *Whistledown* were no different.

'Did you get an up to date chart?' asked Roger.

'Of course.'

'And Dutch charts, did you get the charts all the way up to Den Helder? If we're going to come home that way we'll need a chart to get through the channels.'

'Roger you do go on, of course I've got the charts and the chart plotter card is up to date too. Now I've a question for you.'

'What?'

'Last year you didn't do any washing up.'

111

'Well?'

'I hope you have been practising.'

'I helped my wife on Christmas Day!'

'Christmas Day,' laughed John, 'I think we'll be better off with paper plates and cups. Shall I get some, Skipper?'

Lee and the rest of his crew laughed, the mood was light and hopeful, just how he liked it and the forecast was reasonable. A westerly force four, expected to increase to a five during their first day at sea before swinging round to the southeast and dropping away..

'Weather looks good, we should be able to get the spinnaker flying, for a while at least, and it should be good in Holland all next week,' commented Lee.

It was the day of the race and by mid-day the last of the crews had arrived, stowing personal belongings on board each of the yachts in the few spaces left, and by late-afternoon most of the boats were ready. A large crowd appeared for the start, encouraged by the local radio station, and amidst a carnival atmosphere, the yachts left the sanctuary of the harbour ready to begin the race.

'Have you seen this boat, Skipper?' called John, sitting with his feet dangling over the side.

'Got him,' said Lee, turning the wheel a few degrees to avoid a collision.

'Ease the mainsail a little, Roger.'

'What do you think I'm doing?'

Lee grinned; it instilled confidence when the crew knew what to do without him having to tell them. It took some of the pressure off him and allowed him to concentrate more on the tactics of the race. In the distance, a horn blurted out a signal.

'Ten minute gun,' said John.

'Heard it,' said Lee, glancing down at his watch. The race would begin in ten minutes and he would need to manoeuvre his boat into a good position to cross the start line. He must judge it perfectly: too early, then he would have to come back and start again; too late, and the fleet would leave them behind. For the next few minutes, yachts criss-crossed each other's paths, until eventually they were within a few seconds of the start and, almost as one, like a formation dancing team, the yachts turned for the start line.

As the boats vied for position, the word 'Starboard!' floated across the water more than once. A rule of the road, establishing the right of way of one boat over another, and then, too soon for some, too late for others, the starting horn blared out. Some did start too soon and had to turn back to restart, losing valuable time, but Lee, heart beating madly, was elated to find that he had timed it just right and they were the third boat over the line.

'Next stop Holland,' he muttered to himself.

'Next stop Holland,' said Paul.

The second sunrise saw clear air and a flat sea with a steady breeze blowing from the west and *Whistledown* was making good progress with her spinnaker flying.

'I can see the chimneys at Ijmuiden,' shouted John, sitting with his back to the mast, enjoying the first rays of the early morning sun.

It had been an uneventful crossing; the wind had never risen above 18 knots, steady three or four knots below that for much of the previous 30 hours of the race. They had flown the spinnaker right from the start and for much of the first night, only dropping it when

113

the wind changed direction and made it impossible for them to hold their course, but during the previous afternoon the wind had changed back and they had hoisted that colourful sail again.

'We've made good time,' said Lee, sitting hunched over the cramped chart table, plotting their position. 'You can tell John that what he can see are the windmills of the new wind farm. We have a bit further to go yet before he can have a beer.'

Roger heard him and laughed aloud. He was standing astride the wheel steering the boat and glanced at his watch before hurling abuse at his friend sunning himself.

'Come on big boy, your turn on the helm I'm off watch now and I'm going below to catch an hour's kip.'

John grabbed a line fastened to the mast and hauled himself to his feet, reached for the guard rail and made his way unsteadily back towards the steering position.

'How's it looking Roger?' Lee asked as Roger passed by on his way to an empty bunk.

'No problem, she's sailing well and I haven't seen any other yachts apart from a Dutchman heading out. There's a couple of tankers moored up over there,' he said, pointing into the distance. 'Give me a shout in an hour; I don't want to miss the run in.'

'No chance of that, we will all need to be on deck when we cross the finishing line. No other yachts eh... that's good, we might be first?'

'Might be.'

The yacht passed through the harbour entrance, the crew began the task of dropping sails and setting out the inflatable fenders to protect the hull when they finally moored up and ten minutes later, each crewmember had a can of beer in his hand and a tired looking smile on his face.

'Are we stopping here tonight, Skipper?' asked Paul, dropping his bag on deck. 'I'm off for a shower and want to know what clothes to take to change into.'

'You've only got T-shirts. What's special about a different rig here or in Amsterdam?' exclaimed Roger.

Paul said nothing, simply grinned, his point made. They wore nothing else but T-shirts and jeans on these trips.

'Ha ha,' laughed Lee who saw the funny side, 'I would put your second best T-shirt on Paul, because after a beer in the Yacht Club we'll head straight for the flesh pots.'

'That's the most sensible thing you've said so far this trip,' said Roger.

It was only a brief respite in the Marina, a shower and a change of clothes and then they were on their way again, up the North Sea canal to Amsterdam. The sun was shining on a warm spring day and the boat ploughed effortlessly through the water, pennants flying from the shrouds and damp towels hanging over the safety rails. Each crewmember found a space on deck to relax and with the ubiquitous can of beer in hand dreamed of a night out in Amsterdam and Lee, tired and red faced from exposure to the elements smiled with satisfaction as he steered his boat along the canal.

The day spent at GCHQ had been an exceptionally long, Anita had not returned to her flat until well after midnight, and her head was still spinning when she left for work only a few hours later. Still feeling tired and with bleary eyes, she walked along the corridor towards the Director's office. Stopping outside the door, to take a deep breath she straightened her hair with her free hand and walked in.

'You sent for me, Sir?'

'Yes, the case of the girl abducted from Kiev, er... my daughter. There has been a development. It appears that our man Markov is in Amsterdam and is busy offloading women to the underworld there. We are not sure if Katja is with him, but Colonel Pavlychko has sent a signal indicating that there is a strong possibility that she is.' He paused.

'I have not told you this before and you must be wondering why I am allotting resources to what must seem a personal matter.'

'It's not for me to say, Sir.'

'Quite, but I feel that if you know a few facts you might feel more comfortable with the case. First, Colonel Pavlychko has worked with us for many years, she provided useful information about the Russians before the Wall came down and subsequently, when the Soviet Union became fragmented, she kept an eye on developments in the Ukraine for us. Their system of government, as I am sure you are aware, is corrupt and volatile. Further, we are concerned that the Russians are having an undue influence in the Ukraine. They want to extend the lease for their Black Sea Fleet in the naval base of Novorossiysk, an agreement that will run for 25 years at least, and we are aware the Ukrainians are conducting joint naval exercises with the Russians. That is worrying us. The Ukraine has been talking of becoming a member of NATO, which is upsetting the Russians, and the Ukrainians are working with the European Union on trade matters that will cause other problems with their neighbour.'

'There is more. The Samara oil field in western Siberia pumps its oil west through the Druzhba pipeline in the Ukraine and there are rumours the Russians want to extend it to the German port of Wilhelmshaven. Already there have been problems between Russia and the Ukrainians over the pipeline and the disputes have led to the shutting down of both oil and gas supplies heading west. It has become a serious strategic problem for us. We have become too dependent on these supplies.'

Anita shifted in her chair, her brow slightly furrowed.

'You're wondering what this has to do with my daughter aren't you.'

'Yes Sir. I understand the importance of what you have told me but I admit I haven't made a connection.'

'As I have already said Colonel Pavlychko works for us and has done for many years. I'm telling you this because you have clearance. Obviously this information is classified but I feel you should know, in case you thought you were on a rogue mission.'

'Thank you for that, Sir.'

'Colonel Pavlychko has her ear to the ground; she knows what the leaders of the Ukraine are thinking, she can tell us accurately where the Russian Ukrainian relationship is going at an early stage, which gives us a chance to counter any moves we feel are against our interest and she has asked for help. How the devil she didn't know what Katja was up to with her student friends I do not know.'

'I expect Katja did not know what her mother's job was, Sir.'

'I think you are right. You know even these FEMEN girls are useful to us. They are a thorn in their

President's side and they certainly drew the media's attention with their antics. That in itself is useful because there is no real opposition group in the country, no one to make the leadership stop and think before it's too late. I had a meeting with the Prime Minister, told him everything, and put forward a case for finding Katja and getting her out. He has agreed we should do it but we cannot tell the Dutch for fear of security breaches.'

'I see, Sir, and you want me to follow up my investigation?'

'I do and I want you to recruit the woman our friend Markov was entertaining in Verbier. She has been close to him and might flush him out and if she does you will be waiting.'

Anita left the meeting with Sir Malcolm in thoughtful mood. He was asking a lot of her – and what about the woman, Jane Bennett, would she really be up to it, would she help? They could not force her but Anita felt that during her brief meeting with Jane she had demonstrated to her what kind of man Markov really was, a dangerous, murderous criminal. It had worked; Jane's reaction had been one of horror and revulsion when she saw the pictures of the two dead agents. She would speak to her, try to recruit her and if she declined to help she would use a dose of gentle persuasion to bring her round. Closing her office door, she walked to her desk and picked up her bag, took out the mobile phone.

'Jane this is Mrs Simms... '

The flight from London City to Schiphol took a little under an hour and the two women sitting together spoke only occasionally to each other. Anita had spoken briefly on the telephone to Jane and they had agreed to meet later that day when Anita had been able to explain as much as she could about the plan for locating Katja. They did not have much to go on apart from the telephone number on the napkin and Jane's memory of the man they were looking for. Anita had taken several photographs of Markov, the quality was reasonable but the low light and her distance from him had caused some blurring. She had not dared to look at him directly for fear of arousing suspicion, but Jane had been in his company for several hours and would have a much better chance of picking him out in a crowd.

After the meeting with Jane, Anita had spoken with the travel department to arrange the trip and later had visited the armoury to discuss firearms. There was no way she could carry a gun on the aircraft: she would have absolutely no chance of getting through airport security unchallenged, and so someone from the embassy in the Netherlands would drop a gun off at her hotel shortly after their arrival. Her mobile tracking device was taken from her and returned later that day in the guise of an MP3 player complete with miniature headphones and was not expected to arouse suspicion. Arriving at Schiphol, they took a taxi from the airport straight to the hotel just off Dam Square down the side of Nieuwe Kerk, a short walk from the Red Light district, an obvious starting point.

'Mrs Simms and Mrs Jones,' announced Anita and the receptionist looked at her list, ticking off their names.

'Here are your room keys, number 314 for Mrs Simms and 315. The rooms are on the fourth floor. You can take the lift over there.'

Anita and Jane picked up their bags and walked to the lift.

'Are you all right, Jane?'

'I'm fine, a little apprehensive that's all.'

'Understand this, you are only to confirm Markov's identity. Once we have him in our sights I will take over and you can go and enjoy the sights and sounds of Amsterdam.'

Jane looked at the ground as the lift came to a stop, she did not believe that for one moment.

'Ah, fourth floor, come on, let us freshen up and then we will have a look round. I will give you a knock in half an hour.'

They reached the doors to their rooms and went inside; in room 314, a small package lay on the bed addressed to Mrs Simms. Anita quickly opened it and took the nine- millimetre Berretta Nano out of its protective packet. She held it in her hand, testing its weight and feel and, satisfied, she slipped it into her handbag alongside the MP3 player before casting off her clothes and stepping into the shower.

She finished drying herself and dressed casually in a white blouse and black slacks, took the gun from her bag and slipped it into a small, concealed pocket stitched into her slacks, slipped on her lightweight jacket and left the room.

'I expect we will get a lot of looks if we walk through the Red Light district together and I guess we'll be accosted if we walk alone, so let's find a tourist group and tag along with them.'

'As long as they're not Japanese,' said Jane.

'Japanese?'

'We'll be even more conspicuous amongst Japanese tourists.'

Anita smiled; an obvious joke, but she had not seen it. Her mind was working on another task and wondering where she should start.

The yacht was making steady progress in the warm sunshine, the city of Amsterdam beginning to show in the distance and from below John called out 'Skipper.'

'What?'

'I'm making a cuppa, do you want one?'

'I think I'll stick to a can of beer. It's not wise to mix your drinks you know.'

'Typical.'

The crew were feeling tired after the crossing but excited at the prospect of a night out in Amsterdam. Each of them sitting untidily about the yacht, a can of beer in hand and enjoying the sunshine as the boat nosed its way along the canal.

'Hot news, all of you,' said Roger. 'I've just got a text from the Vice Commodore.'

'Oh... and?' said Lee apprehensively.

'We've won! All the boats are in and the handicaps have been worked out. We've won.'

A cheer went up from the other three; not only were they going to have a night out amongst the flesh pots of Amsterdam but they would have bragging rights amongst the fleet.

'So, we beat those flying machines from Hartlepool, Roger.'

'We certainly did, and you, Skipper, are a star. In fact you have been elevated to the status of a god and as such you can buy all our beer tonight.'

The laughter grew louder, Amsterdam came nearer and by mid-afternoon, they were in sight of the Central

Station and the ferries criss-crossing the river. Time was running out: soon the marinas in the centre of the City would be almost full; it would be a squeeze, but usually they could find a berth of one sort or another.

'I hope we're not up against a big expensive German boat again. Remember last year when that Junker kept chipping at us to move our fenders in case we spoiled his Gin Palace. I bet he has never been any further than Amsterdam. Eh...a caravan on water that's what it was,' said Paul.

'Some caravan, probably cost half a million,' John piped up from below deck, as he watched progress through the small window sited above the chart table.

'Have you seen that barge?' said the ever vigilant
Roger.

'I have now; get ready with the fenders and lines, boys.'

Roger looked at his skipper disdainfully. Did he not have a line ready beside him; was he not the one watching out for river traffic whilst all the others were already partying? It was always the same.

In the City, Anita and Jane were walking slowly along Damrak amongst the crowds of early season tourists. As a tram rumbled past them Anita looked across the road at the glass covered river boats waiting to take passengers on a sightseeing tour of the city's canals and beyond them, she knew, was the Red light district.

'I think all we can do to start with is look around here and see what we can find,' said Anita. 'You can try Markov's number to see if we can locate him. We are fairly sure that they will have brought Katja here to work as a prostitute and she may be in a window by now, though I doubt it. They sometimes have private brothels where they keep the new girls until they can be trusted. Markov's number is our best bet to try and locate him I think.'

'Do you want me to call him now?' asked Jane.

'Not yet, let's have a walk round first and get the lie of the land. If you do manage to contact him you need a plausible story so let's dream something up, why you are here. I don't think it's a good idea for him to think that you are here just to see him. I've told you about Katja, this is her.' said Anita fishing a small photograph from her jacket pocket. 'We'll look in the windows as we go and maybe find a café or bar with a vantage point from where we can ring Markov.'

Jane took the photograph and looked into the flat blue eyes. She was a strikingly pretty girl but so young, too young to be mixed up in all this. She passed the picture back to Anita and for half an hour, the two women walked the streets of Amsterdam making their way towards the Red Light district. They walked down narrow streets and alleyways, looking discreetly at the windows with the scantily clad girls plying their trades. Sex boutiques, bars and shops piled high with pizza slices and other unhealthy delicacies for the tourists completed the scene. Ahead of them, the first of the canals running through the district barred their way and they had to walk along the canal side. Anita looked at the windows as they passed, into the small cramped rooms the girls used and wondered if Katja was already in one. She searched the faces staring out at them, black, brown, various shades of white, each with sad lonely eyes, but Katja was not one of them.

'Look over that bridge, that place has a good view of the street, the Old Sailor, that will do,' said Anita, leading Jane towards its open door.

Katja became fully awake as the effects of the drugs began wearing off. Never again would she trust food or drink given to her by her captors. For a few hours, they had left her to her own devices, her lone guard watching television and barring her path to the door of the apartment. She was famished: she had not eaten a proper meal in two days but still she would not touch the pizza the guard had given her. She rummaged through the cupboards and the fridge in the tiny kitchen of the apartment where she found several tins of tomatoes and one of German sausages. There was a packet of dried pasta, it would have to do, a person as hungry as her would eat almost anything – except that pizza.

She had been a virgin when they had taken her, but no longer. Two men, unknown to her, had come to the flat the previous evening to look her over, to see what her potential might be. She was still a little groggy and at first tried to resist but she was no match for them and from somewhere deep inside her she summoned the mental strength to survive the ordeal, letting her body go limp, closing her eyes and trying to think of anything except what she was enduring.

Since they had abducted her, she had lost track of time, not even knowing where she was and struggled to understand what was happening to her. She was worried about her mother; the last time Katja had seen her she was lying unconscious on the floor of their dacha and she had no idea whether or not her mother was still alive. She spooned her concoction onto a plate and wolfed it down, finishing just as she heard a knock at the door. Her guard jumped to his feet and looked into the kitchen to make sure she was still there before he went to open the door.

'We have come for the girl,' said a Ukrainian voice. 'We are to take her to the flat on Damstraat.'

Katja heard them and prepared herself; picking up a kitchen knife, she stood behind the table and waited. The door opened and she faced the man who had sat in the back of the car with her during the journey from Ukraine.

'Put that down. I don't want to hurt you but if you don't then I will hit you,' he said.

Katja's heart rate picked up, yet she was defiant. He took a pace towards her and she lifted the knife. It was a futile gesture – she was still weak from her ordeal and within seconds he had disarmed her, slapped her hard across her face and sent her reeling backwards. Her head hit a cupboard and for a few moments stars flashed in front of her eyes before her senses returned and she found herself in an iron grip.

'We'll have no more of this or you will be hurt... badly,' he snarled at her. The other man and the guard, attracted by the commotion, came to the doorway and laughed at the sight of Kostyantyn forcibly removing Katja. These men liked violence, particularly against people less able to defend themselves.

'Here, take her arm,' said Kostyantyn to his friend. To Katja he said: 'No more of this, we are taking you to another flat and we go through the streets. Do not struggle, do not try to escape or you feel this.'

He squeezed her arm so tightly that she screamed out in pain. He had made his point: she could not escape their clutches, but she was working on it.

Eager to leave the marina for a night in Amsterdam the crew of *Whistledown* were busy tidying lines and making sure they had secured the sail cover. Below decks, Lee was finishing his chores; Roger picked up a plastic bag containing the day's waste and started to walk towards the gate.

'Come on, Lee, stop messing about,' said John.

'Just a moment, I have to make sure the gas and electric are off,' said a voice from below.

Showered, with neatly brushed hair and weathered red faces, the crew were impatient to be on their way.

'It doesn't take that long, are you sure you're not sending a text to someone?' called out Roger.

Lee quickly pressed the send button on his phone, stuffed it in his pocket and scrambled out of the hatch. His wife would be none too pleased if he did not keep her fully informed of his whereabouts, but he feared more than that, the embarrassment and ribbing he would receive from his crew if they knew.

'How many euros are you taking with you?' he asked, trying to shift the conversation onto a more equitable subject.

'Forty,' said Paul.

'Same here,' said John.

'Ah... good that is what I have brought with me.'

'You'll need more than that, Skipper. Gods might be able to make wine out of water but you're only a beginner and will have to pay for it,' jibed Roger.

They all laughed and in high spirits left the boat and the marina to walk the few hundred metres towards the ferry that would take them across the river to the heart of the City.

Anita and Jane walked slowly along the canal side towards the Old Sailor, through the groups of tourists gawping at the girls in the windows, attracted by the fluorescent lights highlighting their skin and scanty white underwear. Anita walked in first, pushing gently past some drunken youths and ordered two orange drinks from the broody looking barman. Some of the clientèle were ready for pastures new and as they left Anita pointed Jane towards seats just vacated by the window. It was a good position, the view through the open window made it possible to see both ways along the canal. Anita took out her MP3 player and earphones, holding one close to her ear.

'Let's have a go. Try the number he gave you and let's see if we get a response.'

Jane pressed the call button on her mobile phone and waited – nothing, simply a continuous tone. Perhaps the number Markov had given her was no longer in use.

'No answer.'

'Hmm… we'll try again later. It could be that it's switched off or maybe he's dumped that phone.'

Anita was annoyed but not surprised; her visit to GCHQ had prepared her for such an eventuality. They would have to simply keep looking and hope something would turn up that would lead them to Markov.

'Would you like another orange juice?' Jane could see Anita's mind working and thought it best to leave her alone for a minute or two.

Anita nodded and looked out of the open window and across the canal, at the windows opposite where the girls waited for passing trade. Further along the street, in another window, two girls were chatting animatedly to each other, oblivious to the staring eyes of the tourists. The girls she could see were Caucasian; they had passed coloured and black girls in the side streets but here, in the centre of the district, they were all white and that told her that they were probably looking in the right place. The few minutes' peace Jane had afforded her had been priceless; she could see clearly that the City was too big for the two of them to patrol effectively but here, she felt that they were probably not far from Katja and Markov.

'Are you ladies using all these seats?' asked a voice from behind.

Anita and Jane turned from the window to see four men with beers in their hands. The bar was busy, seats were scarce and only a few of them free.

'Er... no, help yourselves,' said Anita.

Jane sat back in her seat, inviting one of the men to take the seat next to her and soon a group of happy sailors surrounded them.

'My name's Roger, this is Lee, John and Paul, are you two on holiday?'

Anita did not really want to become engaged in conversation in case she missed something but it was useful cover to be with a group.

'I'm Anne and this is Susan, we are having a few days looking round Amsterdam, yes.'

'And where do you two ladies hail from, you sound as if you are from the South?' said John.

'And you all sound as if you are from the North,' replied Jane with a grin, happier at some light relief.

'Does it show?' asked Lee in his thick, Yorkshire accent.

'Just a little.'

'So whereabouts are you from?' persisted John.

'London,' Anita stepped in, not wanting to go into detail. To a Northerner, London was London, most had no idea of how large and diverse the conurbation was. To them Slough, Guildford and Luton were all London.

'So what brings you here?' asked Jane.

'We are on a yacht, a wonderful, sleek and handsome yacht just like the skipper here,' said Roger, twisting his fist and pointing with his thumb towards Lee who grinned broadly as he never failed to do when he became the centre of attention, or after too much beer when he was incapable of any other expression. Anita was beginning to feel a little uncomfortable; she wanted Jane to try Markov's number again fairly soon but she could not do much with an audience. Jane though, was resourceful and had become attuned to the situation; she looked Anita in the eye and tried to call the number without prompting. Still nothing but she knew Anita would want her to keep trying.

'Maybe you have a poor signal,' said Paul. 'I tried ringing the UK from here a few minutes ago and couldn't get through either.'

'Yes, that must be it.'

'More beer, lads?' asked John rising from his seat.

'Aye lad.'

'Yes please.'

Roger simply pushed his glass across the table and wondered why John had needed to ask.

Katja's feet hardly touched the ground as she was frog marched through streets teeming with tourists. They had not drugged her this time and her faculties were in full working order; she let her head droop a little in submission but all the time her eyes flicked here and there, as she tried to work out where she was. She heard people speaking as they passed, not recognising any language except English. English was fast becoming the language of young Ukrainians who avidly craved American and British pop music, watched any Hollywood film they could. She must be in the West, she thought; the shops were full and the people well dressed, but where?

They reached Dam Square complete with its tourists, performers and pigeons. She saw two men in uniform and wondered if they were police officers. Could she call out to them for help? Would they help her, or were Western police as corrupt as those back in The Ukraine? She had no time to decide. Kostyantyn nudged them down a side street and away from the crowds, aware that they looked a little out of place and he did not want to draw too much attention. Katja noted a large square building, the hotel Krasnapolsky, but it meant nothing to her and as they carried on for a few more metres, she tried to remember if she had seen the name before. Then they took her away from the square, Dam Square she read on a street sign before threading their way amongst cramped back streets until they came to the rear of a tall building where Kostyantyn banged on a weathered door.

After a short wait, it opened and in they went in, up a flight of narrow stairs and into a grubby room with a worn settee and several chairs. A television almost filled one wall and sitting in front of it Markov and Vladimir were watching a football game. Markov, a half consumed cup of coffee in his hand, glanced briefly at the intrusion before turning back to the game. Kostyantyn and the other man pushed Katja through a door opposite and into a tiny room, locking her in and leaving her alone once more with her thoughts

Chapter 7

The sailors were enjoying themselves at last, consuming large quantities of alcohol chattering incessantly and the company of two good-looking women certainly helped. Jane was particularly good at small talk, laughing at the men's silly jokes and generally enjoying herself. However, for Anita it was different, for her it was a dangerous game of cat and mouse and she hoped that she was the cat and that her mouse would soon appear. She scanned the street looking for a man that she had seen only briefly and was not at all sure she would recognize Mr Kalaman if she saw him again, hoping that Jane would.

'Why do you keep looking out of the window?' asked
Roger.

'I'm fascinated by this City and all these people passing
by. Do you find it interesting?'

It was a searching question leaving Roger a little bemused; the men were obviously drawn by the attractions in the windows but he felt shy in talking about it to a woman he had only just met.

'Very interesting,' he said, changing the subject, 'there's more to Holland than this. Amsterdam is great for a while but you ought to see the little ports around the Ijsselmeer.'

'Ijsselmeer, what's that?' asked Jane.

'It's the stretch of water to the north; the Dutch have built dykes across and are reclaiming the land where they can. We are going there next and spend a few days travelling along its edge until we reach Den Helder in the north and then head back home,' said Lee.

'Sounds nice,' said Anita her attention moving from the street to the conversation. Her task was to locate Markov and from there to find the girl Katja, but she had no plan to rescue the girl if they did find her. Sir Malcolm had said that they would cross that bridge when they came to it, but he did not want to involve the Dutch Authorities unless he had to, and using British Special Forces was not an option in a friendly country. No, he had said, locate them and monitor them, let me know what is going on and I will make a decision on what to do.

'Where do you keep your yacht over here?' asked Anita.

'Sixhaven – it is just across the river from the Central Station.'

'How big is it?'

'Ten metres,' Lee puffed out his chest, obviously proud of his possession, 'come and have a drink on board, we're here tonight and most of tomorrow, you're very welcome.' Anita smiled at him and turned to look out of the open window again, thinking that perhaps it was time they moved on, find another bar or café on the far side of the canal or even somewhere on Damrak, a much busier thoroughfare.

'Thank you for your offer, Lee, but we do not have a lot of time. We are going somewhere else right now.' Anita gave Jane a knowing look. 'Are you ready, Susan?'

Jane stood up ready to leave the bar but before they could, each of the sailors insisted on shaking the women's hands.

'Nice to meet you too,' said Jane, a parting shot to the last of them as she followed Anita out into the street.

Anita was beginning to feel a little anxious; things had not developed as she had hoped. It was always going to be difficult to spot her target in the street; they would have to be lucky more than anything, or the device she was carrying had to work.

'Let's try Markov again.'

Jane tried the call button once more, but still the phone was not in use.

'We'll go to Damrak and find a café with a vantage
point and see what turns up.'

Jane nodded and slipped her phone back into her bag. They walked the few hundred yards from the Red Light district and out onto the busy thoroughfare of Damrak with its teeming crowds of tourists, vehicles and clumsy, noisy trams. They crossed the busy road and walked back towards Dam Square, Jane window-shopping whilst Anita looked at almost every person in the street, searching for a lead of some sort.

'How about here?' asked Jane as they passed a small coffee shop with just a few tables under a wide canopy. 'Yes, this will do for a while.'

They sat at the table and waited to be served, Jane fiddling with something in her bag whilst Anita looked up and down the street. What were they doing, she asked herself. The main thrust of her plan was to make contact with Markov via his mobile phone, failing that she planned to do exactly what they were doing now, keep an eye on the likely places anyone doing business in the Red Light district would more than likely be, but it was becoming a daunting task.

The football match was ending. As with most friendly matches, it had not been overly exciting The Dutch team was one of the best in the world and had proved it on several occasions, with skilful players who could control a game against lesser opposition, conserve energy, avoid injury and collect a large fee for the privilege. Their opponents, on the other hand, were no less skilful on the ball but were less adept at the more refined stratagems of the game. Their best player, Andriy Yarmolenko, had managed to salvage a goal in the dying minutes of the game but the Dutch still beat the Ukrainian team by a couple of goals and it was with disgust that Markov turned off the television and kicked the leg of the sofa.

'How can they expect to be top of the qualifying table with performances like that? They have to beat Poland in their World Cup qualifier if they are going to Brazil. Blokhi will not last long as manager if they don't.'

Vladimir shrugged his shoulders. He preferred boxing to football but if his boss decreed he should watch football then he would watch football.

'The girl, Boss, what do you want us to do with the girl?'

'Caas says he can sell her to an Arab from Bahrain who is here on the lookout for girls. She is young and pretty and has a good figure but she will need some cleaning up I think before we introduce her to a potential buyer. I will ring Caas and ask what he suggests. Make some more coffee Vladimir,' ordered Markov.

Vladimir turned his dark opaque eyes towards one of their men sat by the door, raised his hand and clicked his fingers. The man jumped and went towards the kitchen; it was as much as Vladimir would do to make anyone a cup of coffee. Markov hardly noticed and stood by the window of the second-floor apartment to look down at the crowds shuffling between Dam Square and the entertainment across the bridge.

He put his hand in his pocket and took out a mobile phone, the one he used outside of his home country and switched it on. After a few seconds, it beeped several times and Markov inspected its messages. There was a missed call from Caas – he must ring him immediately, but there was also two missed calls from a surprising source. Jane, the woman he had met in Verbier, what was she doing ringing him? They had exchanged numbers, ostensibly to arrange a dinner date and he had invited her to the Ukraine, but he had not really expected to hear from her again.

'Caas, sorry I missed your call, I was watching your countrymen thrash my countrymen.'

He listened to the reply and forced a laugh to placate his business associate, the contact who introduced him to a lot of money on his visits to Amsterdam. They talked for a minute longer, eventually discussing Katja's fate, arranging her possible delivery to the Arab who could make her disappear forever. He finished the call and looked at his phone slightly puzzled. Jane, where was she, was she in Amsterdam? He recalled telling her in conversation over dinner that he often visited the City and smiled as he remembered her expression when she had believed that he dealt in diamonds. If she were in town, he would complete his business and take her to dinner, perpetuate the myth of dealing in diamonds and then, who knows? He chuckled to himself as he rang the number.

Not far away, on Damrak, sitting outside the café, Jane and Anita sat and watched the world go by until the shrill tone of Jane's mobile phone caused them both to freeze.

'It's him,' said Jane examining the screen.

'Let it ring twice more,' said Anita, diving into her bag and pulling out the MP3 player and by the time Jane pressed the answer button the device was live and searching.

'Hello, Markov, yes, this is Jane. You remember me; we met skiing in Verbier last month. I am in Amsterdam for a few days and remember you saying you were often here so I thought, on the off chance...'

'Ah, Jane, the lady with the winning smiles and the fast skis. How are you, my dear? Yes I am in Amsterdam for two more days.'

Jane swallowed hard and carried on. 'I thought you might show me a few diamonds, I was thinking that I might invest in a few uncut diamonds for my retirement.'

'Ha, your retirement, you are much too young to be thinking of retirement,' he flattered, unable to restrain himself at the thought of a good-looking woman.

'Perhaps we could have dinner, not tonight I'm afraid, but tomorrow, how about tomorrow, say 7.30. Where shall I pick you up from?'

Jane thought quickly, she realised that it would not be a good idea to reveal the identity of the hotel they were staying at and managed to blurt out: 'How about the bar in the Krasnapolsky on Dam Square?'

'Perfect, it is only a short walk for me. I will book a table at one of the best restaurants in Amsterdam and then maybe you would like to visit the casino?'

'That sounds wonderful.' Jane took a sideways look at Anita. 'Until tomorrow then.'

'Until tomorrow.' Anita's complexion faded somewhat as her adrenal gland began to work overtime. She had a signal, a strong signal and the street map on the device showed a small flashing circle not 200 metres from where they were sitting.

'Damstraat, just round the corner. Hmm... I think for a while we should part company. I will find out where he is. He may be on the move or he may be in a building somewhere, the altitude showing here is above street level so I am guessing he is somewhere in a building on Damstraat. Go back to the hotel and wait for me there. I'll call you if I need your help, otherwise I will meet you at the hotel.'

Jane nodded her understanding and left to walk back towards the hotel and Anita quickly crossed the street to make her way across Dam Square towards Damstraat. She smiled wryly as she crossed the square and spotted the diamond exchange. Jane should get Markov to take her there, she thought and then glanced down at the screen to see the circle cease flashing and then it disappeared. He had turned off his phone. Damn. In a flash she memorised the position of the circle, he was probably somewhere towards the far end of the street, but she was still unsure as to from which side of the street the signal had come. She gritted her teeth in frustration, she was so near and yet, it seemed, so far away. She slowed her pace and looked the direction of the windows of the upper storeys of the tightly packed buildings, searching for anything that might indicate Markov's whereabouts, but she could see nothing. Walking past the street café on the corner, she threaded her way through a crowd of tourists and carried on along Damstraat, past a shop selling pizzas. She had not eaten for quite a while and with a piece of pizza in her hand she could loiter without drawing too much attention.

'Just a small slice of that one,' she said.'

The young assistant reached over to scoop up her selection whilst Anita glanced out of the shop window, looking for anything, and there, across the street, she saw a face she vaguely recognised. Vladimir was just leaving a building opposite. She did not know his name but she thought she recognised those dark menacing eyes from Verbier. Was he the thug who had murdered the two men from the Embassy?

'Three euros.'

She watched as he closed the door and began walking along the street.

'Three euros.'

'Oh... yes, here you are,' her hand fumbled in her purse for the money.

She left the coins on the counter top, took the pizza slice from the assistant and, as she left, dropped it in the waste bin outside; she had become more interested in searching the street for the Ukrainian than food. There he was 20 metres in front of her, a big powerful man, one she would do well to avoid but she wanted to know where he was going – perhaps he would lead her to Katja. But what if he did, what would she do, what *could* she do? Her first task would be to inform Sir Malcolm, so that he could decide how they would rescue Katja. But he was in London and from experience, she knew that events could rapidly overtake her.

She looked at her watch. It was half past six, the day was disappearing fast but at least she had an idea where Markov was, and with some luck she might soon discover Katja's whereabouts too. She saw that Vladimir had reached the end of the street and was crossing over the bridge, turning left and heading for the Red Light district. She had better keep well back, not raising any suspicion, but the evening crowds were starting to build up and there was a chance that she might lose him but the road was familiar; she had walked this way earlier in the day. She needed some cover: a lone woman in such a place was not a good idea and up ahead she saw a group of tourists with a guide, perfect. Within a short space of time, she had joined the group and caught up on the Ukrainian, but he was outpacing the group and it would not be long before he was too far in front and again she might lose him.

A group of four or five girls appeared from a side street a short distance ahead of her, noisy youngsters obviously out for an evening's fun, so she left the tourists to tag along behind the girls. They were almost keeping up with Vladimir but as soon as she caught up with the group, he turned down a side street past the windows of more scantily clad women and she had to halt in case he turned and saw her. Half way along the street Vladimir did stop and did look around before he knocked on a door that soon opened and he disappeared inside. She began to feel vulnerable, she

140

was not in a place she where could loiter in safety and looked around for a more appealing place to carry on her surveillance.

There was a sex shop a few doors down and, with some embarrassment, she stopped and gazed in the window, seeing not the array of strange rubbery implements and the stacks of predominantly flesh coloured media covers but the reflection of the building opposite. Thankfully, her ordeal did not last long before Vladimir reappeared with men and between them; they held fast a sullen looking young woman. She waited for them to pass before following at a discreet distance, watching as the trio carried on up the street, turning first along a narrow street of shops and bars running parallel with the canal until, perhaps 200 metres further on, they came to a dark, wooden-fronted bar and went inside.

Another sex shop was her only alternative and for maybe ten minutes, she window-shopped. This time the two men reappeared empty handed and retraced their steps, coming uncomfortably close to her. She felt their eyes on the back of her head and prepared herself for the worst but they passed her by. She decided that perhaps it would be foolhardy to follow them anymore, for even if they did not recognise her face no self-respecting criminal would fail to remember her clothing and realise that she was following them. She needed to go back to the hotel and change.

Ten minutes later Anita reached the hotel and after retrieving her room key, almost ran up the stairs to their rooms. The first thing she did was to tap gently on Jane's door.

'Jane, it's me Anita.' The key turned in the lock and Anita was face to face with Jane.

'I've found Markov, at least I believe I have, and I think I have an idea of what is going on. They keep women prisoners in a safe house before they force them into prostitution and it looks as if they are using the upper floors of a bar on this street here, Kloveniersburgwal I think it's called.' Anita pointed to the street on the MP3 player screen.

'And what about Katja, do you know where she is?

'No, not yet. We're going to go and have a look for her but first I need to change my appearance and you need to as well in case we bump into Markov and his cronies.' Both Jane and Anita set to work applying a little well placed make-up and donning nondescript clothing making them appear dull and insignificant. Flat-heeled shoes, browns and dark-greens from their limited wardrobe, and soon they were back on the street heading
for Damstraat.

'Are you hungry, Jane?'

'Starving, I've had nothing since breakfast.'

'Go in there and get us both a piece of pizza. We can eat and keep a lookout at the same time.'

Jane obliged whilst Anita looked in a shop window to survey the reflection of the building opposite in more detail. There was some movement on the second floor, the curtains twitched and a face peered out. Was that Markov, she wondered? Her memory of him was fleeting, her clandestine photograph the only record she had of his features and then the face withdrew. She looked at the other windows and there, two or three metres to the right, another window, another face, sad and gaunt. There was no mistaking the owner this time. Anita was sure it was Katja, her blonde hair down to her shoulders and those steely blue eyes – it was Katja, she was sure. Her heart leapt and she slowly turned round to get a better view, to confirm her suspicions, and looked up straight into Katja's eyes. Katja recoiled visibly, and then waved. Anita could not afford for an observer in the apartment to notice her, but how could she communicate with the girl?

Katja looked down at the woman opposite, puzzled. Wasn't she the one who had come to her mother's house the night she was abducted, a British woman, a colleague of her mother's, someone who moved in the mysterious world she now knew her own mother inhabited? She waved frantically but the woman turned away, as if she had not seen her, nor recognised her, and yet she knew that she had.

She stopped waving and watched as another woman came from the shop opposite and passed her a paper bag. No, she silently screamed, they were walking away; they were leaving her to her fate. Katja felt deflated. Where there had been a glimmer of hope, she felt hollow, empty and alone. Then the two women below crossed to Katja's side of the street and walked slowly along the row of shops looking into the windows as if they were simply tourists. She pressed her face to the window to catch one last sight of them – and then Anita turned and looked straight at her again. She had recognised her! She was a friend and suddenly Katja understood. Markov was a dangerous man, his men were unfeeling thugs, and women were no match for them. Were these women the ones she had expected would contact her?

From the door came the sound of a key being turned and Katja quickly lay on the bed as if asleep, her mind buzzing with excitement – and fear.

'You come with us now,' said a man's gruff voice and then she felt a hand on her arm, on the bruises making her wince.

'Here, put on this coat, you are going to a new home.'

The man released his grip and Katja did as she was told, slipping the garment over her grubby slacks and jumper. He beckoned her to follow him and they left the bedroom, crossing into the living room where she saw Markov hunched over a laptop. Two of his henchmen sat around reading boys' comics and on the television, some sort of quiz show with the volume muted.

'Take her to the flat; get her cleaned up before Caas brings the Arab to have a look at her.' Markov did not even bother looking up from his computer.

'Okay, Boss. Here, give me a hand with this one,' said Kostyantyn to one of the men.

Between the two of them, they escorted Katja down the steep narrow staircase and out into the street, each keeping a tight grip on her underarm. Further along that same street, Anita and Jane stopped to look in yet another souvenir shop and finish the last of their pizza slices.

'You are quiet, Anita.'

'Yes, I think we have made the breakthrough. I am sure I have seen Katja. I think she is being held in that apartment there, above the ground floor with the newspaper over the windows, the narrow building,' she said, resisting the urge to point.

'Oh, I think I see it. Look someone is coming out,'
said Jane.

Incredulously Anita saw that it was Katja, held between two of Markov's henchmen and heading towards them.

'Quick, down here!'

Anita pulled Jane towards a row of bicycles parked on the bridge over the canal and stood amongst them. Anita placed her hands on the handlebars of the bicycle nearest to her as if it belonged to her and the two of them looked down at the canal, their features hidden from passers-by.

'I'm sure they haven't noticed us. Come on, we will follow them at a safe distance. I have an inkling where they might be going,' said Anita after they had passed.

For ten minutes, they followed the trio, across the canal, down the street towards the Red Light district, through back streets to the same bar Anita had seen Vladimir enter earlier. She was convinced that this was where they housed the prostitutes, close to their work and in a building easily policed by them.

'What do we do now?'

'I need to report to my control, you can return to the hotel and wait for me there if you want to.'

'What, and leave you on your own. I'll stick around for a while if you don't mind.'

Anita looked Jane in the eye, finding a new respect for her. She was tougher than she looked and Anita would be glad of her company but they must keep out of trouble. Jane would be no match for these thugs; at least she had a gun and knew how to use it.

'Let's go to the bar we were in earlier and have a drink whilst I text a short report to my boss and think about what to do.'

Anita turned towards the side street running back towards the canal but before they had gone more than five metres, Jane, walking behind Anita, let out a howl of indignation. Anita instinctively spun around, a small motorbike had come up on them from behind, and the pillion passenger was getting ready to make a lunge at her bag, the one containing the MP3 player. It was a big mistake.

The motorbike drew level, the pillion passenger caught hold of the strap of her bag and tried to wrench it from her shoulder and he would have succeeded if Anita had not run alongside the machine. She held onto the strap and with her free hand grabbed at the peak of the driver's helmet forcing his head violently back and making him lose control. Still keeping pace Anita smartly side stepped as the machine twisted towards her and then she pulled the driver to the ground. His accomplice managed to jump off the bike intact, releasing his grip on her strap, and came at her in a rage, arms outstretched attempting to grab her by the neck, but she was too quick for him. She held her forearm stiff and vertical, and with a swift sideways movement, deflecting his charge, and in that same movement, grabbed hold of his collar to use the man's own momentum to send him flying into the murky waters of the canal. Meanwhile his partner in crime had recovered his senses, and very quickly decided that he did not wish to tangle anymore with this woman and abandoning the motorbike, ran as fast as he could back the way they had come.

'Bloody 'ell,' said a surprised voice as Anita looked up, eyes flashing, ready for further trouble.

'That were some show,' said Lee.

'Are you ladies all right?' asked Roger.

It was the men from the yacht, out once more to experience the sights and sounds of Amsterdam, but not expecting quite such excitement as that they had just witnessed.

'Perfectly all right thank you,' replied Anita.

Jane stood a short distance away looking on with amazement, John and Paul likewise. Roger stood with his hands on his hips a frown on his forehead. He had thought there was something a little odd about these two. Now they had changed their appearances. The dark-haired one always seemed distant, as if there was something on her mind and when he sat with them earlier in the day he had noticed her constantly watching from the open window of the bar. Now this, she was an expert in self-defence. He had never seen anything like it, even in his time with the Leeds Metropolitan Police service and he watched, with some admiration for her, as the pillion passenger hauled himself out of the canal and onto the far bank.

'Anne, what are you two up to? I was a police officer for 20 years and I have seen surveillance teams in action. You look to me as if that is what you are up to and after that performance I see you are one formidable lady,' said Roger as they followed the rest of the group.

Anita snapped out of her thoughts. This was an unwelcome development.

'We are simply having a few days in Amsterdam on holiday – what makes you think anything else? That little incident was nothing, I practise a bit of judo – as a sport, it keeps me fit.'

The two of them began to fall back a little further behind the others and Roger pressed on with his enquiry.

'The technique you used was not self-defence, it was offence. You could have easily killed that man. What are you doing here in Amsterdam, can we help?'

'I will let you know. If you will excuse us we have to return to our hotel.'

'We can escort you ladies.'

'Er...that will not be necessary thank you.'

Chapter 8

Anita's MP3 player lit up: Markov was making a call. Hurriedly she retrieved the earpiece from her pocket, plugged it into the machine and tried to listen in to his conversation. He was speaking in English, she might have understood what he was saying in Russian but still she had to screw her eyes in concentration to understand everything he said.

'Caas, we have the girl in the apartment above the bar on Nieuwmarkt.'

'Good, I will tell our friend the Sheik and call you back once I have contacted him. I will arrange a time for him to view the goods.'

The line went dead but Anita had overheard enough. The machine the boffin at GCHQ had devised was living up to expectations. For the time they were communicating with each other the machine was automatically extracting information from the memories of the two mobile phones so if nothing else, she had obtained some useful intelligence. From what she had heard it seemed that a Dutchman named Caas was Markov's contact in the Netherlands so she would try to monitor his mobile phone also. Who was the Sheik, she wondered – a real sheik or was it simply a nickname?

The screen had shown that Markov was still in the apartment just a few metres along the street and Anita decided that they should hang about the area for a while, meander back and forth to see what they could turn up. For a short time, they wandered round Dam

Square amongst the tourists feeding the pigeons and watching the street performers, but Anita's attention was elsewhere as she concentrated on the tracking device. After the Square, they returned to Damstraat and Jane found a shop window full of fine porcelain to look at while Anita decided what to do next.

It had become clear that Markov was in the habit of switching his mobile phone off for short periods and was proving more elusive than Anita had hoped. It was good security on his part but Caas, on the other hand, was less inclined to cover his tracks and Anita watched a flashing circle on the tiny screen as she observed his movements in the City. He must be in a car somewhere because the flashing circle was moving at quite rapid speeds on occasion and Anita could see that he was well away from the area she was keeping under observation. He had mentioned the Sheik, could it be that he was with this person, could they be meeting Markov later. He had said the Sheik would view the goods. The hairs stood up on the back of Anita's neck and a chill ran down her spine as she made the connection – they were selling Katja to an Arab.

Jane was still engrossed with the shop window, particularly a Japanese porcelain figure of a woman dressed in a long white silk gown with attractive red and black motifs. She had her hair tied in a bun and held a parasol with both hands that rested across her shoulder. Two hundred and sixty euros, Hmm... not a bad price, perhaps she would have time to call back and buy it before they left Amsterdam. She could already see it sitting on the windowsill in the hallway of her flat. She looked fleetingly at the other items on display and feeling pleased with her discovery, turned to speak to Anita when she noticed two men walking towards them on the far side of the street. Her heart missed a beat and she felt panicky, it was Markov and one of his thugs. She turned back to the window as her heart began to beat madly and she reached out to tap Anita on her arm.

Markov must have been in the process of switching his phone back on because at that same moment Anita saw the flashing red circle appearing on the screen almost on top of them and it made her jump. Her eyes looked both this way and that, searching for the source of the alarm; and feeling Jane's touch, caught her eye.

'It's him, he is just over there,' whispered Jane in a terrified voice.

'I know. Keep looking in the window.

The two of them stared at the shop window; Jane seeing nothing, her mind in a turmoil but Anita was calmly watching the reflection from the opposite side of the street. She soon spotted the two men and saw that Markov was intent on making his phone call and his henchman was more interested in a group of female tourists laughing and chattering on their side of the street. She was certain that they were in no danger but still, they must not do anything to attract the men's attention.

'Is that our man, Jane?'

'Yes, definitely.'

'Okay, let's follow them at a safe distance. I have a good idea where they are going.'

Anita leaned closer towards the window, appearing to examine the goods on display, keeping a low profile until it was safe to move. She was quite sure that Markov and his henchman would head for the bar on Nieuwmarkt and glanced down at the screen in her hand for confirmation. The circle began to flash at a faster rate; he was making a call. She listened to him through the earpiece..

'Caas, you said to ring you.'

Markov sounded slightly agitated and even in his poor English it was obvious to Anita he was becoming impatient. What she did not know was that he had off-loaded the women during the day and would soon be receiving payment but there was always the chance of a double cross. He had dealt with Caas for several years and their business had flourished but they were criminals with criminal minds. Once he let Katja go to the Arab Caas would owe him a very large amount of money, enough to end their relationship and that worried him. Katja was the youngest and prettiest of his captives and he expected that she would fetch almost as much as all the others put together, if the Sheik wanted to buy her, and Caas has assured him he would. He wanted to collect his money as soon as he could and return to the Ukraine.

'Stop worrying, Markov, I have spoken to the Sheik and he wants to see her later tonight, about ten o'clock. You will be at the bar?'

'Yes, I go there now, you call me when you ready.'

'I'll call about eight, when I have made the arrangements. How much are you asking?'

'One hundred thousand euros,' Markov said confidently.

'It's a lot of money, my friend, she better be worth it after all this. I do not know if he will pay that much. I'll see what I can do.'

The line went dead and Caas whistled to himself. One hundred and fifty thousand euros was a lot for a girl but if these Arabs took a liking to her, especially one with blonde hair and blue eyes, they would pay anything and he wanted his fifty thousand euros share. Anita heard everything and frowned. So they were trying to sell Katja to an Arab sheik – tonight. She realised that the girl might soon disappear for good; it was time to call Sir Malcolm.

At the far end of the street, a scruffy looking man in orange overalls propped his sweeping brush against his barrow and appeared to rest a while. He had spent hours pretending to sweep the nearby streets and now he had located Markov he would call his section director.

The four yachtsmen had returned to the Old Sailor and from across the table Lee looked at Roger.

'Tha's not drinkin' much Roger, what's up, are you ailing? It's that woman isn't it?'

'Aye, but not like you think you twisted Tyke.'

'Ha, go on then, what's bugging you?'

'I like the little one,' said John in a matter of fact voice.

'If she packs a punch like her mate then I can't see you lasting long,' added Paul. 'Did you see how she handled that mugger, bloody amazing.'

'There's something strange going on,' said Roger, 'I remember when we had a job looking for IRA suspects near Harrogate we had people like her showing up. Quiet, studious types, with gizmos and always on the lookout for something and then they would just disappear. She's like that, something is going on.'

'What?' asked Lee.

'I don't know. We might never see them again so it doesn't matter does it?'

'I'll tell you what does matter,' said John.

'What?' asked Paul and Lee in unison.

'It's time we found a café and had a nice little bun!'

'Ah..., now there's an idea' said Lee, 'space cakes.'

'Are you sure? It's too easy to overdose on those bloody things. You don't know you've had too much until it's too late. I don't think it's a... '

Lee cut Paul short; he had spotted a group of sailors coming towards them.

'Look, there's the crew off that boat that came in behind us.' Lee leaned out of the open window of the bar and called to them.

'In here lads, it's party time.'

During the next hour, several more crews appeared and soon the bar was awash with stories of shared experiences crossing the North Sea. In contrast to the camaraderie of the sailors, a few streets away above a small dingy bar on the corner of Nieuwmarkt and Monnikenstraat, a door burst open and Markov walked into the dirty, untidy room where Katja was imprisoned.

'Get her cleaned up, get her to put on some make-up. Cover that bruise on her cheek with something, I do not want our guests to think she is damaged merchandise.'

'Okay, Boss.'

Vladimir looked over Markov's shoulder at the girl, he would be sorry to see her go so soon; she was young and fresh and he wanted a bit of fun with her but she was worth quite a lot of money to him too.

'Get one of the other girls to come in here and make her presentable.'

Within a few minutes a tall dark-haired girl in a dressing gown appeared carrying a small make-up bag and she looked at Markov; he nodded towards Katja before walking from the room and leaving her to her work.

'I have come to make you pretty for the Sheik.'

'The Sheik,' Katja was clearly shocked, her eyes widening with worry. 'Who's the Sheik?'

'I'm not supposed to say.'

'Tell me,' Katja demanded.

The girl looked at Katja, her eyes showing no pity, only resignation.

'He comes once a month or so and buys a girl for his harem.'

'Harem?'

'Yes, he is very rich and likes Western girls.'

'He can forget me. I'm not going anywhere.' Katja retorted defiantly.

The girl said nothing, simply opening the bag and rummaging for her make-up.

'You can forget that,' said Katja, pointing towards the bag.

'Vladimir,' called the girl.

The door opened and in came an angry looking

Vladimir.

'What is the problem, Sofia?'

'She does not want me to make her up.'

Vladimir took a threatening step forwards, reached across and gripped Katja's arm, holding it tight, staring menacingly at her with his dull, black eyes, killer's eyes.

'You do as you are told or you will regret it.'

Katja relented, afraid, terribly afraid and in that instant the realisation that her life was not her own any more swept over her. Sofia took out a hairbrush and began to straighten Katja's knotted mane before setting to work enhancing her allure for the Sheik.

Katja lowered her eyes to the ground as the wave of uncontrollable despair swept over her and for the first time during her ordeal tears rolled down her cheeks. She had fought her captors quietly, in her own way, defiant, sure that eventually she would be free; she had to be. They had not told her she would have to endure such privation and now her spirit was crumbling. She managed to raise her head a little, as the girl Sofia worked on her face with powder and lipstick to hide bruising sustained when they had raped her.

'Hold still, I need to do something with your eyes,' said Sofia.

Her mind in turmoil, Katja did as Sofia told her. The news that she was to become the possession of an Arab, to live the life of a concubine in a Middle Eastern harem terrified her. She knew very little about the Arabs, but from stories, she had read she was aware that they kept women prisoners to satisfy their every whim. Could she ever hope to see her mother and homeland again?

Sofia seemed to read her mind and held back for a minute to allow Katja to regain some composure. Sofia had herself been duped into leaving the Ukraine for a better life, to work in an office or a factory in the West, and just like Katja, the gangsters had forced her to work as a prostitute.

'You will survive, do not resist them and you will survive. There is no escape, so make the best of it.'

Katja's eyes flickered; her spirit was not completely broken but she felt she could no longer fight them. The finality of it all was horrifying her, weakening her. There seemed to be no escape and so she began to accept her fate and in the living room, Markov had made contact with Caas, impatient to close the deal.

'Caas, yes, ten o'clock. That is good, we are making her presentable and Vladimir tells me that the Sheik will not be able to resist her. Yes, 100,000 euros.'

Markov switched off his phone, slipped it back into his pocket, and stood up. 'Let me have a look at her, she is a valuable commodity and I want to make sure our shop front is as attractive as it can be.'

He walked to the bedroom and opened the door to find that Sofia had already left and Katja was sitting alone on the bed, her eyes staring into space.

'Sofia has made a good job of you indeed, a pity you are to leave us so soon.'

Katja looked at him and curled her lip like a wild animal.

'You will pay for this one day you filthy pig,' she spat
out.

Markov forced a laugh. Normally he would have shown her who the boss was by hitting her but he did not want to spoil her so soon before a sale. He turned away, leaving her alone and crossing the hallway told Vladimir that he was going to the bar for a drink.

The four sailors walked slowly along the narrow street leading to the square where they expected to find a café selling marijuana cakes. They would only try a little, just to say that they had: couldn't do any harm, could it?

'Coffee and buns,' said John, 'no beer here?'

'Don't need beer, we'll have more fun with a coffee and one of those space cakes than a skin-full of beer,' said Lee eagerly.

157

'It's a dangerous place, Amsterdam, if you mix with the wrong people,' said Roger to no one in particular.

'What wrong people?'

'I don't know, but those women are up to something.'

'Come on you two, never mind those women, let's find this café, it's just round the corner if I remember rightly,' said John.

'I've got him again, it's as I thought, they are in the same bar we followed one of them to earlier and the signal is stationary.' Anita gazed at the small screen.

'What are you going to do?' Jane sounded worried.

'Hmm... not sure, but I think we are close to Katja and
I do not want to let her go.'

'Listen, Anita, I am not particularly cut out for this type of work and I'm concerned.'

'Quite right too, you've done all we asked. You can leave me here if you like and return to the hotel, I can manage.' Jane looked at Anita, a woman she hardly knew but already she had a great respect for her ability and courage. She thought about the offer, looked at the ground and blushed.

'I'll stay.'

Anita said nothing. Jane was a brave girl, she was glad to have her along, and she promised herself that if any trouble started she would make sure Jane was well out of it.

'I've spoken with my superior and he has told me that I can attempt to get her out if I think it is at all possible, but I'm not to compromise either the British Government nor you. Do you understand what you are getting into, Jane?'

'Yes I think so.'

158

'Good for you, I will watch out for you, rest assured.' There was a pause before Anita said: 'I want to get into that bar and have a look around, see if I can find out where Katja is being held and figure out a plan to rescue her. Look, our sailor friends are back. I wonder where they are heading. Let's talk them into taking us for a drink.'

'Hello again,' said Roger, the first to spot Anita and
Jane.

'Hello boys,' said Jane, 'where are you heading?'

'Ah..., well, err we are looking for a café for a cup of coffee. We've had enough beer for today,' said John, suddenly embarrassed by their quest for the evil weed.

'Perhaps you ladies might like a cup.'

'Yes, that would be nice. We know a little café bar just over there,' said Anita.

Roger frowned; was she manipulating them, what for, where was it leading? 'The one with the blue and white sign?' he said.

'Yes,' said Anita, thinking that perhaps this ex-policeman was sharper than she realised.

'Why don't you walk with me, I don't know much about
Amsterdam, perhaps you can enlighten me as we go.'

'Years ago this area used to be the commercial district, when boats were smaller and could navigate the canals with the goods brought in from the Dutch East Indies... ' Anita cut him short. She had no interest in the history of Amsterdam; the immediate future was more her concern.

'Listen, Roger, I need to talk privately with you and I need you to promise, under the Official Secrets Act, that you will not divulge what I tell you to anyone without my say so, capiche?'

'Capiche!' Roger swallowed, what the hell was he getting them into?

Markov slid into a stool at the end of the counter in the scruffy, dimly lit bar and summoned the young Dutch barmaid with a click of his fingers. He asked for a whiskey and sat contemplating for a few moments until she passed the drink across the bar top, not asking for payment and Markov did not offer it. She could see that Markov was happy enough and left him to serve a group of noisy British tourists out for a good time, young men in their late teens and early twenties, boisterous from an afternoon of drinking.

'Six beers,' called one, pulling out a wad of euros as the girl passed the drinks along the bar.

The young men were eager to sample the delights of Amsterdam and between drinking and chattering their eyes stayed to the brightly lit windows across the street.

'Hey look at that one,' someone called out, peering through the window at a well-developed girl opening up for business across the narrow street.

'Cor, I wouldn't mind spending half an hour with her,'
said one of the younger members of the group.

'Half an hour, you wouldn't last five minutes with that
one sunshine,' said another, roaring with laughter.

During the next ten minutes other groups of young men entered the bar, filling it with the hubbub of early evening fun. The drinkers were a mixture of

Germans, Dutch, and British with a few Americans mixed in, their drawls, counterpoint to the voluble speech of the Europeans. Markov sat with an elbow on the bar one hand slowly turning his half-empty glass as he listening to the noise around him, periodically glancing down at his watch. It was still only nine o'clock – another hour before the Sheik arrived.

He decided against a second drink because today was to be a big payday and he did not want to lose his faculties until he'd stashed the money safely away. How much would he make this trip? Maybe two, three hundred thousand euros from the women and another five hundred thousand for the cocaine they had brought with them. The men had done well and he would reward them: he had to – anything less and they might go and work for one of his rivals and then what? The drug side of his operation was going well but If the Blue Russian or the Turk learned of the source of the cocaine they would move in and try to take over, put him out of business.

Markov downed the last of his drink and decided he would return to the apartment on the second floor. He slid from his stool and pushed past some of the Germans leaving the bar, almost bumping into a party of older men and two women entering from the street. The British began singing some football slogan and he decided that it was definitely time to leave.

Not more than two meters away Jane's heart missed a beat as she caught sight of Markov and tried to dodge behind Roger. She was just in time, and would have come face to face with him except for the Germans who were leaving and pushing past. She moved with them, managing to keep two of them between her and Markov, just long enough for him to turn away again and leave through an arch at the rear of the bar. That was close, too close, she thought as she once more used the puzzled looking Roger as a shield.

'That is Markov,' she whispered in Anita's ear, 'the one walking through the doorway over there.'

Anita looked along the counter, catching a brief glimpse of him disappearing through the archway and realised that he must be returning to his lair. She did not get a good look at him but at least she felt that she knew the route he had taken and was determined to follow and investigate as soon as she had the chance. She looked at Jane, who was visibly worried and knew that she must avoid exposing her to any danger. The best bet was for the sailors to look after her until she could join them, with or without Katja.

Reaching the top of the stairs, Markov banged on the door to alert Vladimir who opened it to let him into the apartment.

'It's getting too noisy down there, lots of those groups of young men intent on demonstrating their testosterone levels. They wouldn't last long against us, eh Vladimir?' Vladimir managed what passed as a smile and closed the door and at that same time, Markov's phone rang. He took it from his pocket and keyed the receive button.

'Yes...' he listened for a few seconds. 'I see, well I pick you up in the Mercedes... Where exactly to come? I know, where we brought the girls last time, across the river, brothel next the marina, a street called Motorkade. Yes, I know it; the car will be there in 20 minutes maybe half hour.'

Markov finished his conversation and turned to Vladimir with a grin. 'Caas has had his car stolen;

someone will wake up with a bad headache if he catches them I think.'

'Maybe not wake up again, 'said Vladimir, an apology for a smile appearing on his face.

Anita did not hear the whole conversation: she was too slow plugging in the earpiece after the machine began buzzing, but she had heard enough. Markov was leaving to pick up one of his associates and the Arab, the one she believed was coming to look at Katja. It's now or never, she thought.

'Roger, there has been a development.' Anita's heart began to beat a little too quickly. 'I want you to take Susan and wait on your boat. Is it moored near somewhere called Motorkade?'

'Not this year, that's small marina across the main canal. It was too full for us to get into it yesterday so we are in Sixhaven. It's easier to get to Sixhaven. Why?'

'That seems to be one of the places they use, a brothel next to a marina.'

Roger frowned. 'There was a knocking shop alongside the marina, amongst the old industrial buildings, but I've never ventured very close to it.'

Roger was surprised at her question, she had told him briefly that she was working with the police but little else and he was becoming sure that there was more to the situation than she was telling him.

'It looks as if things are starting to move. I don't want Susan around if trouble starts – and that goes for you lot as well.'

'Look, Anne, I can't leave you on your own. I can fade into the background, in here maybe, whilst the boys escort Susan back to the boat. It's a fair old hike you know.'

Anita looked at him; to have an ally would be useful. Perhaps it was not a bad idea.

'Don't you think you ought to tell us exactly what it is you are doing? What trouble are you referring to?' asked Roger, his eyes narrowing a little.

Anita took a deep breath. Roger, Lee and the rest of the crew had been useful as cover but she could not have them around if any real trouble started and she knew there was a significant risk that there could be some. She thought quickly; she would have to tell them something to keep them on side and to be able to use them and their boat if needs be.

'I suppose I should tell you and the others a little of what's going on Roger. Look, tell them I am a police officer on surveillance watching out for drug smugglers bringing cocaine into the United Kingdom and that one of our chief suspects is in here somewhere. I do not want my cover blown, I'm obtaining evidence on their movements and I would prefer it if I am left to my own devices for a while. Please have a word and get them to leave straight away, then go and sit over there and I will join you. I need to keep a watch for a while longer.'

Roger moved towards Lee who was busy chatting to some girls and managed to break him away, briefly explaining what was happening and that he would hang back with Anne and catch up as soon as he could. Lee was a little worse for wear but he had the sense not to argue or ask questions because he was aware of Roger's past life in the police and to do as he asked.

'Lee, make sure that big German boat isn't blocking our way out in case we have to leave in a hurry, you know how awkward Jerry can be sometimes.'

'Right, I will, seems you were right about these two. Good job we've taken it easy on the pop and God knows what we'd be like if we had munched a few of those bloody cakes.'

Roger's mouth curled in a nervous smile. How right his skipper was.

'Come on, let's get going,' said Lee, rounding up his crew.

'Why so soon, where are we going?' asked Paul.

'Back to the boat, come on.'

'What!' exclaimed John.

'I'll tell you along the way. Susan here is coming with us and Roger is stopping with Anne.

John and Paul gave each other a knowing look: after all, this was Amsterdam and as the four of them left the bar. Anita saw Markov coming towards her and stepped back amongst the crowd. She was within touching distance of him as he passed and she felt very relieved that he had not noticed her. He was a powerfully built man, over six feet tall and quite good looking, but he exuded an almost tangible danger. She watched him walk out into the street and hoped that Jane and the others were well out of sight by now. She stepped forwards and craned her neck, checking the direction he had taken just in case she needed to go after them, but it was with some relief that she saw Markov turn towards Damstraat, the opposite direction from Jane and the sailors. She did not know it, but he was going for the car and was busy giving Kostyantyn instructions as to where he should go to collect Caas and his passenger.

Anita had watched them appear through the archway at the rear of the bar, the way to the toilets on the first floor and it occurred to her that it was the most likely direction to go in search of Katja. The last signal had been from an elevated position so the prisoner was probably on one of the floors above and Anita felt that if she could get to the staircase she stood a good chance of reaching the top floor unnoticed because of the noise and ribaldry in the bar.

'I'm going through there, Roger. If I am not back with you in a quarter of an hour, I will not be coming with you. *If* I do not come back, get Susan out of Amsterdam for me, will you?'

'Yes, be careful.'

Anita moved towards the archway. There was nothing more Roger could do except take his drink, sit in the shadows, wait and hope that she would return within a quarter of an hour.

Chapter 9

Katja sat on the edge of the bed, Sofia and the other girls had left for their evening's work, and she was alone in the apartment with her minder. She wondered if she might spoil her make-up, make her face so grotesque that the Arab would not want her. Perhaps if she could put him off they might allow her to remain in the City, working as a prostitute, and then she might find a chance of escape. Maybe she could get out onto the street and call someone to help her.

A noise at the door disturbed her thoughts; it opened to reveal the sinister Vladimir, left by Markov to stand guard over her. He came into the room and for a few moments stared at her before he grasped a handful of her hair and bent her head backwards. She felt a wave of revulsion and fear spread over her as his dark, sinister eyes explored her body and she braced herself for the inevitable, but it never came. Vladimir had a stake in her wellbeing just as much as Markov because his boss had promised him several thousand euros this trip, provided all the merchandise was disposed of profitably and this girl was the most valuable.

'Take your hands off me,' Katja managed to say. Vladimir released his grip and made as to leave the room until Katja called him back.

'I want some water.'

The big man shrugged his powerful shoulders and without a word turned to walk from the room, pausing only to lock the door behind him. He walked along the hallway and began to descend the flight of stairs leading to the ground floor and the bar where he would find a bottle of water for his charge. On the floor below, Anita was moving soundlessly and just about ready to climb the stairs to the second floor, when she heard a noise above her on the staircase and quickly she retraced her steps. Trying the handles of each of the doors nearby she eventually found one unlocked and slipped inside the room. It was a storeroom containing several cardboard boxes and some old furniture. She pulled the door closed behind her, leaving the slightest of gaps between the door and its frame, just enough for her to observe the person coming down the stairs and as the shadow passed she recognised the man as Markov's henchman. He was the same one she had photographed in Verbier and he was looking straight ahead, his simple mind on other matters.

He passed by and Anita was able to carefully open the door and listen. This man was dangerous, she knew, and she felt for the Berretta, pulling it from the pocket in her slacks, gripping the butt and feeling for the safety catch with her thumb. There was a score to settle as well as to find Katja; it was not her brief to avenge the deaths of the two men from the Swiss embassy but given the chance, she would. She pushed the door wider and slipped out into the small hallway, pulled the door closed behind her and moving as silently as a cat, she ran up the two flights of stairs to the floor above. Controlling her breathing, she pressed her ear to the first door she came to and listened hard, but could hear no sound within the room. She tried the handle and pushed her shoulder gently against the door and it opened, Beretta at the ready she scanned the hallway of an apartment – nothing. The hallway had four doors, two on each side and not forgetting the thug on the stairs, she pulled the outer door shut behind her and one by one, she tried each of the door handles in turn. They were unlocked, inside each room she saw a bed and a few female possessions, make-up, white underwear and very little else. These rooms must be where they kept the girls, and of course, they would probably be out plying their trade. Of course, that was why there was no sound – the girls were working and, no doubt, their minders were with them to keep an eye on things. So where was Katja? She must be in the one room she had not looked in and moving to the last door she reached out towards the handle and was about to turn it when she heard a noise behind her. She spun around and sidestepped into the room opposite just as Vladimir opened the outer door and walked in with the bottle of water in his hand.

Anita pressed her back hard against the wall of the bedroom and tried to control her breathing, taking in a great lung full of air as quietly as she could until her body settled down; she listened and heard the sound of a key inserted into a lock and then the gruff voice of the thug.

'Here, a drink for you. Now behave until Markov returns,' he said in Russian.

So, there was someone in the room. Anita was fluent in the language and picked up most of the words, straining her ears to try to hear more. But, there was no more conversation, simply the movement of the man's feet on the thin carpet and then a revelation.

'You can stick your water up your arse, you ugly bastard,' screamed Katja, using up her last ounce of defiance.to throw the bottle of water straight into

Vladimir's face. It landed it squarely on his nose, riling him enough to make him forget that he was supposed to be looking after Markov's investment. He took a step forward and through watering eyes slapped Katja across the face; his first blow was not severe enough to do any damage but as his eyes cleared he drew back his arm for another swing, but he did not get that far. He felt a tap on his shoulder, and he turned, expecting to see Markov, his dark eyes betrayed nothing of the surprise he felt on seeing a woman confronting him. Instinctively he lashed out, catching Anita on the shoulder. The force of the impact enough to send her spinning backwards and then Vladimir caught sight of her gun and reached inside his jacket pocket for his own. He pulled it from the shoulder holster and aimed it straight at Anita's head but she was too quick and dropping to one knee, she levelled the Beretta and fired. Suddenly a third eye appeared in the middle of Vladimir's forehead and in disbelief his existing eyes turned inwards to examine their new companion before his head tilted forwards and he crashed to the floor, dead.

Katja raised the back of her hand to her mouth to smother her scream, terrified. It had not quite dawned upon her that it was the woman she had seen in the street, the one who she had first met in her and her mother's small dacha..

'Ваша мать прислала мне Катя,' said Anita in a calm voice.

'My mother sent you,' said Katja incredulously. 'Who are you?' Then the realisation dawned and she let out a sob.

'Come, quick!' Anita grabbed hold of her hand and dragged her after her out onto the landing.

The two of them raced down the stairs to the first floor where Anita, commanded Katja to halt, took off her jacket, making the girl wear it as at least some sort of disguise. The clothes she was wearing were flimsy and out of place, of use only for attracting the tourists and their money. If she remained dressed in such clothing, then Markov's men would easily spot them. Anita gripped Katja's arm and with her free hand held her gun at the ready in her trouser pocket. She pulled Katja along through the crowded bar towards the exit and from his secluded seat in the shadows Roger sat up in surprise. Anita and Katja reached the doorway and were about to leave when a car, a grey Mercedes, pulled up outside and from it emerged Markov. Anita stopped in her tracks and watched in horror as two more men joined him; one appeared to be the Arab, the other a Caucasian. In mild panic, Anita steered Katja back into the crowded bar and through the archway and from three metres away, Roger watched in disbelief as the two women came past him for a second time and then disappeared. He decided he had to follow them, but by the time he had risen to his feet and pushed through the crowd, they were gone. What was Anne up to: who was the woman with her and why had they turned and gone back through the archway?

He knew from his days with the Leeds Police that drug dealers and pimps were ruthless uncaring people who would stop at nothing in search of profit and from a brief conversation knew that Anne was well aware also. She must have seen something shocking to make her act in the way she had. In the dim light of the bar, no one noticed him as he eased his way towards the archway, wondering what he might find. His instinct told him that Anne was in danger and in need of help but he still had no idea what that danger might be. He looked about him for the threat, at the crowd of people congregated around the bar and towards the entrance. Then he saw the Arab, a man dressed in an expensive looking western suit and wearing dark glasses, accompanied by two tough looking characters and from the little Anne had told him he guessed that these men were the reason for her hasty retreat.

Unsure exactly what to do he pretended to sip from the half-empty glass of water still in his hand and stood back to observe the men's progress. They came within a few feet of him as they made their way towards archway and from there he could see just how mean and dangerous looking they were.

Hurriedly climbing the stairs, Anita and Katja had reached the first floor where Anita once again slipped into the storeroom and this time she closed the door tightly, putting her finger to her mouth, commanding Katja to silence. From the gloom Katja looked back at her with wide eyes, her thoughts only of this woman who had come to their dacha beside the lake, who had recently spoken to her in Russian to tell her that her mother had sent her. Was she Russian? Katja was confused and disorientated. The confinement and the drugs had left her feeling weak. Seeing Vladimir die so easily had shocked her and she had really believed then that it was the end and that she was about to die. Now she started to think that perhaps this was a genuine rescue attempt and this woman was to be trusted, a part of the plan they had led her to expect would happen.

Anita pressed her ear to the door and listened, but the only sound was the occasional drip from an antiquated tap. Then she heard them, footfalls on the stairs, a few mumbled unintelligible words fading as the men went past on their way up the final staircase to the apartment. They only had seconds: she knew as soon as Markov saw what she had done, he would explode with anger and then anything could happen. She took the Beretta from her pocket, held its barrel vertically close to her right cheek and pulled Katja back down the stairs.

'Here, quick,' called a quiet voice, 'this way.'

Anita jumped in mild shock, arching the gun towards the speaker. It was Roger, waving frantically to her, beckoning them towards him with more than a little urgency. He had crept through the archway after the three men and hoping that he would find Anne and the girl he had looked for a way of escape through the back of the building. As Anita and Katja reappeared, there was a great bellow from the top of the stairs, a roar like a wounded lion. Anita knew then that Markov had discovered his dead lieutenant and seen that his captive was missing.

'Here, let's try this,' said Roger, twisting a door handle. He pulled open the fire escape door that led into a dingy, rubbish-strewn backyard and pushing the women through, he pulled the door shut behind him. Their escape route led them across the yard and down a narrow darkened alley towards the street. Above them Markov was recovering his composure, looking down at Vladimir's dark-eyed expression, an expression that differed little in death than in life. The girl, where was she and who had done this, who had visited this mayhem on him?

'You have had a bad experience I think,' said Caas in English. 'I must get the Sheik away; if the police become involved then he could suffer. If it got out that he takes Western girls to the desert it could cause serious trouble for us.'

'I will call my men to get the car and to come back here for you.'

There was no argument, Caas was a big name in the Amsterdam underworld and had a reputation to consider. If the Sheik felt that Caas had compromised him, then it could do his business reputation no end of harm. Markov understood that and became silent, his mind in a whirl as he tried to come to terms with the death of Vladimir and the loss of 100,000 euros he had expected for the girl. He was angry, very angry, but he had not become a successful crime boss by being angry; cunning and guile were the secrets of his success and he needed those attributes more now than he ever had.

The fugitives emerged into the bright lights of the main thoroughfare running along the canal bank, Anita in the lead with Roger and Katja bringing up the rear. Roger had told Anita that they should head for the central railway station and from there they needed to take the ferry across the river.

'Over there, look those bicycles, let's see if we can find three of them unlocked. It will help us get away from here much more quickly,' said Roger, crossing a narrow bridge.

In front of them bicycles were stacked in racks, leaning against each other or against the bridge. They were lucky: they found three machines unsecured by careless owners and they were soon cycling along the bank of the canal towards the Central Station.

Several hundred meters away Markov looked out of the top floor window of the building and down at the yard below, too late to spot Anita, Roger and Katja, but in his mind's eye, he saw something else. Jane, the woman he had met in Verbier and wondered if she was involved. The two surveillance men Vladimir had killed; who were they really working for and why had he still not heard anything about the incident? He had searched the internet, surprised that he could find no mention of a double killing at the ski resort, only the suicide of two gay actors around the same time – could that be it? He did not know. He had presumed that it was a rival gang trying to find out about his business ventures, Russians probably. They were proactive in intelligence gathering, using ex- KGB men who would work for anyone who would pay them. What if it was a government agency, and if it was government inspired then which one? Jane was British, he was sure about that, and the thought now occurred that she might be working for British intelligence. If she were involved, he would find her, kill her and somehow get Katja back, not just for the money; they had severely dented his pride and he could not let such a thing pass unpunished.

The three cyclists crossed the bridge into Nieuwmarkt, almost colliding with a car coming at speed from the opposite direction. Markov had summoned Kostyantyn back to the bar, the urgency in his voice had caused his employee to drive too hastily and he had to step hard on the brake to avoid hitting three cyclists, a man and two women. Still swearing under his breath, he moderated his speed whilst Bohuslav, sitting beside him looked stony faced out of the window.

That was a close thing,' said Roger puffing with exertion. He was out of condition and feeling it.

Anita said nothing, just glad that they had escaped in one piece. Her brain was working overtime and she was looking ahead to the next stage whilst Katja, who was peddling along just behind them, was simply glad to be breathing fresh air again. They rode in silence, crossing back over the canal by another bridge and towards the busy Prins Hendrikkade with its voluminous traffic and pedestrians. In the lead, Roger saw a tram heading their way and halted them until it had passed.

'I am not too happy riding along here; we are likely to have an accident if we keep riding these bikes amongst all this traffic. We must pass through the Central Station, look, just over there.' Roger pointed to a building several hundred metres away. 'Why don't we leave the bikes and walk the last bit?'

Anita was beginning to think the same; it was a fast moving and hectic thoroughfare and she was worried that Katja could not cope – and as pedestrians, they might be less visible to any pursuers.

'Yes let's do it. Katja bring your bike over here, we're going to leave them and walk.'

Katja nodded, following the other two to a bicycle stand where they dumped the machines before crossing the road and walking towards the station.

At the same time, Kostyantyn and Bohuslav pulled up outside the bar to find Markov, Caas and the Arab already waiting for them.

'Kostyantyn, take Caas and the Sheik back the hotel and quickly. Is that where you want to go Caas?'

'I think it will be best.'

'Bohuslav, you stay here for now.'

Caas climbed into the car and within seconds the Mercedes was heading back the way it had come and Bohuslav was following Markov back into the building. As they walked past the bar, Markov hesitated and then spoke to the girl serving.

'Have you seen a girl with blonde hair and blue eyes, about 20 years old, pass through the bar in the last ten or twenty minutes?'

The girl was Caas's niece, her uncle had secured the job for her and she knew a little of his business, knew It was not a good idea to upset these men. She thought for a moment.

'We have had a lot of people in here today. I have not seen a girl as you describe but I noticed two women coming from the toilets not long ago. One seemed anxious, the other I could not see properly. They must still be in there because they actually came into the bar and went towards the door and then I remember they came back and went towards the toilets I think.'

Markov turned and hurried through the archway, taking the stairs two at a time, soon reaching the first floor and there he pulled out his gun. A woman emerged from the toilet: he pushed her aside, ignoring her protests and barged in, kicking open each cubicle, but he found no one. Cursing he left and was about to climb the stairs when he stopped.

Bohuslav was behind him and almost ran into Markov.

'All okay, Boss, I took... '

He got no further; Markov's face was a contortion of fury, his mind trying to piece together the events of the past hour. With a sharp jerk of his head indicated Bohuslav to follow him to the apartment and on the top floor, he vented his anger, not at Bohuslav, but the flimsy plastered wall. With one sharp stab of his clenched fist, he drove it clean through and into the next room. It was enough to relieve the pressure and in a more composed tone said.

'Look in there.' He indicated with his open palm that

Bohuslav should go into Katja's room.

The sight made Bohuslav's blood run cold. He had been wary of Vladimir in life and now, even in death, those black lifeless eyes unnerved him.

'And the girl is gone.'

'Who did this, Russian Mafia?'

'I do not think so, I think British Secret Service.'

'What we going to do, Boss?' said Bohuslav intrigued at this news.

'First I want you to contact the rest of our men here in Amsterdam, tell them to lock the other girls up until we find this one. I will talk to Caas and ask him for help said Markov taking out his mobile phone. 'He knows this town and he has many people working for him. Now get on with it.'

The device in Anita's pocket began buzzing but there was no time to attend to it, they were entering the station precinct. After dodging the trams and mixing with the crowds, she did not want to lose sight of Roger striding away in front and she had to keep close to Katja.

'How are you feeling?' she asked the girl.

'I not feel too bad now I am free,' said Katja.

'We're not free quite yet, we have to hide for a while because they will come after us. Of that I am sure.'

Roger led them into the station building, across the ticket hall, down the sloping precinct, past shops, through crowds and eventually out into the darkening night at the far end. They crossed a road, still busy with people and bicycles even at such a late hour, and made their way towards the ferry that would take them across the main canal to the marina.

'We've just missed one,' said Roger 'shouldn't be long before another one gets here – you can see it leaving the other side.'

Anita looked across the river more concerned that someone was following them. Markov would be angry when he found Katja missing and she guessed that he would not give up looking for them for quite a while. Her plan was to hide on the boat for a day or two until the Embassy or the Service could get them safely out of the country. She wondered what questions the sailors would have, she was not happy sharing information with them but she could not think of a better way right now. If she could get them to stay out on the water just long enough so that they would not be able to mix with anyone – anyone with a Russian or Ukrainian accent, that is. She would ask them to switch off their phones as an added precaution and only hoped there would be no dissent. She was beginning to feel the strain; she had not really stopped for almost 24 hours and was in need of some respite.

The walk from the Ferry terminal to the marina gate was a short one and after Roger had keyed in the code they were through the gate and walking towards the yacht.

'Here they come,' said Paul, coffee cup in his hand and watching Roger fiddling with the combination lock to the marina gate. 'He's got *two* women with him.'

Lee heard him from below and popped his head through the hatch to see what was happening, and behind him, from her seat in the cabin, Jane peered through the narrow window..

'Who's the girl?' asked Lee. 'She looks like one of those girls out of the windows with those skimpy clothes.'

'You're not far off, I think,' said John.

Roger reached the boat first and helped the women to climb aboard, and as Anita followed Katja onto the yacht, she decided that now was probably the time for her to take charge. She needed these men and their boat to hide away from prying eyes and to get some rest. Then she needed to figure out how she could get Katja out of the country? Sir Malcolm's words were ringing in her ears. 'Under no circumstances can you compromise the British Government. The situation is more complicated than you can imagine. If the newspapers get hold of the story it could upset some very delicate negotiations with the Russians over energy supplies.'

The women squeezed into the cabin and sat on the berth next to Jane, Paul sat opposite and John filled the kettle to make them a hot drink. Lee and Roger stood at the foot of the companionway stairs in silence wondering what was going on and then Anita spoke.

'Can you all gather round and listen to me, there are some things you ought to be aware of. I work for the Government back in the UK as I think you may already know. This young woman here is Katja, she is Ukrainian and people traffickers have brought her here. They not only deal in people but also bring in drugs from Afghanistan. I can tell you that there is a flourishing trade in both drugs and white slaves and my job has been to look into this trade and see what we can do to stop it. Two days ago we received information that drugs were coming into Amsterdam on their way to the UK and that some women were being trafficked here as well and I was sent to try and get some of them out by paying off the criminals running the racket. Unfortunately most of the women had already been disposed of and when I arrived, Katja was the only one left; at least I was able to pay them off for her release.'

'So why don't you just jump on a plane and go back to Britain?' asked Lee.

'Because she doesn't have a passport, dummy,' said Roger.

He did not believe Anita's story, but was not sure where all this was leading, then it dawned on him – she wanted them to smuggle the girl out of the Netherlands.

'Bollocks,' he said to himself. It was not too difficult coming and going by sea – all they had to do was fill in a form or two; no one seemed to check much, but there was still a chance they could be caught. He remembered a rubber dingy creeping up on them when they left by the northern route some years before. Three border police had appeared from nowhere and it was lucky for them that all the boats paperwork was in order. The police had made a thorough search of the yacht, everything then had been in order, but it would not be so this time.

'There is one more complication,' added Anita. 'The people who I dealt with suspect that I have a lot more cash on me because I was trying to buy the freedom of more than one girl and they may come after me for the rest.'

'How much have you got?' asked Paul.

'Nothing, I get the money through our Embassy as and when I need it. I have a few thousand euros in the hotel safe that's all.'

Paul nodded, appeared to understand but he was none the wiser.

'These people, what are they likely to do?' asked Lee.

'Probably hurt you quite badly if you get in their way.'

The cabin went quiet, the men became thoughtful, and Jane looked apprehensively at the floor as Katja's eyes turned briefly towards Anita, knowing what she had just said to be untrue. She had witnessed her skill and aggression in rescuing her and more than anyone, knew how dangerous the men following them could be. She listened to Anita trying to convince these men of the seriousness of the situation and felt an urge to help.

'I am Ukrainian, I have been through bad time and this woman got me out. She very good woman, you listen to her.'

All eyes turned to the girl, dishevelled but striking in the makeup she wore and they felt pity for what they imagined she had endured. They had heard vague stories of people trafficking and seen images on the news channels.

'What does tha' want us to do Anne?' asked Lee.

'First we need to keep a lookout for any prowlers. I do not think they will find us here very easily, but I don't want to take any chances. Secondly, I need to catch up on some sleep before we leave early in the morning.'

'How early?' asked Roger

'You're the sailor, you tell me.'

'Where do you intend going?'

'England, of course,' she said in a matter of fact voice.

'Eh…, we are on holiday, we have another week before we need to go back home,' said John a little indignantly.

'If those men catch up with us then you might never be going home,' said Anita, looking him in the eye.

It was enough. They were convinced, and Roger had grasped the situation. He looked at his watch, 11.15, it would be light at six and if they were going to head back home and escape the gangsters, they should really be on their way now.

'Lee?'

Lee, having drawn a similar conclusion, looked straight at Roger and nodded slowly before turning to his chart table.

'Anne, use the forward cabin to get some rest. You two,' he said to Jane and Katja, 'bed down here on these bunks for now. I will work out a passage plan while Roger will try to get us out of this sardine tin. We have a boat rafted up alongside and there are at least two more blocking our way out of the marina. Okay Roger?'

'Aye aye, Skipper,'

Roger beckoned the other two to help him and the three of them went up on deck to size up the situation. They could easily slip away from the big German boat alongside but the passage through to open water was blocked by two other yachts.

'Let's pull her out from under the Jerry first and then we can shift that Dutchman outside him.'

John and Paul set to work, first coiling the shorelines and then dropping extra fenders over the rail to smooth their passage. The German boat was a good couple of metres longer and there was a light on in the cabin. Roger wondered whether to hail anyone on board or simply take it very steadily and hope that if there were somebody he would not realise what was happening. He decided upon stealth, as that seemed to be the name of the game from now on.

'Paul,' he whispered, 'run a line onto the pontoon and hold it ready to pull us out, John, loosen his lines and pull him back in once we're clear.'

The men worked well as a team and were soon in a position to slide their yacht out from between the pontoon and the big German boat. John kept an eye on the fenders, making sure they did not bang into the other boat, while Paul applied some tension to his line and gradually the yacht moved forward. Before long, they were halfway out, it was time to pull the German yacht back alongside the pontoon, and all went well until a brusque voice called out.

'Was vor sich geht?'

Roger's heart leapt into his mouth, dammit, he thought, the bloody German.

'Sorry, wir haben gerade erst von der Stadt and we're a little drunken,' said John.

'Acht, Englanders, always you are drunk,' said the voice with more than a hint of alcohol in it.

Roger looked at John and began shaking with mirth; the tension was getting to him but this interlude was managing to relieve some of it. The German did not look to be coming on deck to see what was going on and they had just about completed the manoeuvre. They would be on their way before anyone could stop them.

'Didn't know you could speak German, John,' said Paul, as they pushed the yacht forward and climbed back aboard.

'He can't! Most of that was in English with a German accent and a few German words thrown in for effect. Anyway it worked. Just these two to move now,' said Roger, slowly coaxing the boat under its own momentum the few metres towards the next obstacle in their path.

'Well done, lads.' Lee joined them just as they cleared the German yacht. 'I've done a passage plan and checked fuel. I don't think we will have enough to motor all the way back, and the forecast looks grim, sixes and sevens from the north-east as the low passes over but at least it's in a decent direction for us. There'll be some pretty big seas for a while till it settles down; I hope these women can cope with it.'

Roger nodded and stepped aside to let Lee take over the conning of the yacht as they drew near to the last of the boats blocking their path. The boats were yachts from their own racing fleet and it appeared their crews were still out sampling the delights of Amsterdam. Climbing aboard each deserted yacht in turn John and Paul pulled them into the space they were vacating whilst Lee and Roger made sure the fenders were doing their job and, with a little puffing and panting, they were finally free.

Markov knew that a huge problem confronted him and called his most trusted men to his side to try to understand what had happened and to find the perpetrators. Bohuslav, the new man, was already with him and Kostyantyn was on his way back as Markov re-entered the room containing Vladimir's dead body.

'Kostyantyn we need to get rid of Vladimir's body, but first I want the person who did this.'

Kostyantyn looked down at Vladimir's lifeless body, fascinated by the bullet hole in the middle of his forehead. In life, Vladimir had been a tough man, a killer and those dark, lifeless eyes reminding him of the times he had seen Vladimir kill. He remembered how he had recoiled in revulsion as he watched him kill the two men they had caught spying on them in Switzerland. The violence as Vladimir's knife had flashed across their throats, their cries stifled by his great hand, and the blood.

Kostyantyn shuddered at the memory, took one last look at Vladimir, afraid of him no more, and looked at Markov who was preoccupied, staring out of the window and down at the small courtyard.

'Boss, I think I might have an idea about this,' he said, gesturing with an open palm towards the corpse.

'What?' demanded Markov, his head turning away from the window. 'What?'

'When I was returning in the car, we almost hit three people on bicycles. It was near the bridge further along the street. I think one of them might have been the girl we kept in here.'

Markov's head jerked round and he pulled out his phone to call Caas.

Kostyantyn gave Bohuslav a knowing smile; he had spotted the fugitives and felt he was demonstrating to Bohuslav why he was now Markov's number two. Bohuslav looked back at him, nodded his acquiescence, and hoped his own feelings did not show.

As the yacht nosed its way between the entrance piles of the marina, Lee spun the wheel and steered the yacht into the main canal. Alongside him, John stared out across the dark water towards the main railway station and sighed at the thought of a holiday cut short. Forward of the mast, on either side of the boat, Roger and Paul were keeping a sharp lookout for the navigation lights of any vessels crossing their path.

'We've done it, lads,' said Lee, pleased with himself.

'Have you seen the ferry, Skipper?' called Paul, pointing to a white, brightly lit shape ahead towards them.

'Got him,' said Lee as he swung the yacht round a few degrees to miss the oncoming ferry.

They were properly underway and had begun to relax a little, the hot drinks had helped and Katja had changed visibly. Gone was the tension from her face, an altogether softer more confident expression replacing the terrified look she had worn earlier.

'Katja, you are safe enough for now.'

'I thank you for rescuing me.'

'You are looking tired, Anita, you should be getting some sleep,' said Jane.

'I think perhaps we all should, it's been a long day.' Anita went to the companionway and looked up at Lee,

legs astride, both hands gripping the wheel and looking straight ahead. He caught sight of her and smiled.

'We're on our way, three hours or so and we'll be in the Sea Lock.'

'I'm going to catch a couple of hours sleep then, I want to be fully alert when we put to sea.'

Lee nodded, transferring his attention back towards their course whilst his crew attended to routine tasks and the yacht glided along through the waters of the North Sea Canal towards the Sea Lock. Anita lay down on the bunk in the forward cabin, instantly falling into a deep and dreamless sleep and in the saloon, Jane and Katja lay on the two bunks. Jane dozed whilst Katja lay there with her eyes wide open, reliving the days since her abduction. Was it all worth it? She hoped so.

'I want two men at the railway station straight away,' said Caas into his telephone. 'One of the Ukrainians will meet them there and help to try to find the girl. It is a long shot but one of our men saw them heading that way. Write this number down and call it when you get there.'

He put his phone down and sighed, it would be like trying to find a needle in a haystack and after thinking about the problem for a few more minutes; he decided to go to back to the bar and try to find out a little more about what had happened earlier in the evening. He called Markov to ask him to meet him there.

'Hello Caas, do you want a drink?'

'Yes, just a beer, hello Greetje,' he said to the barmaid.

'Uncle Caas.'

'You didn't know this was my niece, did you Markov?'

'I had an idea she might be, she's not worked here long has she?'

'I'm working only in my vacation from college,' said Greetje with a smile. 'Uncle Caas got me the job.'

'Tell me, Greetje, were you working here earlier? I didn't notice you when I came in,' said Caas in his native Dutch.

Greetje had heard a whisper about the murder in the apartment and she knew to keep quiet. She had grown up in a crime family; her father was in jail serving time for cocaine smuggling and her mother worked for her uncle looking after one of his 'houses'. She gave her uncle an apprehensive look, she knew something of course, but she did not want to become involved.

'You know a little of what went on tonight, Greetje, I can tell. Do not worry but we need information to try to catch whoever did this. Can you remember much about who was here tonight?'

'I have been thinking about it, your friend here asked me earlier. Then, I could not remember anything but I do remember now; there was a group of people here for quite a time yesterday, four men and two women. One of the women seemed to be always looking round and she did go through there I remember, and she came back but did not leave by the front door I am sure.' Greetje pointed to the archway leading to the staircase. 'She went through there with another woman and I did not see her again.

'These people, what were they like?'

'The men were all in their forties I would say and the women, mmm... probably one was a bit older and the other perhaps late thirties I would guess.'

'Did the older of the two women have green eyes?' asked Markov. He had looked into Jane's eyes more than once, always struck by their unusual colour.

'I think they might have been.'

So it was Jane. He had deliberated about whether he had seen her and now he was sure. He remembered then that he was supposed to have a dinner date with her that evening and thought that if she had anything to do with taking the girl she would probably not answer her phone.

'Excuse me a minute.' Markov flicked through the address book on his phone.

Several kilometres away Jane's phone rang. It was two o'clock in the morning and the ring tone startled her from her slumber. Instinctively she reached for the phone to answer the call, not fully awake, not even looking to see who was calling her.

'Hello,' she managed to say in a sleepy sounding voice.

'Jane, you are awake?'

'Who is this?'

'Markov.'

She was instantly awake, panicking and not sure what to do. 'M... Markov, oh, you woke me up. Why do you ring me at such a late hour?'

'We have a dinner date tonight and I thought I should let you know that I will pick you up at seven but I don't know where you are staying. Which hotel are you in?'

She paused, not answering him immediately, and in that instant he knew she was involved, her and another woman. He waited for an answer that took longer than it should have as Jane thought about what to say and through the silence, he could hear a throbbing noise, a strange noise for a hotel.

'I am in the Best Weston, near Dam Square,' she said truthfully, she could not think of the name of any other hotel in Amsterdam and thought that if she made a name up he would suspect her. He was fishing: why else would he ring her at such a time?

'I am sorry to have disturbed you; I thought a fun loving girl like you would be at some night club or other. Until tomorrow then, goodnight,' said Markov, his face.clouding with anger.

'Is it the time to be chasing a woman, Markov?' asked Caas reverting to English.

'I know who did this.'

'What?'

'Yes, I think I know, but there is a lot I do not know. Greetje, what can you remember about the men with the two women?'

'Not much really, they were sailors I think, British, on a yacht race. The Captain of their boat kept holding my hand and telling me he would like to whisk me off to the Caribbean on his boat, silly man.'

Markov froze: a boat, a yacht, could that be the sound he heard, a boat's engine?

'Caas, where would you keep a boat in Amsterdam?'

'A boat, hell the City is full of them. Sixhaven is the favourite place for visitors.'

'Where is it?'

'Just over the river from the Central Station, why?'

'The woman I was speaking to is on a boat and she is part of this.'

'Of course!' exclaimed Caas, 'we looked for them in the station, which is a thoroughfare to the ferries. So they were heading for the ferry, not the station.'

'What will they do, where can they go?'

'They don't have many options, north into the Ijsselmeer or perhaps a canal, but if they are going to England they will probably travel along the North Sea Canal to Ijmuiden.'

'I'm sure that's what they will do. Which will be the quickest way to England?' asked Markov.

'Ijmuiden, through the Sea Lock and then it's straight across. Take them no more than probably 20 hours.'

'So we might be able to catch up with them.'

'It is possible, but we have to find them first. I will send a man to Ijmuiden to keep watch and see who is leaving. Greetje, can you describe the men that were in here?'

'I think so...'

Chapter 10

Anita felt the wall beginning to collapse on top of her, pressing hard on her shoulders, and what was that noise, she could hear a voice calling her name. She struggled to open her eyes, becoming aware of a hand on her shoulder and gently rocking her.

'Anita, wake up.' It was Jane.

'W... what, what is it?'

'Anita I may have done something terrible. I'm sorry to wake you so soon but I feel that I must tell you.'

'Tell me what?' Anita started to come round.

'I have spoken to Markov...'

She did not finish the sentence, Anita's grogginess cleared in a flash and she swung her legs over the side of the bunk, rubbing her eyes, talking at the same time.

'Markov, how, what have you said to him?'

'Anita I'm sorry, I didn't realise, the phone rang while I was asleep, and I automatically answered it.' Jane was distraught. 'Katja was awake and heard me and now she is upset, she thinks we are really working with Markov. I can see it in her face.'

'Damn, listen, I want you to tell me everything that was said, try to remember everything, it could be important.' Anita slid from the bunk, took hold of Jane's upper arms, and looked at her. 'The damage is done, if there is any damage. Don't worry we will get through this. Let me talk with Katja for a moment.'

Jane nodded and the two of them moved into the main saloon where Katja was lying wide-eyed on her back and obviously disturbed.

'Katja, it looks as if something bad has happened. You heard Jane talking to Markov. Well it is not as you think, we are all trying to get away from him and he's fishing to see what he can find out.

'Thank you, I have been through so much recently, I have become afraid to trust anyone.'

'Jane,' said Anita, 'let's sit down and you tell me all you can.'

Jane told what she could, how she had been fast asleep and not realised where she was nor the predicament they were in when she automatically answered her mobile phone but by then it was too late.

'I tried to sound as if I was simply on holiday, sleeping in my hotel room but when he asked which hotel, I know I gave the game away; I know he didn't believe me.'

'But would he know we are here, here on this boat? I don't know, but we have to believe that there is a chance he could find us. I'll worry about that if it happens. Come on let's have a cup of something hot.'

On the deck, the men were making steady progress in the mix of darkness, navigation lights and the bright lights of the canal side industrial installations. They had sailed during the hours of darkness many times and that experience told as they spoke softly to each other interpreting the meaning of each cluster of red, white and green lights.

'Have you seen that one on Port Lee?' asked John, eyes concentrating on the light cutting through the darkness.

'Yes, got it, can you see the Sea Lock?'

'It'll be a while yet,' said Roger, 'I can only just see the lumen of Ijmuiden, not much in the way of proper lights yet.'

'Aye, should be daylight soon so it'll be a bit easier,' said Lee, straining his eyes.

The yacht plodded on for a further 40 minutes until Paul called out from his position near the mast.

'Sea Lock in sight, Skipper.'

'Good, get the lines ready boys and put the fenders over both side, I don't feel like worrying about which side to lie alongside right now.'

Markov sat on the edge of his seat impatiently drumming his fingers on the table and opposite him sat a silent Caas. Greetje had left them only a few minutes earlier, making both a coffee before she locked up for the night.

'You will pull the latch won't you Uncle Caas, when you leave?'

'Yes, thanks for the coffee and that was gooddescription you gave us of the people we are looking for.' It was drizzling a little when Greetje stepped outside, the few lights still burning reflecting from the wet roadway and she shuddered, not from the cold damp air but in the knowledge of what her uncle was capable of when he was angry, and for some reason the woman they were looking for had made him angry. She pulled up the collar of her jacket and hunched her shoulders, to banish any thoughts of what fate those people might have to endure once her uncle caught up with them.

'Jaap, a change of plan,' said Caas, speaking into his phone. 'We think they are on a boat heading for Ijmuiden. Keep looking around the station and

Sixhaven, but call someone you can trust in Ijmuiden to go to the port and see if they can find a British boat with the people we are searching for on board.'

He continued speaking for several minutes, relaying the description his niece had given of the four sailors and the women. Finishing his call, he drank the remainder of his coffee and looked at Markov.

'There is not much we can do until we get a sighting. I suggest we get some sleep and await developments. My men are scouring Amsterdam for them, we have many contacts and Jaap will get someone in Ijmuiden to watch the canal. We'll find them.'

'All right, I will go to the apartment in Damstraat.' The two men left the bar, pulling the door closed behind them and walked a short way along the empty cobbled streets of the old town before parting, Markov to Damstraat and Caas to his flat in a building near the canal, agreeing that each would call the other as soon as they heard anything.

Outside the Central Station, the ferry with its meagre compliment of late night passengers bumped against the large rubber girdle fastened to the dockside and from it, Kostyantyn stepped onto the landing. He had taken the ferry to the far bank more than an hour before to look around the small marina called Sixhaven. He had walked round its perimeter fence as far as he could, able to see almost everything and cast his eye over the vessels inside. He had watched several people moving about, mostly drunken sailors returning from a bawdy night out in Amsterdam, eventually managing to tag along with one such group. He had followed them in through the security gate and managed to slip away before anyone realised and gone for a closer look at the boats. He knew nothing about boats, but he knew a lot about people.

'Was Wollen Sie,' said a slurry German voice from a large cruiser as he passed.

He stopped and looked for the source of the voice and shortly the man's head appeared, rising slowly up through a hatch.

'Good evening,' he said, in broken German, a language spoken by many Ukrainians. 'I am looking for my friends, some English sailors. I am not sure where they are, can you help me?'

'English, always they are drunk and noisy. There was an English yacht here tonight earlier, but it has gone. I did not hear them go.' A look of puzzlement was spreading across his face. He scratched his head, lifted a can of beer to his lips, and bobbed back into his boat, the conversation over.

So, an English boat had slipped secretly away not long before. Kostyantyn looked at his watch, perhaps he had done enough for tonight; at least he had something positive to report. He walked to the gate, let himself out, and once back aboard the ferry, he had considered calling Markov but there were several passengers on board and he decided not to call until there was less risk of anyone overhearing him but now he was back on the other side he was able to melt into the shadows.

Markov was snoozing in a big armchair when the call came in from Kostyantyn and he had news.

'Boss, I think you are right about a boat and the river. I've had a look round the marina and bumped into a German who said an English boat sneaked out only a few hours ago.'

Suddenly he was wide-awake, it was news he had been waiting for. Caas had told him that a boat would take three or four hours to get to the Sea Lock and once there they might have to wait to get through to the open sea. He looked at his watch – 4.30; he picked his phone up from the coffee table and called Caas.

The morning was at its coldest and the yacht crew's metabolic rate at its lowest as the yacht slowed and inched its way close to the waiting pontoon several meters from the lock gates.

'Looks like there are a couple of barges waiting to go through,' called Paul from his vantage point in front of the yacht's mast. 'The bridge is down.'

'Oh dammit, looks like to be quite a wait before we can get through,' said Lee.

'Might not be, let's see if anything is coming this way first,' said Roger. It was; the working day had already started for the river traffic. It was not long after five 'o'clock and the great barges of the Dutch waterways were already plying their trade.

'We will have to go alongside that waiting pontoon.' Lee pointed to his intended mooring point, reducing the engine revolutions still further. The yacht slowed almost to a standstill and he swung the wheel a few degrees, allowing the boat to slide gently alongside the pontoon. Paul and John jumped ashore and soon had the mooring lines secured to the pontoon. They were tired from the long day, and had anxious looks on their faces after being alone with their thoughts for the past few hours. Both had begun to realise that they were probably getting themselves into a dangerous situation.

Anita felt the boat come to a stop and popped her head up from below to see what was happening.

'Why have we stopped?'

'The Sea Lock is busy. I don't know why they are not using the leisure craft lock, must be down for maintenance or something. We will have to wait until we can go through the commercial lock,' said Lee.

'How long will that take?'

'I've no idea, half an hour, perhaps longer. I'm hoping we can get in with these two in front of us.'

Anita climbed out of the companionway into the cockpit and looked forward, across the boat's deck to see two great barges sitting squarely in the water waiting their turn to pass through the lock. She began to worry that maybe Markov would find them if they hung about here too long and then what would she do? She went back below, passing Jane and Katja sitting quietly on opposite sides of the saloon

'Why don't you two make a hot drink for the boys, it will give you something to do and might cheer us all up a bit.'

Anita was still weary from a lack of sleep. She had managed to sleep for only an hour and a half, enough to keep her going, keep her mind reasonably alert, but her body felt fatigued and now this worrying development. At the rate things were moving, they might be stuck here for hours and that would give their pursuers some advantage. From what Jane had told her, they may have already guessed as to how they were making their escape and any further delay meant more chance of discovery.

Markov's plan was simple: the more he thought about it the more obvious the situation became. They were trying to escape along the canal, towards the open sea and to England. He had learned that it was less than a day's sailing across the North Sea to the nearest English port of Lowestoft and he knew that Katja did not have any papers so it seemed to be the obvious way to try to escape. He would find them somewhere along the canal and retrieve the girl and probably, with the state of mind he was in, kill the others.

'Bohuslav, I want you two to come with me and Kostyantyn in the car. He is bringing it round here at the moment.'

The two henchmen nodded their weary heads, and five minutes later Kostyantyn arrived with the Mercedes as the first feint greyness of the new day showed itself in the overcast sky. They climbed into the back seat of the car, Kostyantyn wasted no time in accelerating away, and soon they were passing through the last of the side streets and heading onto the motorway leading to the coast. Markov checked his gun one last time and slipped it into the waistband of his trousers. He was looking forward to using it.

'You all have your guns? Keep them out of sight; we will need them once we find these people. Remember the girl is valuable, so make sure she at least is unharmed. The others I do not care about.'

The men murmured understanding and Markov slipped into a silent, angry mood as the car sped along, following the line of the canal. The day was breaking and they were in full view of the canal, but still there was no sign of a yacht. Markov called Caas and asked what the best approach was. Caas said to keep going, get to the Sea Lock as soon as possible, and once there he would meet him then they could decide on their next move. All yachts travelling down the canal had to stop at the sluice and judging by the time they had left the bar and the time of Kostyantyn's call, it was more than likely they had not even reached the Sea Lock yet.

The daylight was spreading as Lee looked at his watch and then up at the sky and then he turned to Roger sitting near him in the cockpit.

'Roger, call the lock keeper and see if we can go through with these barges.'

'Aye aye, Skipper.'

Roger got to his feet and climbed down the steps to the cabin, past the women busy making cups of coffee, giving them a grim smile before sitting down at the chart table. He reached towards the radio and turned the knob, switching the radio to the working channel for the sluice.

'Sluis Ijmuiden, Sluis Ijmuiden, this is ya cht *Whistledown*, yacht *Whistledown*, over.'

He waited patiently for 30 seconds or so, the women watching, wondering what was happening and then came the reply.

'Yacht *Whistledown*, diss iss Sluis Ijmuiden, over.'

'Good morning, we want to pass through the lock and wonder if we can go through with these barges up ahead of us, over.'

'I am sorry but diss iss not possible. De commercial traffic has priority. But not to worry I have no traffic coming from de seaward side and once I have let dem through and dropped de bridge for de morning road traffic I let you through on your own, out.'

That was it, no argument; they would have to wait a while longer before they could get through the lock. Anita listened, fully aware of their predicament; time was running out and if Markov had realised what they were attempting he would not be far away by now.

'Here, take the coffee up on deck,' said Jane, 'ask them if they want a biscuit or something.'

Anita nodded and passed a mug of coffee to Roger sitting at the chart table and taking the other three mugs, she climbed up onto the deck to pass them round. Roger emerged shortly after and announced that they would be another hour at least.

'Should we make some food?' asked Jane.

'Bloody right,' said John, not one to miss the chance of a feed, 'I'm starving.'

'Good idea, the wind has picked up a lot this past hour and it will be a bit lumpy out there. We will not want to be cooking if the pots and pans are flying about, will we?' added Paul.

Anita looked slightly alarmed; she had never done any sailing and had never considered that the conditions at sea could be that difficult.

'What will it be like do you think?'

'Forecast is for a short sharp blow from the north-east, up to a force seven, which is not good. Under normal circumstances we would not consider going out in it but you're a special case.'

Anita said nothing; events seemed to be spinning out of her control. She had done all she could, now it was up to these men to get them safely across the North Sea and back home. She left the men with their hands cupped round the warm mugs and returned below to sit and wait patiently for the lock gates to open for them. Jane handed her a mug coffee and between them, the women ate the last of the boat's store of chocolate biscuits until, with great relief, they heard Lee exclaim that the lights on the lock entrance had change to green.

'At last, cast off, lads.'

Lee put his hand on the throttle, made ready to steer the boat into the lock, Roger and John released the mooring lines, and pushed the craft away from the pontoon. Easing the throttle forward and into gear, Lee turned the wheel a few degrees and they slid quietly away from the pontoon and a minute later, to the relief of all on board, they finally hooked their lines over the fixing points and watched the gates close behind them. Below deck, the women sat quietly and above the wind began to howl in the shrouds.

'Roger, we had better see what sailing gear we have for these ladies; we have three spare life-jackets but I'm not sure if there's much in the way of wet weather gear. My wife's sailing clothes are hanging on the quarter berth cabin door; give them to one of them.'

'They won't need to come on deck. We can sail the boat across can't we?'

'We can, but we might as well kit them out as best we can.'

Roger went below to locate the life-jackets and to find what waterproof clothing he could for the women. If they had to be exposed to the elements, it would at least give them some protection and when he handed over the life- jackets, he gave a brief instruction on how to use them.

'It's okay, Roger, I've done a bit of sailing,' said Jane,

'I have a good idea about what to do, I'll look after Katja and Anita.'

Roger looked at her, pleasantly surprised. It would take a lot of pressure off the crew even if only one of them knew a little bit about sailing.

'Susan says she's done some sailing, Skipper, could be useful. How about we work her into the watch system? It would give us another pair of eyes and maybe a better chance of some rest, you know what Paul's like. He could disappear at the first sign of a big sea.'

'Good idea, quiz her when we get moving again. Get ready to cast off,' he shouted as one of the red lights at the end of the lock turned green.

'Susan, how much sailing have you done?' Roger asked as the lock gates began to open.

'I've raced in the Solent for several years and been across to France about a dozen times.'

'So sailing a boat is no mystery?'

'No, I've done a couple of shore based courses too.'

'That's great, you can join the crew for the crossing then, put these waterproofs on and come up on deck and let's see what you can do.'

Jane donned the lion's share of the waterproof clothing and emerged onto the deck just as the yacht began to move out of the lock. She took hold of the safety rail and made her way forward towards the mast where Roger was waiting for her.

'Sit here for a few moments and we'll go through the lines and what they do.'

Jane grabbed a line at the mast to steady herself, sat down, breathed in the cool morning air, and looked about her. Moored up against the riverbank was a barge, a few cars were passing on the main road only a few metres away and leaning against the railings near the bridge was the figure of a man. He seemed to be watching them and then suddenly, his body became rigid, his eyes pierced hers and she realised that it was Markov.

Chapter 11

Markov felt elated; the woman staring back at him was positively Jane, he recognised those same soft features and tousled hair, she was the woman he had met in Verbier. He had found her at last although he still had no idea who she was working for, was it a Russian criminal gang, or was it really some government agency? Whoever it was would pay dearly, particularly for killing Vladimir, he had been his lieutenant for many years and he was feeling the loss personally. Vladimir's death meant a great deal to his operation, the man knew as much about the workings of the organization as he did himself, he was trusted and he would be difficult to replace. He thought about the girl, there, only meters away, she was valuable and the Sheik seemed willing to pay his price. He was determined not to let that amount of money slip through his hands; he would get her back and kill all those on board that little yacht.

There was not a lot he could do without access to a watercraft, he could not get near them and soon the yacht would be leaving the harbour. He stuck both hands into his pockets, turned away from the freshening wind and made his way back to his waiting car, standing for a moment to watch as the yacht made a slow passage away from the sea lock. Looking past it and towards the open sea he caught sight of a pilot boat manoeuvring out of its dock and heading out to sea. The sleek yellow and black hull sliced easily through the water and it was travelling at least four or five times quicker than the yacht. He watched for a while longer as the boat reached the outer limits of the port and then, to his surprise, it suddenly leapt forward, seeming to climb out of the water. Markov knew that if he could get hold of a boat like that he could easily catch the yacht.

'Markov, you have found what you are looking for?'

It was Caas; he had parked his car a few metres away and had walked unnoticed towards Markov.

'Yes, I think so. See that boat there?' he said, pointing.

'There is a woman on board, a woman I met in Switzerland only a month or so ago, she called me a couple of days ago and thought I saw her in Amsterdam last night. She is part of this I am sure.'

'What do you think you should do now?'

'There are fast boats here? Like the one there?' Markov pointed to the fast disappearing pilot launch.

'Yes, I expect so.'

'Then we find one and we go after them.'

Caas fell silent for a few seconds. Where would they get a fast boat like that, no questions asked, at such short notice?

The yacht made steady progress towards the pier ends and headed out into the open sea, rocking gently in the choppy sea. Roger held the wheel in both hands, turning it easily from side to side as he compensated for the sea's movement and below Lee was sat hunched over the chart table setting a course for England. After a few minutes, he returned to the steering position and relieved Roger who talked briefly with the other members of the crew before making his way towards the mast. Bouncing along under engine Lee reduced speed and turned into the wind. On his command, the others began hoisting the main sail, Roger pulling on the line to assist Paul who struggled to winch the great area of canvas into the sky whilst John managed the other items associated with setting the sail. The winds were fair and it looked as if they would take them all the way across the North Sea. Soon there would be no need for the engine.

'Should we be going out in this,' said John, his eye on the distant horizon. 'The wind is picking up.'

'I know, it's up to a five and forecast to increase to maybe a seven,' said Lee. 'Maybe we should turn back.'

'Force seven?' said Anita looking up at him from the hatch. 'You can't turn back. Jane has told me that she thinks Markov has seen us and that he will try to stop us. If we go back now I cannot be responsible for the safety of any of you, and I tell you now these men are ruthless, killers.'

'Killers, what do you mean?' chirped Paul, a worried look spreading across his face.

'I think it is time you all knew a little more of the truth.'

'A little?' said Roger, 'and who's Jane?'

'Oh... yes, I have not been completely truthful I admit. I am Anita and my companion is really Jane. I needed to keep you in the dark about our real identities for security reasons. I can make you aware of the situation we are in, but there are other things you should not know.'

Paul and John looked at each other, Lee looked straight at Anita, and Roger looked at the horizon.

'Katja is Ukrainian and the people following us are her kidnappers but not quite as I have told you. I thought that once we got her out and far enough away, they would turn their attention to other things, but I was wrong. It seems that Markov is obsessed with getting Katja back.' She would be a target for killing Vladimir. None of these people knew about that – only Katja, and she would keep quiet, so perhaps it was better that she did not mention that part.

'This operation has been sanctioned by Her Majesty's Government. I am to bring Katja to safety and Jane has been helping me. I'm sorry I deceived you, but you will have to work to my orders until we reach safety in England.'

The men were silent, they were in big trouble and they knew it. Anita would not let them call the Dutch Coast Guard and so it seemed that their only chance was to run for the English coast.

'Right, let's get some sort of watch system going, the weather is forecast to deteriorate for a while, but once the blow has come through we should be all right. Let's do the five man watch routine. Sue... er... Jane,' called out Lee

Jane's face appeared at the hatch.

'Jane, hmm..., you say you are reasonably experienced at sailing?'

'Yes, that's right.'

'Do you think you can manage to fall in and take a watch?'

'Yes, I think you need all the help you can get, none of us got much sleep last night, did we?'

'I didn't get any,' said Lee.

'What do you want me to do?'

'Myself and Paul will take the first watch starting when we get to the fairway buoy; we'll do two hours on and three hours off to begin with – that should allow us to catch up on some sleep.'

Lee asked Roger to tell each of them how the watch system worked and how they should share the bunks. Anita and Katja would play no part in the sailing of the boat but would keep the crew supplied with hot drinks and any food they had left. Since arriving in Holland, they had not bothered to stock up on food nor fuel. Food was not such a problem for the crossing but fuel was and so they would sail as much as possible to conserve their fuel supply. Lee estimated that they probably had enough to motor half way across but certainly not as far as the English coast and as they passed the fairway buoy Lee set course to Lowestoft.

'Better put a reef in to start with, the wind will only get stronger, we're up to 16 knots already,' he said, looking at the wind instrument. 'We'll reef again if it gets above 22 or 23 knots'

In double quick time, they shortened sail, trimmed it for the wind direction and for the next few hours they settled down to enjoy the ride. Katja had finally fallen asleep in her bunk and Anita was busy making tea without milk, milk being their first casualty. She began to feel the cold, her clothing not particularly suited to the environment she now found herself in. She warmed her hands over the kettle as she looked down at Katja snug in the sleeping bag Roger had given her and hoped to high heaven that they could pull this thing off.

'Henrick, we need a boat, a fast boat, who do you know who might get us one?' asked Caas.

Henrick thought for a moment, he was from the town of Ijmuiden, and was an obvious candidate for Caas to ask.

'I will make a few phone calls. My brother is a fisherman but I think he will not be in port, he told me he was going south for a few weeks after shellfish. I know others, though. Leave it to me for a few minutes and I will see what I can find.'

Henrick took his telephone from his pocket and thumbed through some numbers, calling seamen who might help and before long; he was able to report positively to Caas.

'We have to go to the dock where the Wildcat Work boats are moored, there we will meet someone.'

'Good man,' Caas turned towards Markov. 'Markov, it looks as if we might be able to get a fast boat.'

Markov's eyes lit up, the chase was on, he looked forward to catching up with those that had wronged him, and when they did, he would personally pull the trigger on the one who had killed Vladimir. He signalled to his men waiting by the Mercedes to be ready to move, and soon the Ukrainians were following Caas's car towards the dock. The two vehicles stopped several metres from gates that opened onto an area set aside for the assembly of giant windmills. The operation was vast, with part- built windmills, cranes strewn all over, and in the water alongside these monsters sat specialised shipping for the transportation and erection of the machines.

Caas got out of his car and walked to the security hut, went inside and a short time later, re-emerged with a satisfied look upon his face. He reached the Mercedes and signalled for Markov to open his window.

'We can go in, only four of us and on foot. I will bring Henrick with me; he knows everyone around here and is a good man to have with us I think. You bring your best man, Markov.'

'Kostyantyn, you come with me, Bohuslav you two take the car back to Amsterdam and keep an eye on the women, wait for me at the apartment in Damstraat. If we need the car back here I will call you.'

'Okay, Boss.'

Bohuslav climbed into the driving seat, reversed the car back onto the roadway, and within seconds, was on his way back to Amsterdam his mind racing. Things seemed to running out of control yet again. He would need to find the road sweeper as soon as he could.

Markov and Kostyantyn walked towards Caas's car to join him and Henrick and together the four men marched passed the security shed with some urgency and headed towards the dockside. Markov looked ahead, eager to see what kind of vessel they were going to use and when he saw the sleek lines of an array of half a dozen yellow and black catamarans his face became a picture. If the colours were anything to go by these beauties would easily catch the yacht, and then he would have his revenge. He wondered whether they needed to be in international waters to dispose of the bodies. But then, when had he ever worried about borders and the law?

Waiting beside one of them was a stocky man with a seaman's cap sat jauntily on his head, his hands on his hips.

'This is Tom, he is the skipper of one of these boats and he will take us out, for a price.' said Henrick.

'What price?' asked Caas speaking in his native Dutch.

'He wants 5,000 euros for 24 hours. He can tell his company that they are doing sea trials after repairs to the engine, which is true.'

Caas whistled and turned to Markov and in English said, 'It will cost 10,000 euros, Markov. Are you prepared to pay that? The price is high because she is a fast boat and burns a lot of fuel.'

Markov was busy looking over the vessel and was only half listening.

'He wants the money before we go and he has to get at least one of his regular crew back aboard to keep an eye on the machinery. And there is one more complication,' said Henrick.

'Complication?' queried Caas.

'Yes, the weather. He will not take us to sea until the weather calms down.'

Caas looked up at the clouds accelerating across the sky, dark, angry looking and even he could feel the wind freshening, but not being a seaman did not fully appreciate the significance.

'It is not that bad,' he said.

'Here is Tom, you can ask him yourself,' said Henrick. He knew the conditions were worsening and was glad to let the skipper explain the situation.

'You are Tom?' asked Caas.

'I am.'

'You will take us after the yacht that has been stolen?'

'I will, for 5,000 euros. I could lose my job if the company finds out, but for 5,000 euros I take the risk.' Caas looked at Tom's weather beaten face, a confident and capable looking man whom he decided he could believe. Caas knew very little about boats, especially sea going ones and that whatever the man told him about boats and the sea he would have to accept.

'Henrick says you will not take your boat out because of the weather.'

'Not yet. The front coming through will bring strong winds for a time. I expect the seas to build up and that is not good news for us, these boats are more useful for speed than coping with heavy seas. We could finish up in trouble if we go too soon. Give it six or eight hours and then we go, it will give you time to get the money – cash.' Caas frowned, cash, 10,000 euros, could Markov get hold of the cash so quickly?

By ten 'o'clock that same morning the yacht was clear of the coast and passing near to the offshore wind farms. The crew had changed watch; Lee and John were below fast asleep in their sleeping bags and on deck Roger was gently turning the wheel to keep them on course for Lowestoft.

'The wind is picking up Paul, it's above 20 knots, the gusts are getting stronger, and we need to think about that second reef.'

He looked up the mast, the sail and then the wind instrument at the very top of the mast. It was spinning so fast it was becoming a blur. The seas were beginning to build, the waves growing in size by the minute, their tops starting to trail white spray as the wind increased and so the boat's motion became more noticeable.

Below deck, Katja was still fast asleep, curled up in a foetus position, snoring gently and hardly moving. Across from the sleeping girl, Jane sat at the table poring over the chart. It was several years since she had been to sea in a small boat and she was beginning to enjoy the experience but underneath she was worried about Markov. He had recognised her, of that she was sure, but would he really be able to follow them? She looked out of the cabin window amazed at the sight of giant windmills no more than a kilometre away, a forest of white trees, their giant blades slowly spinning. She watched them for a minute or two before turning her attention back to the chart. She took the dividers from the receptacle in front of her and stepped off the distance from the windmills to the English coast. They still had a long way to go, 20 hours she estimated, at the present rate.

Anita had gone into the forward cabin to try to sleep for a time but she was finding it increasingly difficult as the waves built up and the motion of the boat became ever more uncomfortable. The storm was upon them and the boat was beginning to struggle through waves that lifted them up and then crashed them back down again with such force she felt the boat would fall apart. She was not a sailor, had never ventured out on a yacht, she was beginning to feel seasick and had to close her eyes tightly to try to hold back the feeling of nausea.

On deck, the waves were beginning to crash over the side, cold, angry water washing past the two sailors and streaming over the stern of the boat.

'It's time for a reef, Paul, give Jane a call to come and help.'

Jane heard her name called, interrupting her thoughts and she slid off the chart table seat to look up through the open hatch at the two men in the cockpit.

'We're going to reef the sails, Jane, and we need your help,' said Paul.

'Right-oh,' said Jane zipping her oversized jacket right up to her chin. She had found a woolly hat in a cubbyhole and now she pulled it down firmly over her ears. She was ready.

'Those waves are a bit much, be careful whilst I try to ride over them. Jane, take the main halyard whilst Paul puts the reef in to shorten sail. Are you ready?'

Paul and Jane both nodded at him and took up their positions.

'Remember what I told you, Jane, don't forget to put the clutch back on when you have dropped the sail or the line could slip and the sail could come right down and then we'd be in a fix.'

Jane said nothing, looking over the assortment of lines, her eyes following their paths through pulleys and up the mast to make sure she had hold of the right one. Paul hooked his safety line into the safety wire running along the deck and shuffled on his backside towards the mast. A wave broke against the hull sending cold seawater cascading over him and he had to hang on for fear of slipping over the side but as the water streamed past him, he was able to continue and begin reefing the sail. Between the three of them, they finally managed to reduce the sail to half its original size and once they had re-set it the boat eased its bucking motion considerably. But the effort had got to Paul. As he climbed back into the cockpit, grasping a cleat with one hand and the nearest winch in the other, his face looked ashen.

'Can you cope, Jane?' asked Roger looking both of them over.

'Yes, I'm fine,' answered Jane, and then he turned his attention towards Paul whom he knew was prone to seasickness. 'Get below, Paul, you're no good up here, we can manage.'

He looked up at the sky, the dark clouds were swirling viciously overhead announcing the imminent arrival of the worst of the bad weather.

'The blow that was forecast is coming through right now. Once it has passed things should settle down a little but I think we're in for a rough ride.'

Jane looked at Roger, following his eyes skywards to the furious sky above them.

In the wheelhouse of the big yellow catamaran, Tom, the skipper, had just finished a mug of coffee when the outer door opened and in walked Caas.

'You have the money?' asked Tom.

'Not yet, my friends are getting it from Amsterdam and should be back shortly. There is something you should know, my friend.'

Tom eyed Caas apprehensively, knowing very well the man's reputation.

'I look after the business interests of my Ukrainian friends here in the Netherlands and as such I earn a commission on all the deals we are involved in. This is such a deal. Markov will pay you your fee plus my commission. Do you understand?' Caas had a steely, threatening glint in his eye.

Tom knew from Henrick that he was dealing with one of the Netherlands' most powerful underworld figures and Henrick had warned him not to cross Caas. 'You can make a lot of money in a short time if you give my boss what he wants,' he had said, and Tom was heeding his words.

'I understand, Mr Bleecker, how much is your cut?'

'Five thousand and another 1,000 from you for introducing you to my associates,' he said with the steady look of a man who got his way, no question.

'As you say, 6,000 euros,' said Tom, a little uncomfortably but 4,000 was still good money for one day's work.

Caas nodded; pleased he had cleared that hurdle. He was a man of violence; he would stop at nothing where money was involved, but these Ukrainians were just as bad. If Markov ever thought he was taking him for a ride, he might have a serious problem himself, but then he had to make a living, didn't he?

Caas turned away smiling to himself and looked out of the wheelhouse window to see his car pull up at the dock gate. Markov and Kostyantyn emerged and walked through the gateway towards the catamarans. Markov carried a briefcase in his hand with the 10,000 euros, a high price to pay but he had a good chance of recovering most of it; perhaps they could put the price for Katja at 120,000 euros and he would get his money back and more.

'Here you are, count it.' Markov opened the case on the chart table.

'I do not need to count it.'

Markov handed Tom the money and asked when was the earliest that they could put to sea after the yacht.

'Not yet. This front is already passing through and the wind should drop off quite significantly. We wait two or three hours for the sea to calm down enough for us, then we go.'

'Hm,' grunted Markov, 'they will have got away by then.'

'No, I don't think so, look at this chart. They were heading out between the wind farms, here look,' he said, indicating the position of the farms on the chart. 'They will make eight knots maximum I think, maybe only six in these seas, and they will have an eight hour start on us so they will be no further than this line look, maybe 50 miles ahead, we can make that distance in less than two hours at full throttle. The sea will calm down enough for us to make thirty knots to their five or six I think. When we get here,' he said, indicating to a point on the chart, 'we can use radar to find them. The radar on board will pick them up even if they are 5 or 10 miles away. There will not be any other small boat out in this weather I think.'

Markov nodded, reassured; it looked so simple and the boat could go as almost as fast as a car.

'I can take you all if you wish,' said Tom to the assembled gangsters.

'Not me,' said Caas in Dutch, 'I don't do boats. Henrick, you can go with them and look after my interests. When you return, Tom will have something for you to give me, won't you Tom?'

Tom nodded nervously and Markov watched, unhappy that they were speaking in Dutch, a language he knew little of.

'What are you saying?' he asked in his broken English.

'I was telling Tom that I will not be coming with you because I am many things but a sailor is not one of them; but Henrick here is from a fishing family and will be at home on this boat. I wish you luck in your hunt my friend.' He shook Markov's hand, turned and walked towards the gangplank, and left the boat.

'We rest for a couple more hours then I look at the sea. If it is not too dangerous for us then we go. Make yourselves at home; when my crewman arrives we can eat something hot and I find you some waterproof clothing and tell you procedures,' said Tom.

Roger looked out across the deck, at the waves rolling towards them and then down at his wristwatch.

'Jane, go and wake Lee and John, it's time for them to take over.'

She unclipped her safety line and climbed down the companionway, hanging onto anything she could to steady herself in the violently rocking boat and went to find Lee who was curled up in his sleeping bag in the aft cabin. With so many people on board, the Skipper's double bunk was the only space available and there she found Paul to, sprawled out beside Lee and snoring heavily.

'Lee, wake up,' Jane shook the stocking clad foot protruding from the open zip of the sleeping bag.

'Uh... what?' he said with a start.

'It is time to change the watch. I have already woken
John'

'Okay,' Lee looked his wristwatch, his bleary eyes not believing four hours had passed so quickly and that it was time to go back on deck.

He noticed Paul for the first time and managed to crawl past him and off the bunk to pull on his jacket and boots. Holding onto a grab rail, he made his way unsteadily into the saloon, sat at the chart table and read some numbers from an instrument in front of him. Taking the ruler and a pencil, he carefully plotted their position on the chart and studied it for a time.

'We are well past the wind farm, only 70 miles to go.'

'How long do you reckon, Skipper?' asked John.

'At the rate we're going, I would say we'll be just off Lowestoft at about one o'clock in the morning.'

Their movements and the noise they made talking disturbed Katja and she opened her eyes wide. For a moment, she was unsure where she was, and then she saw Jane holding herself steady by the companionway and Lee sitting at the chart table and was relieved she was not still in the hands of her countrymen.

'So, you have finally woken up,' said Lee, looking down at her, 'and where is Anita?' he asked Jane.

'In there I think,' she said, indicating the forward cabin.

Lee frowned; he knew the forward cabin was not the place to be in heavy seas. He went forward, holding on tightly to the grab rail running the full length of the saloon, and listened at the door. He could hear moaning and guessed that Anita was having a bad time of it.

'Hello in there, are you all right? 'He knocked on the door.

He pressed his ear to the wood and heard nothing but moaning and decided to investigate. He pushed the door open to find Anita curled up and letting out a low moan, which increased in volume each time the boat smashed back down off a wave.

'Bloody hell, she's in a bad way, here help me move her onto Katja's bunk, tell Katja to get up.'

Jane understood and together with Lee managed to get Anita out of the forward cabin and onto the saloon berth where the boat's motion was less violent.

'I should have given you all seasick pills before we put to sea. Here let's give her one now. Get some water Jane. The pills are on the shelf behind the chart table, you can't miss them.'

Jane found a cup and with some difficulty managed to half fill it from the galley tap; she located the packet of pills and made her way back to Lee and between them they forced a couple of pills and some water down Anita's throat. She was suffering badly, her face was a deathly white and her eyes were rolling, but as they lay her flat on the bunk Lee could see that she was feeling better already away from the slamming in the forward part of the boat.

'You had better have some as well,' he said to Katja.

'What about you Jane?'

'I'm okay.'

Lee, grim faced, looked around the saloon, at John and then at the women. The storm seemed to have increased since he had come off watch; the faces looking back at him were drawn and worried and if the gangsters were after them then things could not get much worse, not unless the boat sustained damaged. He swallowed hard, forced all thoughts of disaster to the back of his mind, and climbed on deck to take over from Roger.

'We've reefed both sails, the wind got up to more than 30 knots for the best part of an hour but seems to be easing now. You will need to watch the waves, they are coming across our beam and I've had to ride the bigger ones,' Roger said, handing over the wheel to Lee.

'Okay, Roger, I have put our position on the chart, we are about 70 miles out and I reckon another 10 hours or so should see us safely across.'

Roger told Lee about Paul feeling unwell, said Jane was capable of helping them sail the boat. She could take Paul's place until he felt better then he unclipped his line and climbed down the steps into the cabin to find Jane and Anita already asleep in the saloon bunks. He grunted as he realised that his only option, unless he wanted to brave the forepeak, was to crawl in beside the sleeping Paul to try to get some rest. It had been a hard few hours but they were through the worst of it, and with that thought in mind, he crawled into Lee's sleeping bag and fell into a deep sleep.

Chapter 12

Tom sat in his swivel seat in front of the catamaran's control console, pressed the start buttons and several metres below, almost inaudible to him, the two Detroit diesel engines burst into life.

'We have a range of 120 nautical miles,' he said to the three men watching him. 'Your friends cannot be more than 60 or 70 nautical miles from Ijmuiden even now. We might be lucky and find them straight away, two hours maybe three.'

Markov nodded approval, he and Kostyantyn would be ready when they finally caught up with the yacht; they had Henrick with them and Caas had instructed him to follow Markov's orders. The three of them and this powerful machine would easily catch and overpower that puny yacht and her crew.

Tom reached forward, lifted the telephone receiver on his control desk, and waited for the engineer to answer.

'Jos, how are the engines? I am going to cast off in five minutes; I see the shore-men walking towards us. Yes, we have all tanks full, yes, five minutes, I will call you when we are moving away from the dock. Henrick, you can help me cast off; are your friends seamen?'

He turned to Markov and asked in English if he or Kostyantyn could help with the mooring warps. Markov looked at Kostyantyn and told him to help.

'Henrick will show you,' he said.

'Good,' said Tom, 'let's get to it. Henrick, you take the forward line and your friend here can take the one aft. I can keep an eye on him from here,' he said looking through the side window.

Henrick and Kostyantyn left the bridge and climbed down the ladder to the foredeck where Henrick showed the Ukrainian the technique of casting off. Two shore-men arrived and made ready to let go of the mooring warps and as Henrick moved towards the forward part of the deck, Tom came from his bridge and leaned over the rail to keep an eye on the inexperienced Kostyantyn.

'Cast off forward, cast off aft,' he called out and the two lines fell loose against the boat's hull.

Henrick and Kostyantyn hauled them aboard and coiled them neatly whilst Tom hurried back inside to call Jos in the engine room and slowly the boat swung round into open water.

'Caas said you have been up all night. If you want to catch up on some sleep there are two cabins on the lower deck with berths, feel free,' he said to Markov.

Markov was feeling the lack of sleep, he had been on the go for more than 24 hours and a nap would be very welcome.

'You tell me when we find the boat.'

'I will.'

Tom watched as his guests disappeared below and then turned his attention back to conning the boat and the big yellow catamaran moved slowly out of the harbour entrance. Tom had spent the last year and a half in these waters and he knew them like the back of his hand. He guessed that the yacht would follow a course towards the north-west, passing between the wind farms, but once they were far enough from the coast, they could go anywhere. None of the gangsters seemed to have much idea where the yacht was going to other than across the North Sea to England and he wondered where that might be.

He glanced down at the chart plotter, bright colours showing the geography of the sea around him, the depth of water, the buoyage and lights. He pressed a button and zoomed out to reveal a larger portion of the southern North Sea, the green of the land, yellows indicating shallow water and out in front of them the vast blue expanse of the North Sea. The sea was not empty: far from it, oil and gas installations were dotted about all over and he decided to give them as wide a berth as possible to avert prying eyes. That was a thought. If they came upon the yacht within view of a manned rig there would be witnesses, and what about their radio? They could easily send out a mayday.

Caas had told him that they needed the catamaran to find a yacht, the people on board had stolen diamonds from Markov and then the yacht and that a show of force would probably be enough to make them give up the diamonds. Once they had retrieved the diamonds, they could leave the yacht because Markov had no real interest in it, adding that it was unlikely they would call for help. 'These people are criminals, they will not want the authorities involved, do not worry.'

The sea was still rough as the catamaran passed the fairway buoy, the waves swinging it wildly about but at least the wind had dropped significantly and Tom was confident that the sea would soon drop away as well. He looked at the chart plotter and decided on his course. He would head for Lowestoft, the nearest port on the English coast, an obvious destination for the yacht, and he would push the catamaran along at no more than 15 knots until the seas subsided. He knew that, apart from Hendrik, his passengers would not know what was going on, and by the time they came back to the bridge he could well be up to full speed and they would be none the wiser.

Many miles ahead of the big yellow catamaran the yacht was coping well with the seas, the waves were beginning to reduce in size and intensity as the storm passed over. The wind had dropped to less than 18 knots, they had shaken out the first of the reefs in the mainsail, Lee, and John had settled into their watch and below, Katja sat at the chart table. Anita lay semi-conscious on her bunk, on the bunk opposite lay Jane, curled up, and fast asleep and in the aft cabin the snoring of the two men resonated.

Suddenly the boat heaved up and over a large wave, the biggest wall of water that had engulfed them all day, but it seemed to be the last – after that the sea was noticeably calmer, the horizon a little straighter and an hour later Anita stopped dozing and tried to get up from her bunk. She swung her legs round to sit up, but the feeling of nausea immediately returned and she slumped back against the side of the boat. She closed her eyes tightly trying to fight off the sickness, she felt physically useless but her mind was still active and she began thinking of a way out of their predicament. On deck, a happier and more relaxed Lee looked out towards the horizon. The waves were slackening visibly and the wind was down to 12 knots. There was nothing in sight, not a ship nor a rig of any kind and they were well clear of any wind farms, they were more than half way across the North Sea.

'John, give Roger and Jane a call will you and see how Paul is before we change watches.'

John stood up, much steadier than he had during the previous four hours and made his way below to shake Roger gently on the shoulder. Paul was still asleep and moaning softly so John decided to leave him where he was for the time being. Roger was soon awake and struggling into his jacket and boots and John went to Jane's bunk and tapped her on the shoulder.

'Did you manage a plot Roger, how far to Lowestoft?'.

'The wind has blown us too far south and we've been sailing well below our course. I reckon we'll be another eight or ten hours at this speed.'

'Oh, that's a blow, I knew we were going a little south but it didn't seem that bad,' said Lee

'Things are unlikely to improve unless the wind blows from a more favourable direction; we could use the engine.'

'I think that maybe we can.' Said lee, 'the fuel is low because we did not manage fill up after the race but I think we might have enough to get us in from here. I'll check before I go off watch.'

Roger looked up at the sky. The clouds seemed friendlier, white instead of black and were moving across the sky at a sedate, steady pace. Areas of blue were beginning to appear and the late afternoon sun was just about managing to break through.

'Looks like the wind's dropping right off, shall we shake out the first reef, I think we can cope with more canvas before you go off watch, Skipper?'

'Yes, let's do it.'

Jane appeared in the companionway.

'Can you drop the main for me whilst I go and take the reef out?' Roger asked. 'It looks like John is already in his bunk.'

Jane grinned; she had felt guilty after her mishap with Markov, if had she not answered her phone they would have probably got clean away. Still, the yacht seemed to be making good progress and finding herself useful as a temporary member of the crew made her feel a lot better and helped push her worries about the Ukrainian to the back of her mind.

'Of course, just tell me when.'

Lee swung the boat round towards the wind and between them, Roger and Jane shook out the final reef and as Lee brought them back on course, the big sail filled with the breeze. The wind still had plenty of power in it but the direction was not as favourable as they would have wished.

'We had better use the engine. If we carry on sailing like this we will have to tack and we could be another 12 hours out here,' said Lee finally agreeing to Roger's suggestion.

'Aye, I'll start the engine. Do you really think we have enough fuel to get to Lowestoft, Skipper?'

'Maybe, we're a bit low for my liking but there should be just about enough for eight or ten hours' motoring, I will go and check it.'

Lee left Roger and Jane to sail the boat and went below. The gauge on the electrical panel had come to life once the engine started and he could see that the fuel tank was less than a quarter full. It would be touch and go and then he saw Katja looking at him.

'Are you all right?'

'Yes I am fine.'

'Do you think you could make us a cup-a-soup? We haven't had anything for ages and I think cup-a-soup is all we have left.'

'Yes I think maybe I do that.'

'Good, make one for yourself and Anita as well. How are you feeling?' he asked Anita.

'A bit better, I don't know if I should eat anything though.'

'The sea's dropping right off; we're through the worst of it and in deeper water. I bet its flat calm soon.'

'How far away are we from Lowestoft?'

'We reckon about eight hours. We have started the engine to try to get there a little sooner. Drink some soup; I think you might feel better for it. Here, let me fill the kettle,' he said to Katja, lifting the utensil and putting it in the sink.

A small smudge suddenly appeared on the radar sweep and startling 'There it is,' he thought to himself. It was slow moving and for a few minutes, he watched it, checking the target's course. It seemed to be heading more for Lowestoft just as he had predicted and no more than twelve miles. He could be upon them easily within less than half an hour; it was time to rouse Markov and his two associates.

'Jos,' he said into the telephone, 'can you wake our passengers; I think we might have found our quarry.'

Five minutes later Markov, Kostyantyn and Henrick trooped into the bridge a little worse for wear. They had been awake all of the previous night, and now, after a brief rest, they were bleary-eyed and still a little groggy.

'Jos will make you some coffee and breakfast if you want. There is plenty of food in the galley, bacon and eggs eh? Make some for Mister Markov and make me some to,' he said to Henrick.

It was a mistake on the part of the Dutchmen, because as Henrick grinned at the prospect of some hot food and coffee, in Markov's tired mind a primeval reaction took hold.

'What are you saying in your undecipherable talk, what are you saying about me? I hear my name,' he said in his poor English.

Tom was alarmed, the last thing he wanted to do was alienate these dangerous men and he swallowed hard, more than a little fear welling up inside him.

'Mister, I am looking after you, not pulling you to pieces. If you think I am then I am sorry. I was telling Henrick to call Jos and make you coffee and a hot breakfast. It will make you feel better and look,' he said, pointing to the screen in front of him. 'Look that is a slow moving boat and could be your yacht.'

Markov's anger abated as fast as it had appeared and he followed Tom's finger to the small smudge on the screen, seeming to come closer with every sweep of the radar scanner. He looked hard at the screen, mesmerised by the colours and icons and that one blip in particular. Tom looked at him from the corner of his eye and noted his reaction and he felt more than a little relieved.

It was a difficult few minutes until Henrick came back onto the bridge carrying four mugs of steaming coffee and behind him Jos carried a tray with a pile of hot bacon sandwiches. It did the trick; tucking into the food and downing the fresh coffee left Markov feeling better and he managed to forget about Tom, his thoughts turning to the developing situation. What was he going to do when they finally caught up with the yacht?

'There it is,' said Tom, his eyes peering through the binoculars towards the horizon.

230

Markov swallowed the last of his food, swilled down his coffee and took a pace forward to look over Tom's shoulder. Tom passed him the binoculars and Markov saw, in the distance, a yacht. Instinctively he felt for his gun; someone on that boat had shot Vladimir and it was likely that one of them might try to kill him too. Nevertheless, he was ready for them; he would not be the one to go to the bottom of the sea.

Anita had lain still for two hours, looking at the ceiling and thinking through the situation and as the sea gradually became less intense, she managed at last to leave her bunk, swinging her legs over the side and sitting up.

'Here I make you hot soup,' said Katja watching her.

'Thank you, Katja,'

Katja handed Anita the hot mug and for a time sat quietly rolling the mug gently in her hands, she managed a tentative sip and before long she had consumed it all, felt its warmth spread through her body, rejuvenating her.

'We have not had chance to talk, Katja.' Katja looked at Anita, her eyes hooded and tired. 'You remember me don't you? I came to your house by the lake in Kiev.'

'Yes I remember you; you are friend of my mother.'

'That's right, your mother asked my Government to find you and to reunite you with her. Soon, I hope, you will see her again.'

A tear formed in the corner of Katja's eye and rolled down her cheek; hastily she wiped it away and took a deep breath.

'Thank you for rescuing me, those men horrible, you shoot the big one,' she said, her voice faltering, as she recalled the horrors of her captivity. She had not realised until very late that they were going to sell her to an Arab and that she might never see her mother again. The thought had horrified her for that was never part of the plan.

'We are not completely safe yet. I do not know if those men are still following us. Lee says we should reach Lowestoft in the next few hours and then we will find your mother.'

Anita's words tailed off as she thought of Kateryna. It seemed that powerful people wanted her silenced – they had proved that already. She wondered that perhaps the time was fast approaching for her to talk to the lawyers at The Hague. But she could not make that decision, that would be Sir Malcolm's prerogative.

'Bloody North Sea, look,' said Roger pointing.

'What?' asked Jane sitting with her back against the life-raft.

She could not see over the top of the spray hood and gripping the rail, she pulled herself up for a better look. The wind had dropped completely, the sea was almost flat and the sun was coming out as she looked towards the horizon but there was no horizon. Not three miles away, stretching as far as her eye could see was a fog bank.

'Have we got radar?'

'No.'

'How will we manage without?'

'With difficulty, it's the one thing that scares me out here, fog. Lee could never afford to fit radar on this boat, but at least we have a decent chart plotter and we can avoid hitting the rigs.'

'What about ships?'

'Ah, now there's the problem, if they don't have radar and they don't see us, then watch out.'

Roger stood up and stretched his legs, his back was aching from sitting on the hard wooden bench and the tension he was feeling was getting to him. 'Jane, I think that fog bank isn't getting further away and the wind is down to five knots. Can you roll up the foresail?'

'Yes, no trouble, just tell me when.'

'Let's do it now.'

Jane heaved on the line, the foresail rolled tightly round the forestay, and Roger reached down to the lever beside him and increased the engine revolutions. The wind had become almost non-existent and increasing the engine revolutions was the only way they could make progress. At the back of Roger's mind was the fact that they were low on fuel and once engulfed by the fog they would be vulnerable if the engine stopped.

Anita's head appeared in the hatchway, her complexion paler than usual but she seemed in better spirits.

'How are you feeling?' asked Roger.

'Better, a lot better. Can I come up on deck? I need some air and I want a look around.'

'Yes, for a while anyway. Put on a life-jacket first and sit here,' said Roger pointing to a space close to the hatch.

'What about Katja,' asked Jane, 'does she need some air? She's been cooped up down there all day.'

Roger sighed. 'All right, but only for a short time, we will be in the fog very soon and when we do I want the other watch up here with us. I think we will need

233

to go slow and keep our eyes peeled but that's up to the skipper.' A minute later Anita and Katja were sat in the cockpit and staring at the great wall of white fog in their path. Anita had put on one of Roger's thick jumpers she had found when they were waiting in the lock and Katja was in John's oversized fleece. They sat quietly as Roger concentrated on the fog and Jane leaned against the spray hood. Anita scanned all around just in case Markov was somewhere out here and still chasing them.

Chapter 13

Lee pulled on his sea boots and rubbed his eyes for the tenth time and still feeling groggy, made his way to the chart table. He noticed the bunks were empty and had a quick look round and through the hatch saw that everyone was on deck. The sea had calmed so much so that the movement of the boat had reduced to nothing more than a gentle swaying motion and from the speed of the engine, he knew the wind must have dropped significantly and Roger had them on engine power only.

'What time is it?' he asked Paul, who had recovered from his bout of seasickness and was busy looking through their meagre store of food and drink.

'Coming up to seven o'clock, Roger asked me to wake you because we will be in the middle of a fog bank soon and he thinks you should be on watch to take charge, Skipper.'

'Phew, fog, I never considered we would get caught up in fog, blast it.'

'Where's John, still in the forward bunk?'

'Yes, we can leave him if you like.'

'And the women, all on deck?'

'Yep.'

Lee grabbed his life-jacket, fastened the straps and climbed the steps through the hatch. The sight that met him reminded him of a pleasure boat at the seaside. Sat on one side of the cockpit were Jane and Katja, opposite sat Anita and in between them Roger stood, legs apart, holding the wheel as if he were taking day trippers out for a sail.

'Looks like everything is under control, Roger?'

'Aye, just about, look at this,' he said nodding his head in the direction in front of the boat.

Lee climbed out onto the deck and turned to look forward. Not 100 metres away a great white wall of fog awaited them, thick fog, the kind in which you cannot see much more than a few meters.

'We'll need to keep a sharp lookout in that stuff,' said Lee.

'Aye,' was all Roger could say.

'What do you want us to do, Skipper?' Jane asked.

'Go below and stay there I think.'

Jane's eyes dropped, she had enjoyed the chance to sail the boat and now, when she felt that they needed her most, Lee was sending her away.

'She is a good hand Lee, could be a useful pair of eyes I reckon, why not post her forward of the mast as a lookout with one of us?'

Lee blew out his breath through half closed lips as he considered his options. The first thing he needed to do was get all the regular crew on deck and position them to keep a good lookout. He stuck his head forward and looked back down the hatch.

'Paul, give John a shout will you, and get up here.' Turning back to Anita he said, 'I want you and Katja to go below and stay there until it's safe to come up.'

'I don't think so,' said Anita.

'What...'

'I said I don't think so – you seem to have forgotten the danger we could be in if we are being chased.'

'Don't be daft, there's no one after us.'

'Look over there, what's that bearing down on us?' Lee and Roger both turned to look back and saw, two or three kilometres away, a boat travelling at high speed and coming straight towards them.

'Sugar,' said Lee, 'You don't think... '

'I do,' said Anita.

Markov had a wry grin on his face as he lowered the binoculars for the last time because they were close enough for him to observe the yacht with his naked eye. His breathing increased slightly as the excitement of the chase got to him and reached inside his jacket to feel for his gun.

' You catch them up quick, Tom,' he said,.

'We should be up with them inside ten minutes, but they are heading into a fog bank.'

Markov's head jerked up, his face resuming a veneer of controlled anger.

'What you do if they are in fog?'

'Watch them very carefully, on the radar. I don't know how thick the fog is but one thing is sure, I will have to drop our speed right down. Don't worry, we will find them but it might take a little longer than we thought,' he said, not taking his eyes off their course, both for safety and to avoid Markov's glare.

Lee decided to cast caution aside and left the engine on high revs; they would have to keep a good look-out and hope that any boat likely to cross their course would have radar or at least see them soon enough to avoid collision. He steered the yacht towards the white wall and they slid effortlessly into the fog bank, the rays of sunshine fading to a dull grey the further in they went. Everyone on board was silent, worried, and Katja noticeably shivered from the abrupt drop in temperature.

Anita's heart rate picked up as her adrenalin began to kick in and her mind turned over their predicament, their strengths and, more to the point, their weaknesses. She was the only person on board that knew the true extent of the situation they were in and, together with Katja, the lengths the Ukrainians might go to. From her brief glimpse of the yellow boat following, she knew they were in trouble and she was sure it was Markov. From what she had seen of him it was obvious that he would stop at nothing to get Katja back and she also suspected he was out to seek retribution for Vladimir's death – which made her a target.

'They'll find us with radar,' said Roger. Our best bet is to send a mayday, or at least tell the Coastguard what's going on.'

'No,' said Anita abruptly. 'We cannot tell anyone, we must try and get out of this situation ourselves.' Questioning eyes turned towards her, she knew that she was denying them a chance of escape but could see no alternative.

'Listen lady,' said Paul, 'I don't know who you think you are but if these people really are after us, then I am going to call the Coastguard, whether you like it or not.' He stood up and began to make his way below to the radio. As he made to push past Anita he stopped abruptly as a small black disc at the end of Anita's arm came into focus and he realised he was looking down the barrel of a gun.

'Wha... what's going on?'

'Sit down, Mister; you have all done well under the circumstances, all of you. Unfortunately, I have mixed

238

you up in something you do not understand, something the outside world does not need to know about, not yet anyway. You are aware that those men following us kidnapped Katja; you know I got her away from them and now they will believe that you are all part of it. I was not going to tell you any more than I needed to, but it seems a little more explanation is overdue.

'Katja is part of an organisation in the Ukraine that is a thorn in the side of her Government and her mother has inside knowledge about criminal gangs, smuggling drugs into the West and infiltrating the governments of smaller countries. Katja's mother has also offended powerful people and they arranged for her daughter's abduction, and now her mother has asked us for help. So please bear with me and I will try to get us all out of this. You must understand that we are involved in an operation instigated by the British Secret Service and once you are ashore you will be asked to abide by the Official Secrets Act.' She paused her eyes engaging each member of the crew in turn to reinforce the gravity of the situation.

Jane's eyes rolled upwards, she had been with Anita long enough to realise that she clouded some truths with lies, but she had witnessed her ability and intellect and had to admit she deserved respect. If anyone could get them out of this mess, it was Anita.

Katja listened to Anita talking about her mother and remembered the night at the dacha, when Anita had visited them. Her mother had told her things then that had shocked and surprised her. She had revealed that she worked for the Ukrainian Secret Service, a colonel no less, and of her early days as a secret agent working in London. But Katja was feeling exhausted by her ordeal, the lack of sleep and food taking its toll, leaving her feeling confused and vulnerable.

Roger saw nothing of the confrontation, standing square against the mast and peering into the thick mass of fog, listening, worrying. There may be danger following them into the fog but the immediate worry was the fog itself.

'Don't you think we had better keep a better lookout? If there is anything in here then we might not have to worry too much about that cat following us.'

In the cockpit Paul looked at the gun, then at Anita's face and, lost for words, joined Roger to keep a lookout. The swirling mist was so thick that Lee could hardly see them at times and decided that perhaps he was being a little too reckless and pulled the accelerator lever back to slow the boat speed. At three knots they could not out run the catamaran, their only hope, it seemed, was to find a gas rig or one of the guard ships circling the area but the last time he had looked at the chart, he had seen nothing within five miles. Beside him, a grim looking Anita slipped her gun back into the pocket in her trousers. Had that been a mistake, should she really have pulled out her gun to stop them using the radio? Now they had all fallen silent, each alone with their thoughts. She knew that they would be worrying and combined with their lack of sleep and sustenance it was cause for concern. Any one of them could become unpredictable, she could not afford for any of them to fight against her, she had done all she could and she needed them to work together to shake off their pursuers.

Tom eased back on the throttles just as the catamaran approached the fog bank and the two powerful engines became barely audible, the vibrations of the powerful engines dying away and from his vantage point could see the front of his craft becoming invisible as the thick fog swirled and enveloped them. He was a seaman and had a great respect for fog and even the most modern of his instruments could not help him overcome his natural caution. He eased the two engine controls forward a little more, the fingers of his left hand loosely gripping the joystick, all he needed to steer the craft. He glanced at the radar echoes on the screen, nudged the boat round five degrees more until the reflection of the yacht was directly on his course and began to close in on it.

Markov was staring hard out of the window expecting the yacht to appear at any second from out of the mist. He had decided to hit them hard when they did appear, threatening at first and if that did not work, he would put a few shots into them.

'How far away, how soon we catch them?'

'Not far, maybe a mile, less I think. We can be on them in less than half an hour, but we need to be careful with this fog. I will hold her at four knots, a safe speed, one that should give us time to see them before we run them over. I will bring us alongside and then it's up to you.'

Tom looked again at the screen and coaxed his boat steadily towards the yacht. His stomach was churning as he watched the yacht's radar reflection; it was getting nearer with each sweep of the antenna and he thanked god that there was nothing else in sight. He pressed a button, zoomed in to make his task easier, but by mistake his finger pressed the opposite zoom and the range of the radar went from two kilometres to nearer ten. A blip appeared, it was a ship not more than five kilometres away, an automatic signal broadcasting its name and position. It was a guard ship, the *Maggie M*, standing sentinel over the gas rigs, ready to deter any ship from coming too close to them. But there were no rigs anywhere near. He let the radar sweep three times more, establishing that the ship was motionless and of no danger to them, and zoomed the radar back to a one-kilometre range, focusing his attention once more on the yacht.

On the yacht, Roger slowly turned his head from side to side, straining his ears. 'Hear that?' he said.

'What?' said Lee.

Roger put his finger to his mouth to warn all on board to be silent, listen. Lee eased the lever into neutral for a few seconds and switched off the engine. In the silence and blinded by the fog, each of them strained, concentrated, and there it was, the low throb of the twin diesels.

'I think we have trouble brewing,' said John. 'I'll bet a pound to a penny it's your friends arriving Anita.'

Anita stiffened and felt for her gun. The last thing she wanted was a shoot-out. Her brief was to locate and rescue Katja, but not cause an incident or to risk lives. She knew that this was the end game; she knew they were in a desperate situation and she began to make some decisions.

'Look, I've got you all into this and it's my responsibility to keep you all as safe as I can. Katja, you might have to go with them. I will do what I can, but I'm sorry, I can't risk everyone's lives.'

Katja looked down at the deck, devastated by the thought that Markov might take her back with him. She could not go back she would rather die first.

'They're here,' called Jane who was looking back along their track.

In the swirling fog she had not really seen the boat approach, more a change in the fog's hue from white to yellow, the yellow of the catamaran. All heads swivelled in that direction and watched as the boat slowly morphed from a yellow smudge into the bulk of the catamaran.

'Well, that's it lads,' said Lee. 'We'll see what happens now.'

'You down there,' called a voice, in English with a strong East European accent. 'You stay where you are, stop your ship.'

They were already drifting without power and Lee pushed the lever back into neutral, watching as the boat came to rest alongside them, the low throb of its engines the only sound and then Markov's head appeared. He leaned over the rail of the catamaran glowering down at them and slowly, menacingly spoke again.

'I want the girl back, give me the girl and I let you all go.'

Anita watched him, watched his eyes, would he let them go? She was not so sure.

'What will you do with us?' she asked.

'Who are you? Oh yes, you are friend of Jane. Ha, Jane, I see you are sailor now!' he joked.

'I want girl and I want person who killed Vladimir.'

'Markov, throw them a line,' Tom had appeared outside the wheelhouse. 'Get a couple of lines aboard and secure them to our side.'

Markov did not have much idea about what to do but Henrick, standing further along the deck, did, and he moved towards the front of the catamaran to find a rope to throw to the yacht. Kostyantyn appeared from the doorway at the back of the saloon, went to find a second line and Tom went back to his steering position. They were beginning to drift away from the yacht and he did not want to start manoeuvring in such a restricted area and at low speed. The catamaran was excellent at rapidly coming alongside but he knew from experience that if he made a mess of it he would struggle to get her alongside again without a good run at his target and in this fog, he did not really want to try. Reaching for the twin throttles, he give the boat a gentle kick forward, watching the radar screen to judge his position. What was that? For a brief second a black smudge appeared not more than a hundred yards away and then it was gone; he looked again, it must have been a rogue wave. He dismissed it and turned his attention back to manoeuvring the boat, bringing slowly back alongside the yacht and feeling satisfied, he went back outside to see how his makeshift crew were coping when suddenly, a shrill scream pierced the air followed by a splash and below him, Markov cursed.

'Katja,' shouted Jane, 'Katja has gone over the side,' and then she screamed at the others to help her.

Sure enough, Katja had jumped over the back of the yacht and into the sea. Jane had seen her, watched her disappear under the surface and then, with relief, seen her re-appear as her life-jacket inflated and bobbed her back to the surface. However, she did not seem to be helping herself and began to drift away from the two boats, soon she would disappear into the fog and they might never find her. Without thinking, Jane sprang into action. She jumped from her position against the life-raft and dived straight over the side without a thought for her own safety. She hit the water with a loud splash and as her life-jacket inflated began striking out towards Katja Her arms thrashed at the water as she fought against the drag of her clothing and slowly managed to reach the girl and grab hold of one of her wrists.

Anita did not wait any longer. She whipped out her gun and fired at the nearest target, Kostyantyn, hitting him in the chest and sending him sprawling backwards. For an instant Markov was taken by surprise and retreated towards the cover of the saloon whilst Henrick pulled out his gun and took cover behind a winch looking for a target to shoot at.

'Roger, quick grab this,' said Lee, unhooking the life- raft.

Roger saw what he was attempting to do, and jumped from the deck into the cockpit to help Lee unclip the raft and with a mighty heave the two of them sent the canister over the side. They did not wait to see the outcome, leaving the raft to inflate automatically whilst they dived for cover. Lee fell head first into the companionway followed close behind by Roger who let out a yelp of pain as several shots from Markov's gun sprayed the cockpit and one caught him on his buttocks as he tumbled after Lee. Paul and John had already scrambled into the yacht's interior and Anita was crouched in the cockpit with her gun at the ready.

Tom heard the gunshots and took a quick look through his starboard window to see mayhem unfolding below. Was it worth it? All this shooting and what about the diamonds? Markov had never mentioned diamonds; he only seemed interested in a woman on board the yacht. Tom began to feel decidedly unhappy and regretted ever getting involved, so much so that his concentration wavered and he did not notice the rapidly moving smudge that had reappeared on his radar.

On the port side of the catamaran, invisible in the fog, a high-speed rib with a silenced engine, glided along the side of the yellow hull and from it two grappling hooks arced up and dug into the rail. Even before the lines became taut two of the four-man team were scrambling aboard, dressed in black diving suits, their faces obscured by rubbery hoods. Each of the Special Forces troopers carried a Heckler & Koch G3 KA4, their stubby barrels making it easier for killing at close range in a confined space.

The first man cleared the rail and landed silently on the deck, shuffling towards the sound of gunfire coming from the stern and keeping a low profile as his partner covered him. The remaining two soldiers performed a similar manoeuvre, making their way forwards and as Markov reached out to fire once more at the yacht, he felt the cold, hard steel of the Heckler & Koch against his temple. The surprise was absolute. Markov froze, not daring to turn; he knew very well what was pressing into his head.

'Drop your gun,' said a voice in Russian.

The next thing he felt was a knee smashing into the back of his leg and his body buckled, an arm swung round his neck, holding it in a vice like grip and forcing him flat onto the deck, forcibly pulling his hands behind his back. Whoever it was crossed his wrists and then he felt something pulling tightly against them, tying them together and he was helpless.

Not far away Kostyantyn lay moaning, his hands held together by a plastic cable tie and a Special Boat Service soldier was applying a field dressing to his wound. On the forward part of the deck, Henrick was in a similar state to Markov and on the bridge Tom stood with his hands aloft, a look of horror on his face. The only person on board still free was Jos, sitting in the engine room poring over a glossy girly magazine, oblivious to the issues being resolved above him.

In the sea, Jane reached with her free hand, grabbed the line hanging loosely from the canister, and pulled with all her might. There was a hissing noise as the life-raft began to inflate and within seconds, she was forcing Katja up over the side and to safety. As Katja's feet disappeared inside she tried to pull herself up but she was exhausted from her exertions and the cold and fell back.

'Katja, help me,' she called, but Katja was in a worse state, cold to her core and unable to move.

Jane began to feel desperate. The cold water had penetrated her flimsy clothing and succumbing to the cold she could feel numbness spreading through her limbs and she began to say a prayer. One last try, she thought, one last try to get into the life-raft, she had to do it this time. Reaching up she grabbed hold of a line attached to the raft and heaved with all her might. She rose a few centimetres from the sea, reached into the raft, feeling Katja's trouser leg, it was all there was. She reached out and gripped it with her weakening hands but it was no good, she could not move and a feeling of desperation began to engulf her. It must have been no more than seconds she hung there but it felt an eternity. The life-raft was drifting away from the yacht and soon they would be invisible in the fog. She knew she was going to die and all she could think of was her dog pining for her. Her consciousness became clouded but through it, she heard the sound of gunshots and then a splash and she wondered what was happening on the yacht. Had Markov started killing them, was he throwing the crew overboard? And then she felt a strong arm around her waist, felt warm breath in her face and someone lifted her bodily up and over the sill of the raft to where she collapsed alongside Katja. The soldier kicked out hard with his legs and slowly the raft began to move back towards the yacht.

'What kept you, you had me worried, I thought I wasn't going to get us out of this one,' said Anita to the dripping wet soldier.

'We couldn't let you know what we were up to. We hoped that we could get to you before this lot showed up and transfer you to the guard ship. But at least we got here in time.'

He smiled at Anita and unclipped a small waterproof pouch on his belt, pulled out a radio attached to a lanyard and pressed the transmit button.

'Small Boy to Big Boy, Small Boy to Big Boy, over.' The radio crackled into life.

'Big Boy to Small Boy, reading you loud and clear, over.'

'Code one, I repeat, code one,' he looked down at the radio, its miniature screen indicating their position on the planet. 'Our position is... '

Jos's eyes had become wide with surprise when the black figure had appeared as if from nowhere and without ceremony, pinned him to the wall and frisked him for weapons. After tying his hands behind his back, the soldier hauled him roughly up the staircase and into the saloon where Tom and two others were lying prostrate on the floor. The big Ukrainian bodyguard was slumped against the saloon wall with another of the black clad men applying a second bandage to stem the flow of blood from his chest and then Jos fainted.

On the yacht, Roger was lying face down on the saloon bunk as another of the soldiers dressed his wound. He had caught a bullet in his buttocks and was grimacing with pain.

'You were lucky there, Roger, it could have taken your balls off,' said John, his black humour a cover for the relief he felt knowing they were all safe.

Roger said nothing.

'Big Boy this is Small Boy, we need urgent medical assistance, two gunshot wounds and two suffering from hypothermia, over.'

'Small Boy, we will be with you in a few minutes, stand by.'

The Special Forces soldiers did not stay long, in and out quickly, leaving no evidence of ever having been there, except for a wounded man and four bound captives on the catamaran. They had patched Roger up and left him as comfortable as possible before their leader had crossed back over onto the catamaran to make sure the captives were secure and then they were gone. For a short time Anita was in charge and she looked over her charges, the women in the sleeping bags their cold bodies slowly warming back up and then at Roger lying on his stomach and staring at the wooden panel six inches from his face. Paul and John sat quietly on deck and Lee was standing motionless, hands on the helm. She checked her gun just in case any of the men on the catamaran managed to escape and come looking for her, and then she sat back against the cockpit bulkhead.

No one spoke; each exhausted and shocked by their ordeal, they were tired and hungry, ready for a hot meal and some rest and it wasn't long in coming. At first bright lights cut through the fog and gathering darkness and then a ship appeared, towering high over the yacht, the guard ship Tom had seen on his radar had finally arrived on the scene, the mother ship for the rescue operation. Crewed by Royal Naval personnel speedily assembled on orders from the highest authority, they had commandeered the ship as soon as Anita's last messages had reached MI6. Soon a boat was lowered and from their position holding onto the yachts rigging, John and Paul watched in fascination as it approached.

'Hello,' said a polite, military voice, 'who's in charge here?'

'I suppose I'm still skipper, but this lady here has been doing most of the organising for the past day or so,' said Lee

'Ah yes,' said the man a knowing look spreading across his face.

Anita looked up and nodded to him. She felt unable to speak, the excitement of the last hour had drained her both mentally and physically.

'We have a wounded man down below,' said Lee

'Yes I know. I'm Surgeon Commander Volans and I've come to take a look.'

The doctor waited a few moments as the sailors secured their boat and then he climbed on board the yacht, two marines followed and climbed aboard the catamaran to take charge of the prisoners.

'Now then where are the patients...? ' he said as the tender pulled away, returning a few minutes later to evacuate the wounded from the yacht and to deposit an officer and several sailors on board the catamaran.

The officer busied himself looking over the vessel and then gave orders for his men to take over its running, before he stepped over the guardrail to salute a still bewildered Lee.

'Compliments of the Captain, we're here to help you get to port. The Captain thinks you are all probably a bit shell shocked after what has just happened and you could do with a hand.'

Lee sat down on the seat next to the wheel and let out a great sigh. 'How are my crew, is Roger all right, and the girls?'

'They are in good hands, have no fear, Surgeon Commander Volans knows what he's doing. If he can't get them right then no one can.'

The Lieutenant was not privy to all that had gone on, but from the small operations room they had set up on the *Maggie M* he had seen events unfold and learned of one or two names. 'You must be Mrs Simms,' he said with a smile.

'Yes.'

'Well done is all I can say. My name is Lieutenant Mills and my orders are to get you aboard the guard ship as soon as for a debriefing. I think that is now. Any of you others want to leave?' he asked the remainder of the crew.

'No thanks,' they said in unison.

'We signed on for the whole trip,' said Paul.

John looked at the naval officer and with a grin asked, 'have you got any beer?'

Lee wearily cradled his head in his hands and, after a brief silence, looked up grinning.

'What a crew.'

Epilogue

It was a bright and sunny June day when Anita drove her little sports car into the underground car park for the first time in almost two weeks. She felt good, the mission had been a success, Katja was safe and her kidnappers were behind bars. Events of the past few weeks cycled through her mind and she felt her only regret was that the two Embassy staff had died but then Vladimir, as she now knew him, had paid the price. The conclusion of the operation at sea was swift and efficient; the navy had transferred Jane and Katja, the wounded men and prisoners to the guard ship and Lee and his remaining crewmembers, together with Navy personnel had sailed the yacht the last few miles to Lowestoft.

As soon as the Naval commander was satisfied everything was in order he had ordered the Captain of the guard ship to steam at high speed to an area clear of fog where a Lynx helicopter had winched her aboard and whisked her away for her debriefing. After a gruelling few hours of interrogation and a medical examination, the doctor ordered her to take a few days' rest and now she was back. She left her car and presented her clearance to the security personnel before walking along the familiar corridor towards her office. The mission had been secret but there were people in this building who had been privy to her signals and reports, it was their job, and one or two gave her a knowing look as she passed. She turned the corner towards the offices of her section and was surprised to see a security officer waiting outside her office door.

'Morning, Ma'am.'

'Good morning... ' Why was he here?

'I've been asked to escort you to a meeting in H section, Ma'am, could you come with me please.'

This was an unexpected occurrence; 'H' section was on the floor below the director's office, a place from which the most secret operations of the day were controlled. She followed the man towards the lift and together they ascended three floors.

'This way, Ma'am, this way to the conference room.' They reached a set of oak panelled double doors, where he indicated she should enter and then he closed them behind her. The sun was bright, streaming through the bulletproof windows and it blinded her for a time. Her eyes adjusted and at first, she did not notice the figure standing by the curtains looking out across the river until the person spoke.

'Good morning my friend.'

Anita was a little taken aback until her eyes adjusted and the person turned to face her. It was Kateryna.

'Kateryna, what are you doing here?'

'I am British citizen, why not should I be here,' she said with a grin and reaching out to take hold of Anita's hand.

'British citizen! let's sit down, tell me all about it.'

'First I speak; I thank you from the bottom of heart for what you have done. You have brought me my Katja back from hell. The President of the Ukraine should go there one day, one day soon I hope.'

'What has happened to you, why are you here, why are you British citizen?' She need not have asked, in truth she had played the game long enough but she wanted to hear it from Kateryna.

Kateryna became serious. 'My position in the Ukraine

Secret Service was becoming, un...

'Untenable.'

'Yes, untenable, the President's office began to hound me, I was followed everywhere and I know if I do not get out they maybe they send me to labour camp, or kill me. I worry about Katja and when I hear from Sir Malcolm my Katja is safe I put plan into action. I have a meeting in Stockholm only two days later so I tell my people I need prepare documents and I will work from home but instead I catch first plane to Stockholm and from there I contact Sir Malcolm and catch plane to London. I bring very important, secret documents on the Russians with me and I ask for asylum.

'Sir Malcolm takes memory stick and begins to view documents, whistles, and says no problem. I ask him to let me see you to say thank you and here I am, in the headquarters building of MI6. I never manage that before,' she said with a wry smile. 'I not free to wander about though, Sir Malcolm has security man with me always and anyway I spy no more.'

Kateryna chuckled softly to herself and looked Anita straight in the eye as if to make her point.

'Where are you staying? I presume the department will have found you a safe house.'

'Oh yes, very safe. I and Katja are stopping with Sir Malcolm for a while,' she said, a twinkle in her eye. 'I am to ask you to dinner at his house tonight. A car will pick you up at seven and we can all relax for a while and talk. He is overjoyed to have his daughter here and wants to get to know her better and he still likes me I think.' She chuckled again and Anita frowned.

'Here we go again; this is how this whole thing started, you sending a car for me,' said Anita

She stayed with Kateryna for a further ten minutes engaging in small talk until there came a knock at the door and the security officer said he was to escort her back to her office.

'I must go now, Kateryna, it looks as if we have been allotted only a short time together.'

'Not to worry, I have debriefing all day and then we will meet again tonight and you can tell me more of how you rescue my daughter. We both look forward to seeing you at Sir Malcolm's.'

They shook hands; Kateryna's grip was warm and firm and after they had parted, Anita began organizing her thoughts – she had her report to write. She wondered what she would say. There were important issues associated with the case not least the fact that Katja was the illegitimate daughter of the head of the Secret Service. Should she mention it? She was supposed to disclose everything; leave nothing out and with this problem uppermost in her mind she turned the handle of her office door and stepped into the room. For the first time in what seemed an eternity, she sat behind her desk, leaned forward and rested her chin on her clasped fingers. Where should she begin? A tap on the door interrupted her thoughts.

'Come,' she called out and a clerk walked in with a large file containing her signals, photographs from Verbier, Jane and Markov having dinner together, the corpses; there would be others she had taken in Amsterdam, images she had not yet had time to view, images she had forgotten and she had to put them all in order.

She dismissed the clerk and reached across for the telephone receiver to ring for some coffee, strong, black and full of caffeine and then she opened the file. Sifting through the papers and images, she wrote one-line notes in chronological order as near to their correct sequence as she could remember and by lunchtime, she had enough to begin the report in detail. Pausing to ring for more coffee and a sandwich, she lifted her glasses, sat them on her head and rubbed her face with both hands to try to order her thoughts.

After the coffee arrived she began to look deeper, speculating – she could not help it, it was how she thought – it was one of the reasons why she had taken the job with the organisation in the first place.

At 6.30, she showered, put on her dressing gown and sat in front of her mirror to apply the little make-up she forced herself to wear on these occasions. The flat was quiet; the only sounds those of passing vehicles, deadened by distance and the thick stone walls of the building. She liked it when it was quiet, it allowed her to think deeply and right now, her mind was working overtime. She glanced at the clock; the car would be here soon so she left her thoughts for a while and dressed in her best blue party dress and stood in front of the mirror to fiddle with a pair of silver pendant earrings. She took one last look in the mirror and feeling presentable, went to the door of her flat and watched through the lace curtains for the limousine from the car pool.

She did not have to wait long, only seconds after the hour a shiny black limousine came into sight and she picked up her bag, let herself out and a minute later the car whisked her across London to the secluded mews cottage tucked away in an exclusive corner of Knightsbridge. Sir Malcolm had lived there for least 20 years; she knew that, because during the Cold War she had followed Kateryna there on more than one occasion.

A man from the department opened the door and took her coat; he was one of several staff on loan for the evening. Sir Malcolm was a stickler for security; always very careful with whom he encountered, always aware of situations that might compromise his position. To have two women from a previously Soviet dominated country as his guests could raise a few eyebrows and he had not entered into the evening's celebration lightly. Convening a meeting of his policy committee that same afternoon he had discussed effects and opportunities the situation might present.

He was dressed in a smart evening suit and wore a broad smile across his face as he stepped forward to greet Anita.

'Welcome to my humble abode, err...Mrs Simms,'

Anita smiled shook hands with him and then her attention turned to Kateryna and Katja sitting side by side on the sofa.

'Mrs Simms,' queried Kateryna, a puzzled look spreading across her face. 'I did not know you were married.'

'I'm not,' said Anita.

'Oh, I understand.'

'Well, ladies, shall we have a drink before dinner? The Department's finest chef is preparing the food for tonight. From your record I see you are a fan of Bombay Sapphire, Anita.'

'Oh, yes please.'

'And you two, not vodka I hope.'

Kateryna's face was unsympathetic and Anita guessed that the reference to the Russian drink had offended her and as if to confirm it she said.

'Now that I am here in England I should drink an English drink – perhaps a whiskey,'

Sir Malcolm and Anita smiled at the misnomer and everyone began to relax. Sir Malcom poured Kateryna and Anita's drinks and handed them to them.

'And what about you young lady, a whiskey with some ice perhaps? Or are you still a vodka drinker even after all you have been through?'

Katja's hesitation took just long enough for Sir Malcom's to feel his suspicions were confirmed and then she compromised.

'I will have a Bombay Sapphire the same drink as Anita.'

He poured the drink, placed a slice of lime in with the ice before handing it to Katja, a pleasant, friendly smile on his face and then he turned to Kateryna. It seemed his hunch was probably right.

Several days later in the small Yacht club on the North East coast, Roger and Lee sat with a beer in front of each of them. They had not recovered fully from their experiences, physically yes, but their minds remained troubled by the events of the recent past. When the officer in charge of the rescue had asked, no, ordered to them to take an oath on the bible to abide by the official secrets act, they had become fully aware of the gravity of the situation.

'It's bloody hard not being able to tell anyone isn't it Roger.'

'Aye.'

'I can't even tell Sharon. She keeps asking me why we went to Lowestoft on the way back and why we returned home so soon. It's worse than the time I had an affair, at least no one else knew much about it and I could change my story. She's suspicious already.'

Well it is your own fault you dirty little Tyke. If you did not go chasing after other women all the time you could tell her you thought the tulips from Lowestoft are better than Tulips from Amsterdam.'

'Daft sod. Look here's John. My turn, do you want another beer?'

At practically the same time in a half full, dimly lit restaurant bar in London, Surgeon Commander Volans was ordering some drinks.

'Two large G and T's please,' he said to the barmaid who turned to mix the drinks.

'That will be eight pounds ninety,' she said placing them on the bar in front of him.

The Navy man passed a ten-pound note to the girl and looked round for his date and saw a smartly dressed lady emerge from the ladies room at the far end of the bar and thought how different she looked than when they had first met. With both hands full, he used a movement of his head to indicate where to sit and with a twinkle in his eye, he said 'it's a large one I'm afraid, naval tradition you know.'

Jane smiled, reached out to take her drink and said, 'well I think I should be an honorary naval officer after our last meeting, don't you.'

Over 2,000 kilometres away, a man in a dark-blue suit sat behind a large oak desk and opposite him, the head of the Foreign Intelligence Service of Ukraine waited patiently.

'Well, now that the operation seems to have come to a conclusion what can you tell me.'

'Mister President I think we were lucky that the British M.I.6 had such a good operator in the field. Markov Kalaman became a liability, more obsessed with his own profit than letting the operation run and he almost wrecked our plan. The British have him in prison but my sources suggest that the authorities over there will release him and his men without trial to avoid any adverse publicity. What do you want me to do about him if they do release him? I have a field agent working within his organization and might I suggest we leave him in place and use Mister Kalaman more advantageously in the future.'

The President nodded. 'As you say, Markov nearly destroyed the operation, but he knows very little of its real purpose. His organization was a good cover and he is dispensable. Perhaps we can use him again in the future. Leave the file for me to read and if you will excuse me I have a telephone call to make.'

The general took his leave and the President looked at the clock on the wall; it was precisely ten o clock East European time. The secure phone on his desk began to ring and the President of Ukraine drummed his fingers lightly on the desk, composed his thoughts for a few seconds and then picked up the telephone.

'Yes, Mr President... I am very well... yes we are pleased with the agreement and I look forward to coming to Moscow. '

The two men spoke for almost half an hour, covering matters of importance between their two countries, the prospect of the new gas pipeline across

Ukrainian territory, the problem of the impending membership of the European Union. The Russian's were applying pressure and he felt that perhaps he needed to show some sort of solidarity with them.

'Mr President, you are aware, I am sure, of our covert presence within the British state, you will know of our agents in the United Kingdom because of their contacts with your people. I am able to tell you now that we have inserted a spy with connections to the highest level of their Security Service... a woman... we have worked very hard on her cover. Without boring you with the details, it was a complicated operation and it did not run as smoothly as we had hoped, but then how often do these things, and we expect results in a year or two. She has first to convince them of her sincerity and her controller has to believe the plan will work. Yes Mr President I can assure you that the British are not suspicious.'

A minute later the conversation ended and the President replaced his receiver, let out a sigh, rested his elbows on his desk and thought about Katja. She was a brave and clever girl and he hoped that she would realise the potential she had shown in training.

Other Books by
Kelvin Robertson

---

iGoli City of Gold
Published September 2014

Set in the goldfields of post union South Africa the
story charts the trials and tribulations of an immigrant
family searching for a better life. Greed and deception
become the twin drivers of the head of the family when he
becomes embroiled in a scheme to take money from
unwitting American investors.

Pickpockets and Zulus
Published January 2015

The harsh reality of Victorian London leaves Georgie
an orphan with the very real prospect of deportation to
the colonies until a friendly recruiting sergeant rescues
him, enlisting him as a boy soldier. In the army he
befriends Patrick and they campaign together, fighting
the Zulu army of Cetshwayo as mounted infantrymen